Published in the United States by:
Spaceboy Books LLC
1627 Vine Street
Denver, CO 80206
www.readspaceboy.com

Cover design by Clark Allen

ISBN: 978-1-951393-31-1
First printed February 2024

Praise for **Dead Broke in the Yonder Void**:

"In this propulsive tinderbox of a novel, Michael J. O'Connor has captured the beautiful, dark corners of San Francisco with its deeply evocative sense of place. *Dead Broke in the Yonder Void* is a vulnerable and ecstatic portrait of a troubled young life in all its hilarity and heartbreak.

— Thea Chacamaty, Henfield Prize recipient

"Some of the most engaging and encompassing prose I've read in a long time. This book will make you feel uncomfortable and alive all at the same time, right alongside the main character. Highly recommend this book if you want to get a little lost for a while—you might find more in common with the void than you'd think."

— Chlo Connaughton, Editor-in-Chief of *Zaum Literary Magazine*

"*Dead Broke in the Yonder Void* is a dark reminder of what happens to the human beings our society decides no longer matter. From petty, power drunk landlords to institutions ready and willing to condemn the main character, Matty, to death, sympathy is scarce and often unravels rapidly. As society looks away, embarrassed, or in fear, Matty is compelled to remain small and invisible, lest he inspire rage and retribution. O'Connor is a gifted writer that gives us a raw and visceral account of a hellish downward spiral. You can smell the endless pints of cheap whiskey, the sweat-drenched anxiety, and the matted clothing, stiff with misery. By the final pages, any decent human will vow to never look the other way again."

— William M. Brandon, author of *Eternity: The ~~Long and~~ Short of It, SILENCE & Selene, The Exile The Matriarch & The Flood*, and *Welcome to Spring Street*

"A witty, honest work of autofiction, *Dead Broke in the Yonder Void* is the story of a young man stranded at the intersection of adulthood, addiction, and the search for meaning. The desert island is the Mission and Tenderloin neighborhoods of 2000s San Francisco. The shipwreck is a series of misfortunes and misadventures. Our protagonist can only struggle to survive by blending urban camping, odd jobs, and a glimmer of hope that the next day will be better, or just won't come at all. This is a story of redemption. It's a story of faith. This is a story about the empty space inside us that we have to fill, the ways we find to try to fill it, and the moment we understand that we are full."

— Nate Ragolia, author of *One Person Can't Make a Difference* and *There You Feel Free*

DEAD BROKE IN THE YONDER

VOID

A NOVEL

MICHAEL J. O'CONNOR

Denver, Colorado

For everyone still out there.

Chapter One

For a while, everything was perfect. Lola found me while she was on vacation in Seattle, where I was living in a wet basement and eating from the dumpster of a vegan hot dog factory. I was like a raccoon that crawled out of the trash and followed her home to San Francisco. I had lived there briefly years before but quickly hit the road, traveling around the country and playing in bands, but mostly washing dishes, and eventually ended up in that basement in Seattle, broke and eating garbage. She was excited about the idea of me coming back with her. I must have seemed like a good idea at the time.

"What about your stuff?" she asked.

"I don't really have anything."

⟵〰

The first month of us living together in her apartment in the Mission went well, but when it came time for her to go on a camping trip she had been planning and she didn't invite me, I knew she was glad to get away.

"I'll take care of the place while you're gone," I said.

"Just please don't..."

Her eyes darted around the apartment, taking a good look at the neatly arranged bookshelves weighed down with chemistry textbooks and picture frames filled with college memories. Then she settled her gaze on me; pale and graying at the temples at age 24 from too many years at sweaty jobs with screaming bosses and bloated from cheap beer and ramen noodles, like something dragged from the bottom of a lake. Her face scrunched up, half hopefully.

"I'll see you in a week," she said.

⟵〰

The morning Lola was due to come home, I woke up

2

with a start and was sure of only two things: I had overslept and I had pissed in her bed. I jumped up and swung my legs to the ground violently, knocking over four empty beer bottles on the bedside table and sending broken glass all over the room. I started to gather up the sheets and noticed that the floor was also wet, as were the walls and the ceiling and the curtains. I scanned the space, trying to understand, before landing on a box fan whirring in the corner. All the pieces of the puzzle, as well as some vague, half-asleep-half-drunk memories, started to come together. Apparently, in the middle of the night, I had thought it prudent to sleepwalk over to that fan and piss directly into the back of it, spraying the entire room with urine composed mostly of malt liquor. As I dragged the sheets off the bed, I knocked over more bottles I had left sitting on the ground, fully intending to clean up before Lola's arrival, one of which was half full of beer and cigarette butts, which drained out and under the bed with a sickening glug. I dropped the sheets and watched as the thick brown liquid seeped through them.

"This is a nightmare," I said out loud.

Then I heard the front door open.

When she walked into the bedroom, the first thing she saw was me, her month-long boyfriend whom she had met in another state and had inexplicably brought home, naked on the floor, kneeling over her sheets, which were stained brown and covered in broken glass. I'd like to think she was stunned, but she wasn't. I watched as all the red flags of the last month came flooding back to her. The fact that I hardly had any clothes and had moved to a new city with her simply by grabbing a guitar case and a backpack. The fact that I wore the same filthy, crunchy socks for days in a row, and had mostly sat around her apartment, reading her books and drinking her booze; all of these things clicked together and made up the disgusting image she was looking at on her bedroom floor.

"Matty," she said calmly, brushing her blonde hair out of her face, dirty from the woods. "Get up and get dressed."

"I can finish cleaning," I said.

"Matty, just get up and get dressed." She stood still for a moment and smelled the air. She looked like she was going to throw up. "I'll be in the living room."

She closed the door behind her and as I put my pants on, I looked out her window to the sidewalk below. It was only the second story. It wasn't close enough to the ground to sneak out and run away or high enough to kill myself. I was going to have to go out there.

She was picking up the few articles of my clothing that were strewn all around the living room and putting them in my backpack when I finally worked up the nerve to go out there. She handled them with a caution usually reserved for bags of dog shit, then zipped the backpack up and handed it to me.

"I'll give you money for a bus ticket back to Seattle," she said. "This was a mistake. This was a big mistake"

"No, no it's fine," I said, reaching for the backpack and slipping on my shoes. "It's fine. I'm sorry. It's fine."

We stood by the front door for a moment, both holding onto the bag and looking at each other. I could tell that she was not mad that I had peed into her fan, or if she had figured out that happened yet, or if it even mattered. I could tell she was upset that I had turned out to be just what she was afraid I would be. I had not surprised her at all and she blamed herself. I had been exactly as advertised. I knew this was why she was upset because I had seen that look on the faces of friends, girlfriends, and family before. I had been disappointing people for a very long time.

"I'm really sorry, again," I said, "I don't know what's wrong with me. I think I'm just an asshole."

She laughed a little at that.

"You're not an asshole, you're just confused."

She let go of the backpack and opened the door for me, and I stepped out into the late morning of the Mission District with my socks crunching in my torn Vans.

I immediately thought of going to Caleb's house. We had been in a band together for a couple of years and had traveled around and lived together in some truly terrible conditions before he settled in San Francisco. He understood what it was like to be down to nothing and at the end of the line. He lived just a few blocks away from Lola and I was sure he would let me sleep on his couch for a bit. I would, and had, done it for him. My phone was almost dead considering I had been too busy spraying Lola's room with piss in my sleep to bother plugging it in but Caleb and I had met up a couple of times since I'd been in town so I knew where he lived and which doorbell was his. I checked my wallet. I had two hundred and fifty dollars left of the six hundred I got when I sold my guitar. I did it right when I got to town and regretted it immediately. I kept the pawn ticket in my wallet, but I knew down in the very bottom of my gut that I was never going to redeem it and it was gone forever.

The light in the Mission was bright and I could feel my pale skin absorbing it like hot, cracked earth taking in a first rain. It was good to be outside. Steam rose off the wooden fences and porches of the houses I passed. It was eleven in the morning on a Monday in April of 2009. I stopped at a liquor store and bought a pint of Ancient Age whiskey, a bourbon with a large scroll on the label that made it look fantastical and magical when really it was just the cheapest kind they had. I stepped back out onto the sidewalk and took a pull before sticking it in my backpack. It coated and calmed my stomach, which was still spinning with nervous energy from the morning. Lola was no doubt mopping up the bedroom now. I hoped that she knew to watch out for broken glass. I considered calling her. Then I thought again and kept walking. She was probably having the whole place fumigated. Or maybe just moving out altogether.

I started formulating a plan for asking Caleb to let me stay with him. We had taken care of each other a lot over the years but he had more or less gotten his act together, unlike me. He was tall and spindly and had always had a nervous energy but when we got together I noticed it got much worse. He seemed manic and fearful now and it made me uneasy. He was the only person in town that I knew besides Lola, though, and as I walked, I rehearsed my speech to him and tried to anticipate what he might say. I practiced out loud as I strolled past fruit stands and grandmothers and colorful murals and more liquor stores before finally turning a corner and stepping up to the doorbell at Caleb's house.

I rang the bell, which was the only button on the front of the cage surrounding the porch, and stepped back to look up at the windows above. For the first time, it occurred to me that he had never invited me inside, so I didn't know what the situation was in there. I didn't know if he had roommates or if he even had a couch that I could sleep on. I stood in the middle of the sidewalk, scanning the windows. I thought for a second that I saw Caleb's paranoid, darting eyes peeking out but it could have been the glare from the sun, or perhaps someone else altogether, or just the whiskey. I stomped up the steps and rang the bell again. This time I put my ear up against the gate, straining to hear anything, and enjoying the feeling of the cool metal on the side of my face. I rang the bell two more times before sinking down onto the step, feeling suddenly tired and immeasurably sad. He wasn't there. I stood up after a few minutes of feeling awful and took another sip of rotten bourbon. It hugged me and curled up in my stomach, and I started walking toward the park.

On the hill in the park, people were tanning and hula-hooping and smoking weed and drinking and blasting music and banging on drums. I picked out a patch of grass and took out the Ancient Age as I sat down, taking big pulls from it and people-watching in the sun. Caleb would have to let me stay with him. I had let him live with me for two months in my shed in Portland. It was tight and tense at times but we got through to the other side. He owed me this much. I may not have seen the inside of his place, but I was fairly certain that it was bigger than the shed. Further up on the hill, two dogs started fighting over a discarded hamburger and I watched them snarl as each of them went blind with fear at the thought of giving it up. Clouds were starting to roll in from the ocean and a breeze picked up, so I put on my hooded sweatshirt, which left three T-shirts, three pairs of boxer briefs, and five pairs of socks in the backpack, all filthy. I took another sip of whiskey and laid down on the backpack, looking up at the clouds. The breeze blew harder and it swept up everyone's loose sandwich wrappers and brown paper bags that they had been using to disguise their cans of Tecate. It all blew up into the sky and scattered itself along the sidewalks and gutters below the hill. I closed my eyes, and soon I was slipping into a sun- and wind-battered sleep, clutching what was left of the bottle in one hand, with the rest of my belongings tucked under my head.

⋘〜〜〜

When I woke up, it was dark and I was shivering and curled up into myself, trying to keep warm in the hooded sweatshirt. A spot behind my eyes throbbed and my skull felt like it was getting sliced in half. Stomach acid bubbled up into my throat and my face was raw and sunburned. The park was empty except for trash left behind by the crowd and I was terrified for a brief moment before I remembered where I was and what I was sleeping outside. Then I was a little more terrified. I had no idea what time it was since my cell phone battery was long dead, but judging from how empty the sidewalk below was, it was late. There was no way I could show up at Caleb's docr now. There was also no way I could spend the night in the park. It was too out in the open and I was already pleasantly surprised to find my wallet still in my front pocket. No one had thought to rob me while I slept drunk on the crowded hill. If I stayed in the park, there was no guarantee I would be so lucky again. I stood up and took the last swig of the bottle of Ancient Age, cringing as it burned its way down my throat, and tossed it into the shopping cart of a man collecting recycling as I left the park and headed down Dolores Street.

The bars were closed, so I knew it was after two o'clock, and everyone who was going to go home that night seemed to have already gone there. The fog had come in while I slept and a fine film of water settled on my face as I walked. I could feel the last bit of booze working its way to the spot behind my eyes and cushioning it so it didn't hurt as bad when my skull bobbed with my steps. I put my hood up and considered walking around all night until a good time came to show up at Caleb's house. Not too early, but not too late in case he had a job or something to go to in the morning. I didn't want to miss him again. The prospect of walking all night started to seem less enticing the further I went. After only an hour I was exhausted. I hadn't eaten anything except bourbon all day and all I wanted to do was lay down. My feet were heavy, and my mostly empty backpack was cutting into my shoulders. I stopped at a crosswalk, and even though there were no cars on the road at that time of night, I waited for the light anyway, just to take a rest. When it turned green, I just couldn't cross. The other side seemed too far away. Instead, I limped to a traffic island separating the two lanes in the middle of the street, landscaped and lush with bushes and a small tree. I kicked around on the damp soil to make sure there were no syringes or broken glass and I laid down, hidden from view by the bushes. Cars passed on either side, but their headlights didn't shine onto me. I pulled the hood tight over my face and started laughing on the dark dirt.

⟵〰〰

"Mr. DeYoung, did you know that this will be the one-hundredth funeral that you have served as altar server?"

I stopped tying my dress shoes and sat up straight on the iron bench in the vestibule.

"Really?"

Father Wade picked up the incense burner and lit it with his cigarette lighter. His white collar was loose and hanging off his neck, and he was still wearing his Members Only jacket.

"Either you're just doing it to skip school, or you really love funerals, but either way, I think that's too much death for an eighth-grader."

11

It seemed impossible at first, but thinking back, I had served about one funeral a week during the school year since the fifth grade when I became an altar boy. The math added up. It made perfect sense to me to join the altar servers, seeing as I had to go to church anyway. I figured I might as well be involved in the process and make myself useful instead of passively kneeling and sitting and standing like the people in the audience. I was a big kid, so I could carry the heavy gold cross down the aisle, sweating and red-faced in a white gown that was too short. It felt important. The funerals were just a part of the package that I hadn't considered when I joined. However, the priests and funeral directors were so business-like and relaxed about the process that I just acted like they did and eventually, I got used to it. I blessed bodies with the soccer ball-sized incense burner and helped funeral directors lift coffins onto a silver cart that closed up like an accordion. I was always surprised by how heavy the coffins were. It made sense since there was a human being in there, but it never failed to surprise me when I felt the weight shifting and jostling inside. I served funerals for old people and young people and children. I helped bless more than a few tiny coffins. There was no cut-off and no age limit. Some of the services were packed to standing room only, with family and well-wishers weeping and screaming in the aisles, and others were completely empty. Those were usually paid for by some distant relative who could get the cash together to clear their conscience but couldn't get on a plane or maybe even in the car and get down to the church.

Father Wade was right in that I had continued being an altar boy partially because it got me out of class. I would often get to miss an hour or sometimes two of school. Sister Pat, the nun who ran the front desk, would poke her head into the classroom and interrupt Sister Nelson, or any of the other squat, mean-spirited nuns, and apologize profusely before pointing to me and waving me over.

"Matthew is needed at the church," she would say.

I would stuff my hands in my pockets and make my way across the playground to the gothic, stone cathedral that sat on the other side of the school. Broken free from the bonds of the nuns, I was moving freely about the grounds, no adults questioning me because I was so obviously of their world. I was needed at the church.

I would meet Father Wade in the back vestibule and we would set up the incense burner or the giant gold cross or help the funeral director with anything he needed. The sparsely attended funerals weren't the ones that bothered me. Those were the ones where it was our job to make sure that the person was sent off with some scraps of love and respect. Those were the ones where it was enough to be present. There weren't going to be any more chances after that. Mostly, those were the ones where I felt like there was something I could do. By performing all the same rituals and moves I would at any other funeral, I left those feeling like I had some control.

It was the funerals that were packed to the rafters with friends and family that left me with a bad, helpless feeling for the rest of the day. Standing up on the altar, there was a buffet of suffering on the faces of the guests in the pews. Parents and husbands and wives and children wept and screamed and clawed at the coffin as the funeral director and I pushed it down the aisle to put it in the hearse and drive it to the cemetery. People lost complete control. Some of them vomited. Others sat in stony silence, their faces gray and empty, looking like they could just open the wooden lid of the box on the cart and crawl right in. It was not like this was something horrible and rare that had happened to a very small sample of people. This happened to everyone. The empty funerals were comforting and peaceful, but the services of the people who were loved greatly during their time on earth left some of their attendees broken and weeping on the steps of the church long after everyone else had left. The depth and breadth of their love terrified me.

"They just told me I'm the oldest one so I can deal with it," I said, finally answering Father Wade and leaning down to tie my other dress shoe.

He took a cigarette out of his pocket and stuck it in his mouth, then leaned on the door of the vestibule to go outside for a smoke break before the service.

"Can you?" he asked.

⟵〰〰

It wasn't exactly sleep that I got on the traffic island that night. It was a fitful start and stop of being jolted awake every time a car passed by. I kept thinking in my half-awake haze that I had fallen asleep in the middle of the street. Which, of course, I had. In the morning, I stayed crouched down behind the bushes and made sure the coast was clear before emerging, dirty and hungover, from the brush. I could barely remember where I had aimlessly walked and had to take a second to get my bearings. I was on a quiet corner of the wealthy Noe Valley neighborhood, which featured tree-lined streets and homes with large glass picture windows made for watching people walk by from a safe, warm, and dry distance. I noted the traffic island. It was a good thing to keep in mind, just in case things went bad.

I stayed away from the sunny side of the street, trying to blend into the sidewalk and storefronts. I didn't want to stand out to anyone. Neighborhoods like that have a good memory. They aren't like The Tenderloin downtown, where you can be at the end of your rope anonymously. People who live in big houses in San Francisco know who is walking around their neighborhoods. I climbed to the top of a steep hill, sweating out brown liquor the whole way, and at the crest, The Mission came into view. I cut through the park, which was starting to fill up with people again. It had been cleaned since the day before, the recyclables having been picked up by someone willing to put in the work for a nickel, and the rest of the trash had just blown out to sea. People were opening up bracers of PBR and pouring mimosas into little plastic cups, starting the cycle over. It would be new again the next day, too.

I kept walking until I got to the tiled, mosaic-inlaid 16th and Mission BART station. People were shoving each other to get on the bus and a small woman in a purple beanie and a leather jacket was standing on the corner screaming at somebody on the bus and banging on the window and I realized that I was walking to Lola's apartment. It had been automatic. I started laughing like I had the night before under the tree on the traffic island. The idea of me showing up at her apartment, hair dirty and sticking out on the side, wearing a black hoodie with what I hoped to Christ was mud running up the back of it, and smelling like I had been aged in a barrel, was so absurd that I couldn't help but laugh out loud. After the atrocities I had committed in her bedroom, not to mention the fact that I owed her a new fan, showing up and saying "Hi honey, I'm home" was the worst idea I could possibly imagine. She had suffered enough. I turned around and started walking back toward Caleb's house. Caleb would have to let me stay with him. He would remember the shed in Portland. He owed me big time.

Chapter Two

Caleb kicked me awake on his couch. He started doing that on day three and we were now two weeks in. The blanket he gave me was a brown, wool, army-issue electric blanket that hadn't had a plug in years, which was probably for the best. I often had nightmares that I was being electrocuted by the thing in the night, wrapped up tight and unable to escape as it jolted me. I couldn't imagine how much of a fire hazard it would be in real life. I could see the kitchen from the couch and watched Caleb get ready for work from under the brown blanket. His place was cluttered with neatly arranged piles of books and papers and art supplies. Old photographs were meticulously arranged on a coffee table in front of the couch but I could never figure out how they were organized or what he was doing with them. Some of them were of anonymous families standing in front of suburban houses and old cars, smiling. Others were much stranger. Darker. One was a Polaroid of an old man in a bed, clearly deceased. On the white paper part of the Polaroid, it said "Dad" in ballpoint pen. I picked up the photo and looked at it as Caleb shot me a sideways glance, making sure that I hadn't fallen back asleep.

I, of course, had to remind Caleb about the shed. I didn't want to, but he hesitated for too long when I asked him if I could crash on his couch for a little bit. The silence built up while I watched him search for excuses, so I had to use it before he was able to come up with something.

"It won't be for nearly as long as when we lived in the shed," I said.

His face dropped and he knew that he was cornered.

He had a roommate. A German student who never left his room except to go to class. I only knew his name because Caleb would often cite him as the main reason why he was so anxious to get me off his couch.

"It's just that Knut is kind of a control freak," he

would say. "I don't know, he's weird."

He wanted me out as soon as I got there, and his nervous energy seeped into my bones and made me tip-toe around the house. I would stay out all day, wandering the streets or reading in the park until it was late, and I would open the front door with the spare key he reluctantly gave me as quietly as possible, hoping not to run into him. Then I would slip under the brown army blanket and try to sleep until getting kicked awake the next morning, long after Knut had hurried himself off to class. Before leaving, Caleb never failed to stand in the doorway between the kitchen and living room and ask me what my plan was for that day.

When we were playing in bands and traveling around together, Caleb was always wild-eyed and loose. He was tall and wiry and seemed to fall instead of move. He lunged when he walked and when he played the drums his arms carried themselves with their own momentum like he was a machine that had been cranked up and let go. Now though, it seemed that he had been wound up and simply put away. Everything about him was tight and controlled. I watched as he poured himself coffee and opened the refrigerator. It almost looked like it hurt him to move. It was like a big elastic band had been wrapped around his waist and connected to his head, and it was ready to snap at any moment. I didn't want to be the one that snapped it.

That morning, when he asked me what my plan was, I was thankful to finally have an answer for him.

"Caleb, tell Knut that I'm going to be out of his hair tomorrow," I said.

His eyes grew large and for the first time since I had been in town, I saw him smile.

"Oh, man we're going to miss you," he said, lying. "Did you get a place or what?"

"Better," I said. "I found a van."

⟵〰〰〰

I found the van on Craigslist while using one of the computers at the Mission branch of the library. It was a green Chevy Astro with no windows or seats in the back. It was almost my civic duty to buy it since it would prevent someone else from buying it, who would surely use it as a murder van. Its most enticing selling point was the fact that it was only a hundred and fifty dollars. I could almost smell it just from the pictures and it didn't go in reverse but it started up and could drive a little bit, which was perfectly fine with me. I only had to move it from parking space to parking space since I was going to be living in it. I had already gone by the carpet wholesale place and picked up some samples out of the dumpster to line the back of it with. I could picture myself waking up every morning in a different spot, rent-free but still staying out of the rain. The current owner was a man named Diego and I had spent all day at the library the day before emailing back and forth with him. He was happy to be rid of the stinking thing and we arranged for me to pick it up at his house in Merced Heights, a neighborhood way on the outskirts of town, close to Daly City.

"I'm picking it up tomorrow morning," I said to Caleb, who was trying so hard to contain his excitement that I almost wanted to give him permission to go ahead and celebrate.

Instead, I just let him stand there, grinning and nodding, suddenly relaxed.

I got up the next morning at five. Diego had to meet me before he went to work and it was going to take about an hour and a half to get all the way to the edge of the city that early. I got up with the slow, sickly feeling that comes with being awake before anyone else, even Knut. I could hear Caleb snoring in his room. He had not slept that sound since I had been staying there. I often heard him get up in the middle of the night and mutter to himself or pace, but that night he hadn't stirred and was sleeping the sleep of the just. When I turned on the lights in the kitchen, the windows were suddenly giant black mirrors, and I studied my face for a while. I was sunburned and peeling from spending so much time in the park drinking Ancient Age and napping or reading a book from the thrift store. Whatever kept me away from

Caleb's prying eyes and nervous, jerking movements. I got dressed and thought about how life was going to be after that morning. It was possible that whatever was wrong with the van that made it so cheap could be fixed. I could always go to the library and research auto repair. I could take it on the road. Get a cheap guitar and go on a permanent tour. Me and my green Chevy Astro van. I started to think about nicknames for it. The Green Monster. The Green Machine. I was just spitballing, though. I would have to spend some time with it before I could come up with a good one. There was no way I could do that before I lived in it for a while.

I made sure that I had everything in my backpack and took an inventory. It didn't take long. I had the foresight to go to the laundromat, so everything was at least clean. I folded the brown army blanket nicely and placed it on top of the couch. I took one last look at the table with the photographs on it and tried in vain one more time to understand what he was doing with them or what order they were arranged in. I picked up the "Dad" Polaroid. The man in the picture was lying in a hospital bed with the same gray complexion of the bodies I had swung the incense burner over so many years ago. For a moment, I felt compelled to put it in my pocket but I set it back down exactly where it was and put the spare key on top of it. I briefly considered writing a note thanking Caleb and Knut, but I knew that my leaving was thanks enough. I looked through the holes in the bottoms of my shoes before putting them on, swung the backpack onto my shoulders, and turned off the kitchen light before heading out the door, locking it behind me.

Outside, there was an early morning mist left over from overnight rain. Cars drove by and made a whispering sound on the asphalt, which was shiny and black in the street lights, just like the kitchen windows. The rain fell and soaked into the streets, dredging up the dirt and grease that had penetrated the concrete, making everything slippery. My backpack was light on my back and I put my hood up and my hands in my pockets, walking carefully and trying not to slip in the filth. The bus stop at 16th and Mission was bustling, even at five-thirty in the morning. Some people were still out and about from the night before, stumbling and grabbing at each other as they teetered into the street, but others were heading to work. I tried to hide my slightly trembling hands from them. I would have to drive the van somewhere to park it after the purchase and the last thing I needed was a DUI. So there I was, awake and sober before the sun was even up. I almost felt like a productive member of society until I remembered that I was going to live in a van.

I got on the bus when it pulled up and sat in the back, looking out the window and watching the sun come up as I got tossed around on the hard plastic seat every time the driver hit a bump or made a turn.

Caleb's happy face from the day before bobbed around in my mind. He was afraid of me now. I was the ghost of his younger self, tossed away and left to crash around in the waves before finally showing up soaked and gaunt at his doorstep, asking to sleep on his couch. I wasn't an old friend; I was a terrible vision of how he could have ended up if he hadn't gotten his act together. I didn't blame him for being frightened. We were on different roads now.

The second bus I had to take was packed, and it rumbled up and down the hills and winding roads, throwing my stomach around as I braced myself, trying not to lean on anyone too much. I was sweating now. The bus made a sharp turn and the woman next to me scowled as I tried to lean with it and give my stomach a break from all the movement. She elbowed me hard and scooted as far over on the seat as she could. She hated me so much, so quickly, that it made my face hot with embarrassment. I reached up without looking and pulled the "Stop Request" cord. I had time. I would walk the rest of the way.

Junipero Serra Boulevard stretched out in the sun when I got off. I had to squint to keep my eyes from stinging with sweat as the bus rolled on without me. Everywhere, people power-walked around and crossed the busy street. This was much different from the chaos of The Mission, however. This was organized. It's proven that the better your living conditions are, the longer you live, and if you're going to live longer, you'd better be nice to your neighbors. I started down the street, feeling small and walking on the long stretch of highway that chokes itself once it gets into the city. Car horns blared and I moved along the sidewalk, glad to be a part of something that would take me somewhere.

Diego lived at the top of a hill off Junipero Serra that seemed to go on for at least another mile. I sighed and started up it, already drenched in sweat and with my hands still trembling. I coughed my way up to about the halfway point, where a few suburban-style houses were nestled against the hill. There, perched on top of two trash cans that hadn't yet been picked up at that early hour, were two gigantic ravens. Their size struck me. They looked real, but not quite. One of them was digging through the garbage while the other one squawked at it. It picked up tin cans with its beak and tossed them to the ground, angry when they were empty. The sound of the cans echoed out off the hill and down the street and one of them rolled into the gutter. The bird that had been squawking quickly spread its wings and started screeching. The other one lifted its head out of the trash can and was holding half of a sandwich in its mouth. It also spread its wings, both of them huge and terrifying. It felt like I was watching something that I shouldn't be seeing. Something the animals did in secret. The loud raven started pecking at the sandwich in the other one's mouth and they both toppled off the trashcans and rolled on the ground. The sandwich dropped too, so I didn't know which bird was which anymore, but they fought hard, pecking and kicking until one of them got to it and flew off. The loser went back to digging through the trash. Picking up empty tin cans and throwing them on the ground, where they would be picked up later by a furious homeowner. I wiped the sweat out of my eyes and continued up the hill, trying to be quiet so the ravens wouldn't know I had seen the entire thing.

Diego's house was just like the ones the birds were vandalizing further down the hill. The front porch stuck out onto the road and there was a small driveway with a new black sedan parked in it. I had pictured myself cresting the hill and slowly catching a glimpse of The Green Ghost, or The Green Goblin, whatever my new home was going to be called, sitting there waiting for me patiently, but it was nowhere in sight. I checked the numbers on the house a few times to be sure it was the right one. It dawned on me that the van was probably parked somewhere else. There wasn't nearly enough room in the driveway and Diego obviously wanted to park his new car where he could see it, so he must have stashed the old van a few blocks away. Maybe he knew of some good parking spots where I wouldn't run into trouble. I sniffed my armpits and shrugged, then stepped up to the front porch to ring the bell, but before I got to it, the screen door flew open and a man with a tightly braided ponytail stepped out into the light.

"Matty?" he said, searching my face and shutting the screen door behind him.

"Yeah, yeah," I said, startled. "Diego, good to meet you."

He shook my hand and didn't let go.

"Totally, totally, listen man it's been stolen."

"What's swollen?" I asked, either mishearing him or not able to process it.

"No, no, it's gone. The van. Someone stole it."

Neither of us let go of the other one. We just stood there for a while shaking hands and he watched as my face fell and all of the consequences of what he said slowly dripped into my mind.

"Diego," I said, "Diego, what are you saying to me?"

"The van you were gonna buy. Someone took it."

"Diego...Diego."

I didn't know what else to say.

"Diego."

"Yeah man, I know, I'm sorry. I emailed you last night but I didn't hear back from you."

"I don't have a computer," I said, as I finally let go of his hand. "What happened?"

"This guy came over," he said, "and he wanted to test drive it. I told him it was sold but he offered me six hundred if he liked it."

"Oh, Diego," I said.

My face was now completely fallen and I could

feel furious blood rushing to my cheeks.

"I figured once he got in there and the smell hit him he'd change his mind," he said. "He told me he'd be right back but he never came back."

I stood on the front porch for a long time not saying anything. Feeling like crying. The Green Goblin disintegrating and slipping through my fingers.

"They stole my house," I said. "I was going to live in it."

Diego made a face.

"You would have changed your mind once the smell hit you."

←⌁⌁⌁

Walking back down the hill toward Junipero Serra, I picked up a stray can that one of the ravens, both of which were now long gone, had thrown on the ground. I started to go to the trash bin to throw it away, but as I got to it, I turned around and hurled the can off the hill and into the small parking lot below. I left the rest of the trash scattered on the road and headed toward the bottom.

There was a liquor store on the corner and I went inside and went to the back, picking up two 24-ounce cans of Olde English malt liquor and bringing them to the counter.

"And two small brown bags, please," I said, not

making eye contact with the man behind the counter.

I knew how this went. His judgment barely registered. I gave him the money, keeping my hands as steady as possible, and stepped out onto Junipero Serra. I cracked open the first can, concealed by one of the brown bags, and gulped down the first sip. It was golden. People stepped around me on the sidewalk and I stared straight ahead as I walked, chugging the beer while keeping one eye on where I was going. I finished the first can by the time I got to the bus stop and opened up the second one while I sat and waited under the glass canopy. Caleb's face again appeared in my mind, but it was the reverse of earlier on the bus. I watched it as it fell in disbelief. I would tell him the story, but he would already know the ending before I even got to it. I would have to watch him mull it over and I would have to watch him open his door to me, and then I would have to watch him get the brown army blanket out of the closet even though he didn't want to.

I could see the bus a few blocks down so I lifted the can of Olde English to my lips and tipped my head back as far as it would go, letting some of the beer run down the side of my face and onto my shirt. It was starting to get hot out. I tilted the can into my mouth one more time and the last bit caught in my throat, going down the wrong tube. I coughed and sputtered, before turning and seeing that a young woman had joined me in waiting at the stop and was staring at me in disgust. She must have been standing there for a while. I set the empty can on top of the trash can for someone to grab and make their nickel, and when the bus pulled up, I got on first so she wouldn't have to worry that I was going to sit next to her.

It was only about eight-thirty in the morning when I got back to Caleb's place. I was tipsy and loose. It felt like I was walking through jelly as I paced in front of the house, trying to gather up the courage to ring the doorbell. He didn't leave until nine so I knew he was there. He would be making his coffee and probably looking over to the empty couch every so often and smiling to himself. When I finally did ring it, and he answered, I didn't even give him a chance to say anything. I avoided looking at him as I told the entire story of the morning, even the part about the ravens. As I talked, I moved my arms and acted things out, thinking that if I just kept going I wouldn't ever have to look at his face and he wouldn't have to say anything. I also told him the story of what had happened at Lola's apartment. When I had first shown up there a couple of weeks prior, I just told him that she broke up with me. I glossed over some of the more disgusting details, knowing they weren't going to do me any favors. As I talked, I could see in my peripheral vision that he had closed the door behind him and sat down on the steps. He just nodded and stared off across the street as I slowly ran out of material to stall with and finished my story.

"...so I don't know. I don't know where I'm going to go."

For a second there was silence and I panicked. I almost brought up the shed again but knew that I had already cashed in that favor. Finally, Caleb turned and looked up at me and I gathered up the courage to look back.

"When my dad died, I went crazy," he said. "I needed help. I called you over and over again. I emailed you a bunch of times."

I remembered. It was two years ago. I didn't know how to respond to his first voicemail and spiraled, avoiding his calls and messages because I was ashamed of not being able to be there for him. I was always a mess.

"Hey, I'm sorry," I started.

"It's fine. You have problems of your own," he said, cutting me off. "And he was not a nice guy. Before he died he told me that I was killing him faster than the cancer."

I sat down on the steps with him.

"We're both nice guys, Matty," he said, "but you can't bargain your way through life just by being a nice guy. Especially when you can't hold up your end of the bargain."

His face didn't look at all like I thought it would. It was a new one. It was just tired.

"I can let you stay another two weeks," he said, getting up. "Knut is going to freak out."

I watched him open the door for me. Then I watched him go in the closet and get down the brown army blanket, even though he didn't want to. He left for work and I got under the blanket and closed my eyes, dreading the afternoon hangover I would have when I woke up. The next morning, I would have to find a job.

Chapter Three

When I tried to hand the two dollar bills to the girl behind the counter at Muddy Waters, she just stared at them. I inched them further toward her, but her hands stayed at her sides. There was no one else in the coffee shop, seeing as they had just opened, and I looked around to make sure there wasn't someone secretly robbing the place. She stayed firm, and eventually, I set the money down on the counter. She used the tip of her index finger to flick it into the cash drawer. She picked up my fifty cents of change and gave me a look that pleaded with me not to make her touch my hand.

"Keep the change," I said.

I had gotten up before Caleb and Knut to wait for the thrift stores on Mission to open. If I was going to get a job, I would need some new clothes. My jeans had big holes in the knees now and I was certain I was going to get jungle rot in my feet from the holes in my shoes and only having five pairs of socks. Luckily, I had at least gotten a haircut at a Super Cuts downtown right before Lola kicked me out. When it was done, the barber started shaking his head and apologizing, having given me a high and tight haircut that would have been given in an eighteenth-century insane asylum and was only just now, weeks later, starting to look normal. Some new-to-me clothes were going to set me right and maybe at least make me look like I was allowed to be walking the streets on my own.

I sat down and looked out the window at 16th and Mission, which was just starting to get lit up from the blue glow of the sun coming in from the East Bay. When the girl behind the counter wasn't looking, I poured a little bit of Ancient Age from my backpack into the coffee and celebrated the fact that I was taking this step. Even if I only found a dishwashing job, I didn't have to do it forever. I could be a line cook or even a chef if I could pull things together a little bit. Stay in one spot for a while. Keep my head down. I sipped the bourbon coffee and watched as the intersection slowly filled up with people, who were replaced with new people, who were then replaced with new people. All of them were working their way up, or spiraling down. I was interested in finding out which one I was doing.

I opened the lid of my cup and started to unscrew the cap of the Ancient Age to pour some more in when I heard the girl behind the counter's voice cut through the quiet behind me.

"Hey, you can't do that in here! Get out of here!"

I tossed the bottle in my bag, got up, and left without turning around or saying anything. I made a note to come back later in my new clothes and ask if they were hiring.

By the time Thrift Town opened, I had been walking around and drinking bourbon coffee for an hour and my head was being pulled in opposite directions. Possibility pulsed in the store's violent fluorescent light as I walked in. There were suits and ties as well as button-down shirts lined up behind a rack of undergarments; a section that had never made any sense to me. I had to think that even in my darkest hour, I would rather wear no underwear at all than someone else's. As I looked through the racks of Sans-A-Belt slacks and short-sleeved, button-up mustard shirts, a woman in a turquoise apron walked up to me.

"Are you finding everything okay?"

She was in her fifties and she said it in a bored

but genuinely curious way and the bourbon and coffee were making me talkative and anxious to connect.

"Yes, thank you," I said. "I have a job interview so I need some new clothes."

"Oh," she said, "where at?"

"Well, I will. I'll have a couple soon."

"I'm sure you will," she said.

She seemed to mean it, but something about the way she said it made me want to prove it to her.

"I will," I said, defensively. "I can find a job quick. I once got fired from a restaurant and just walked across the street to another restaurant and got a job there."

"Why did you get fired from the first restaurant?" she asked.

"For drinking at the second one during a slow day," I said. "Then, when it was slow at the second one, I went back to the first one and drank there."

The story had always seemed funny to me, but this morning, the look on her face told me that it had failed to find its audience and instead came off as sad. She sniffed the air much like Lola had and I could tell that the coffee had not fully covered up the smell of the bourbon. She looked at the shirt I was holding.

"I like this one better," she said, and she handed me a blue shirt.

Then she reached into her pocket and pulled something out, handed it to me, and walked away. It was a small comic book with the words "This Was

Your Life" printed on the front and a story inside about an alcoholic businessman who dies and is shown all his sins. It was part of a series I had seen at school and church growing up and the sight of it made me uncomfortably nostalgic and angry. I quickly gathered up the clothes I wanted to try on and asked the man at the counter for a key to the dressing room. When he eyed me up and down and didn't answer right away, I put the comic book on the counter and placed my right hand on it.

"I swear to God I won't steal anything," I said.

The dressing room was a small, partitioned box next to the jewelry case with a door that didn't go all the way to the ground, and I could hear people talking and shuffling outside. It smelled like someone had peed in there. Not necessarily that day, but recently, and I understood why he had been so reluctant to give me the key. Taking my clothes off with so little privacy proved difficult. At one point, someone's foot appeared under the door as they browsed the costume jewelry in the big locked case, and I froze, feeling exposed and vulnerable. The wall had a big mirror hung on it that was too close, and I glanced up, disappointed in what I saw. I was sweating and red in the face as I tried to pull the pants up and over my waist. My gut flopped out over them, and I couldn't tuck it in enough to snap the button. I realized that I hadn't looked at myself in the mirror in a long time. At Caleb's house, I would rush past it to pee, and when

I was sober enough to brush my teeth I did it in the kitchen, long after everyone else had gone to bed. If I had to walk past a reflective surface, I would push my chin out and forward and lift my eyebrows, trying to hide the bloat that had settled in my cheeks and under my eyes. I had always assumed that living on the margins of society would at least give me a svelte, chic look, but instead, I was carrying water weight from salty top ramen and thousands of extra calories in syrupy malt liquor and cheap bourbon. It had not been good to me. I started getting gray hairs in high school, but now they were everywhere, and the white flecks were poking out underneath at the roots, threatening a complete takeover very soon. I tried on another pair of pants, and then another, and all of them stretched and strained at my stomach, as I sweated harder and harder trying to snap them closed. Someone banged on the door.

"Hey there's people waiting out here," someone yelled.

I didn't say anything back, but I rushed to try on the shirt that the Christian lady picked out for me. Before even putting the second arm in, I could tell I was too fat for it as well. Despair rained on me as there was another bang on the door.

"Yeah just a second, Christ," I screamed.

I struggled to put my own pants back on, which I could now see were stretched at the waist and barely holding on at the little metal clasp. When I threw the door open, I was drenched in perspiration and breathing heavily with wild eyes. The two people waiting, an elderly lady and a middle-aged man, who I assumed was the one who yelled, jumped back with surprise and fear on their faces.

"I'm not the one who peed in there," I said.

They both looked to the man behind the jewelry case and he nodded.

"It's true," he said.

I went back to the racks to put the clothes away, making a mental note that I was at least one size bigger now and I got deeply depressed. I considered buying a bad sci-fi book from upstairs for a quarter and just going to the park and drinking beer for the rest of the afternoon. I was flustered and the clothes I was putting back on the rack were damp with the bourbon seeping out of my filthy pores.

⟵〰〰〰

I tried to remember the last job interview that I had gone on. It was at least six months ago. I had answered an ad on Craigslist for a maintenance worker at the Kingswood retirement home in the Fremont neighborhood of Seattle and they wrote me back right away. An hour and two buses later, I found myself sitting in a plywood-paneled office attached to a garage housing two ride-on lawnmowers and various other lawn care equipment. The man sitting at the desk across from me had introduced himself when I got there but I immediately forgot his name and was now too terrified to ask.

"You're a pretty big guy," he said. "How tall are you?"

"Six-foot-five," I said.

"Nice, that's gonna come in handy, how are you with ladders?"

I didn't know if he meant climbing them or carrying them or maybe building them.

"I think good."

"Great, come with me."

I followed him out to the garage and he handed me a hazmat suit with a full head covering and a clear plastic window to see out of, then we got in his truck. We drove out to a hillside on the far end of the property and he stopped. He pointed at the hill from the driver's seat.

"See that hillside there?" he said.

"Yep."

"That's all poison oak. I need you to clear it today. Just pull it up and put it in a few big piles and I'll come pick them up at the end of the day."

"Sure thing," I said. "How much of it?"

He turned to me and laughed.

"All of it. Get out."

He drove away as I put on the hazmat suit and got to work. After about five minutes, I was starting to get itchy and the poison oak had already made its way to the inside of the head cover. I tried clawing at my face with gloved hands but pressing on the clear plastic just pushed the poison oils into my eyes. I trudged down the hill and walked back to the office.

He was still sitting at the desk when I got there but he wasn't really doing anything. It was like he was waiting for me.

"Do you need something?"

I set the hazmat suit in front of him.

"Sorry, I can't do this."

"Oh, the big man can't handle it?"

"I guess not," I said, and I reached out to shake his hand because it seemed like the thing to do. "Thanks for the chance, though."

He looked at my hand like he could smell it and crossed his arms over his chest.

"No thanks, big man."

↞∿∿

I shook my head and tried to chase away the humiliating, awkward memory as I put the wet clothes back on the rack at Thrift Town. I didn't know where I was going to find the energy to put myself through another string of demeaning interviews just to have some poor asshole agree to yell at me every day for a couple of weeks until I quit and ghosted. At that point in my life, I had worked at over thirty jobs, a few for a year or so, but most of them for less than a month. It was the same every time. My alarm would go off and I would lie there, unable to get up and go through another day of washing dishes, or laying carpet, or cleaning up construction sites. Then I would turn off my cell phone for a couple of days and erase all the angry voicemails without listening to them. I knew that no matter what, I was just going to do the same thing again.

I put back the last pair of pants and was just about to leave when I saw the shoes and stopped short. They were a beautiful pair of low-top Doc Martens that looked to be almost brand new. They could work for a job interview and last a long time as day-to-day shoes to replace my torn Vans. They were only half a size too big for me, which after a morning of clothes being disappointingly small I was thrilled about, and they were only ten dollars. I was able to talk the Jesus lady down to six plus a two-dollar donation to her church and, after adding a tattered copy of a Timothy Zahn Star Wars novel for a quarter, I left happy that at least something had been accomplished for the day. I put them on right on the sidewalk outside and carried my Vans under my arm. I would wait until they were completely destroyed to get rid of them. I was in no position to be throwing away shoes.

The Doc Martens were already broken in and

comfortable, and as I walked down Valencia, I realized that I was coming up on Muddy Waters. Without thinking, I walked in. The same girl was behind the counter changing music on an iPod and when she saw me, her eyes got wide and furious. I put my hands up and slowly placed a five-dollar bill out of the change from my new shoes in the tip jar by the register.

"I should have tipped you more this morning."

I looked her in the eyes.

"I'm sorry," I said. "It's been a rough... It won't happen again."

She kept her frown but relaxed her shoulders.

"It's cool," she said, and she went back to the iPod and I left.

I went back to Caleb and Knut's and stashed the Docs under the couch quickly, hurrying to get back out of the house in case one of them decided to come home for lunch. I put my Vans back on and left to go to the park and read. I was exhausted.

⟵⋀⋀⋀⋁

When I opened the door to the house late that night, I was fighting a throbbing in my head from the excitement of the morning and half a bottle of Ancient Age from the afternoon. As soon as I closed the door behind me and the cold air from outside was shut out, I was hit with the smell. That was the first thing. It was rotten and dead, like old garbage but more human. It stuck to the inside of my nose. Inescapable. The second thing was the noise. It was a screeching, lacerated voice that I had never heard before, screaming. Then I heard the spraying and stomping around. The third thing as I came down the hallway and rounded into the kitchen was the sight of Caleb and Knut, each with two cans of Lysol bathroom spray in their hands, spraying it into the air and squinting against the thick mist that formed and almost blocked out the light. I was startled by the sight of Knut in stasis, holding still long enough for me to get a good look at him. He was normally rushing in and out of his bedroom and I had never noticed how muscular he was. I could see his arms now and they were vascular and taught, ready to strike. His veins bulged out of his skin and I saw one in his neck pulsing with the rhythm of the Lysol spray. I held my nose, shocked and still half-drunk, getting even more light-headed as the kitchen filled with lemon-scented particles, which got in my mouth and coated my throat. I could see that Knut was the one doing the screaming, but I couldn't process it, and couldn't make out any of the words. I had never seen him move his arms quickly or even talk, let alone yell. When he saw me, he dropped an empty can of Lysol and crooked his finger at me, contorting his face and letting his voice crack.

"You," he said, "get out."

"Caleb," I said, coughing from the smell which wasn't being covered up by the spray at all. "What is that? What's happening?"

"The shoes. The god mother fuck fucking shoes." Knut croaked, running out of breath at the end.

Caleb pulled a broomstick from behind the stove, then went out onto the porch and came back with the Doc Martens hanging from it, tied together by the laces.

"Oh get them the fucking fuck out of here," Knut said, retreating to the living room as if he could get away.

I pulled them off the broomstick and could immediately tell that they were the source of the smell. Whoever had owned them before must have had a serious medical problem with a foot fungus or a completely dead toe. It was apparently dormant in the store but was activated by my wearing them home. I wretched and held them at arm's length.

"It's going to be in fucking everything. We'll never get rid of it," Knut said from the couch, covering his eyes and nose. He quickly sat up and looked at me.

"Well, what are you waiting for? Get the fuck out."

I looked to Caleb, who immediately broke eye contact and went into the living room, coming out with my backpack and handing it to me.

"Sorry, Matty."

I could still hear Knut screaming in the living room as Caleb ushered me down the hall. The smell from the shoes seemed to have a weight to it. It was like they were glowing with the odor and I held them as far away from my face as possible. At the door, he stopped me.

"Wait one second," he said.

He went back down the hall and I heard more screaming and arguing in the living room. The cloud of spray was wafting out of the kitchen doorway, and after a minute or so, Caleb burst through it, backlit by the living room light and rolling up the brown army blanket in his hands. Knut screamed at him down the hall.

"Don't give him shit."

He handed it to me and opened the door. I put the roll in my backpack and the zippers strained, trying to keep the top flap closed.

"Call me. Check in," he said, and then I was out on the porch, Knut's screaming muffled almost to silence by the closing of the front door and completely gone by the time the gate crashed closed behind me and I was out on the street.

I held the Doc Martens far out ahead of me. Even outside, their stench was thick when it hit my nose. People approaching me in the opposite direction on the sidewalk looked curious at first when they saw what I was holding and would give me perplexed looks until they got within two or three feet. Then I watched the connections being made in their brain as they smelled why I was holding them like that. I didn't know where to go but I was walking quickly and weaving in and out of people like the shoes were on fire. After a block or so, I realized which way I was heading. I shoved through a crowd of people waiting at the corner and crossed against the light, holding the shoes out, barely touching them at the laces, and finally stopped in front of the neon sign of Thrift Town. They were closed, of course, since it was well past ten o'clock, but I searched their storefront for any kind of night mailbox or package delivery. I wanted to throw the reeking things back in there along with the Jesus comic book and let both of them fill the place with their horridness for the crew that opened the next morning. I walked all around the outside of the store, which took up an entire city block, and finding no such entry, I gave up and walked off through The Mission. It wasn't their fault. It wasn't the Jesus lady's fault. It wasn't Caleb or Knut's fault. It wasn't even the previous owner of the shoes' fault, though I did hope they got whatever professional help they needed to get rid of what was clearly a terrible affliction. It was just bad luck, and I was certain that there was more on the way.

I wandered through the neighborhood for a little while, whipping the shoes at fences and sides of buildings as I walked. People crossed the street to get away from the smell and I was glad for it. I found myself walking toward Bernal Hill, a small mountain of undeveloped walking trails and park land on the south end of The Mission that loomed high in the night sky, keeping watch and set black against the glow from the street lights behind it. I grabbed a few free newspapers from a box on the way and hopped the yellow traffic gate at the bottom of the hill, then started stomping upwards, trying to breathe heavily through my mouth so I couldn't smell the shoes. I could still taste them, though. The smell laid on my tongue even with the misty air washing over it. At the park on top of the hill, I found a big cast iron barbeque grill cemented into the ground and threw the Doc Martens in along with the free newspapers. This was the only way to truly be rid of them. I lit the papers with some matches from the liquor store and they quickly burned into the leather of the shoes. They didn't catch on fire so much as they melted, but they did it steadily, and I took a seat on a picnic table and watched as the noxious, disgusting smoke wafted out over the city.

There were no more places to go. The end of the road had come upon me much faster than I imagined it would. I figured I could run from myself for a few more years, but it appeared that I had finally caught up with me in San Francisco, and I was exhausted and barely functioning at the top of a mountain. It was all downhill from there. For a minute that morning, everything had seemed so possible, but now the morning felt like a dream and that mood seemed ridiculous. This made more sense. The man walking around with the sun shining in his face and making amends with people at the coffee shop may have been a brief glimpse at my best self but that wasn't who I was on the hill. Burning rotten leather in a park where I was going to be sleeping was feeling more and more second nature and normal to me by the minute and the speed of the transformation frightened me. The Doc Martens melted into a gooey black glob that hung onto its smell until the very last moment but finally gave it up when the soles curled and the last bit of sickening smoke puffed out and dissipated. I pulled the army blanket out of my backpack and got under the picnic table. With my hood pulled over my head, I rolled up in the blanket and fell asleep, the smell of the shoes still clinging to the inside of my nostrils.

Chapter Four

Some of the afternoons after I was kicked out of Caleb and Knut's house wore on slowly and seemed to fade directly into the next morning. Other times, it would feel like it was night for days and days, and I couldn't remember the last time I had seen the sun. I would go to Muddy Waters now and then to charge my phone, but after the second or third time of turning it on after several days and seeing no messages, I let it stay dead. Without the phone, I had no way of telling time and everything stretched into one long day, or week, or month. I would leave The Mission and walk up to Noe Valley to sleep on the traffic island. It was always just how I left it, and while I considered finding some cardboard to lay on the ground and leave for the future, that seemed like a step toward making a home there, and I wasn't quite ready for that.

I also had a spot that I had staked out while I was staying at Caleb and Knut's house. I was always waiting for the other shoe to drop there, which it had, in the form of some reeking Doc Martens, so I kept an eye out for good places to hide and sleep should that situation inevitably arise. There was a little wooden staircase on the side of the house that led up to the laundry room with a perfect square of concrete underneath. Hidden from the view of the street and the house itself, it was butted up against the wall where the dryer vented, and what it spat out in moisture, it made up for in warmth. In the morning, there would be a big wet spot underneath me and the brown army blanket would be soaked and heavy, but I figured that I was less likely to get shot if I were to be discovered there rather than under some stairs at a stranger's house. Knut was insane and would probably scream at me again, but I would be able to leave without a bullet in my head.

I split my sleeping time between those two places and my waking time sitting in the park and reading. I bought loaves of white bread and little jars of peanut butter from the same liquor store and the owner, Ray, would always give me a plastic knife when I bought them together.

"For protection," he would say, winking.

I watched people in the park drink bottles of champagne and then go back to their apartments. The crowd would thin and dissipate and I would find myself alone on the grassy hillside sitting among the trash as the fog and cold started to roll in and blanket the neighborhood. That's how I knew that it was time for me to move along to one of my hidden spots in the shadows of the city.

After what I figured to be a couple of weeks, I started to long for a place where I could consistently go and be out of the sun. The summer was in full bloom, and I was starting to feel like a baked ham, walking aimlessly around The Mission for hours with the hot light reflecting off the beige and yellow stucco of the buildings, or falling asleep full of warm malt liquor under the open sky of the park. My eyelashes were burnt and crisp, and they stuck together when I blinked. There was no plan. This was what I was doing until something else came along or the little bit of money I had ran out. That day was coming quicker and quicker. I only drank Ancient Age or the cheapest malt liquor I could find and lived off peanut butter sandwiches, but I was still down to eighty-four dollars. Once that was down to zero, I didn't really know what was going to happen. Maybe I would just walk into the ocean.

Now and then I would get a text from Caleb letting me know if he had come home from work for his lunch break. If my phone happened to be charged, and I caught it in time, I would meet him there, and with Knut gone, I could come in and take a shower. The showers were lifesavers and quickly became the only thing I looked forward to in my days spent wandering and frying in the sun, killing time. The meetings between Caleb and I were often quick and filled with anxiety for him and they broke my heart. I scared him before, but now I just made him sad and he always looked like he wanted to tell me something but then remembered that he couldn't. I would try to take the fastest shower I could and get out quickly so he could get back to work, making sure to leave the bathroom window open to let the vapor escape so Knut wouldn't get suspicious.

One day, as I was leaving freshly showered and Caleb was going back to work, we started to part ways on the sidewalk and I turned to him.

"Hey, you don't have to text me anymore, it's okay I'll figure out a shower."

"Oh," he said. "Okay, cool."

I hugged him.

"Thanks, buddy."

Then we went opposite directions on the sidewalk, and I had to figure out a new place to shower. I just couldn't do it to him anymore. I thought back to us living in the horrible, dilapidated shed together listening to the battery-powered radio or eating peanut butter sandwiches and laughing by the light of the poisonous kerosene lantern. We weren't ever going back to that. I wasn't even serving as a grim reminder of how things could have been for him anymore. My life was in way more of a shambles than he would have ever let his get.

I spent more and more time at the library. I started going to the Mission branch at first but it felt too homey and clean for me to dirty up its books with sticky malt liquor and the filth under my fingernails. Everything was earth-toned and padded and I always felt horribly out of place there. The Main Branch downtown, though, was a different story altogether. Located right on the edge of The Tenderloin, a neighborhood thick with death and hopelessness and a rare, deep humanity, The Main Branch was a sweeping, operatic building that seemed to sparkle like it was in a vintage ad for the city of the future. The sound of footsteps inside echoed and clacked against the hard, white surfaces, and the whole place looked like it could be hosed down like the back room of a butcher shop. It was probably for the best because it was a popular hangout and bathing place for people who were so much worse off than I was. It made me feel worse for Caleb because I didn't even know these people and seeing how far someone could fall terrified me. There was almost always a smell of stale booze and sickly dried cigarette butts, and I loved it. It was air-conditioned and dark, and if I could get a chair, I could sit there all day reading old collections of Peanuts comics and sneaking swigs from a plastic bottle in my backpack.

At night, when it was getting near closing time, a big electronic voice would shatter the quiet and announce that the library was closing in ten minutes. The wooden chairs at the tables would squeak, and the high-backed plastic ones would scrape along the floor as dozens of sad old men and strung-out young women with pet mice in their pockets packed up whatever they had and started to head out to wherever they were going. I would get up too, my feet aching and throbbing as soon as I put any weight on them. I had not replaced the Doc Martens that had ultimately been my undoing, so I was still wearing the Vans, which had a hole on the left one where my toe stuck out, and another, much bigger hole worn in the bottom of the right one. All my socks now had holes in that exact spot as well and I felt nervous about walking around on the syringe-sprinkled sidewalks of The Tenderloin.

Everyone would file out from the top floors and down the stairs to the tiled lobby. Some would use the bathroom monitored by an angry security guard for one last indoor pee and the rest of us would mumble to ourselves and shuffle out the brass-handled doors into the arms of whatever was waiting for us out there. Almost everyone left the library empty-handed at the end of the night. To get a library card, you had to have an address. For the people who had friends and family who might let them use their mailbox, this wasn't a problem, but the ones who were out there on the edge alone had to do their reading during the day and dream about it at night. I wasn't exactly in either camp. My library card situation, like everything else in my life at that moment, was of a slightly tenuous nature and required a delicate balance.

Lola and I had been sitting on the small back porch of her apartment where the sun came streaming through the slats of the porch upstairs and dust sparkled in the bars of light. I had only lived with her for a week and her plants were already starting to die, but every evening when she came home from work we would sit out there and drink wine and she would try to tell me about her job and I would try to understand while I tried not to gulp at the small amount of pinot noir that she had poured into my glass. She had once asked me to get her a glass of wine and when I came back with a pint glass filled to the brim, she sighed.

"Only you would think that counted as a glass of wine."

That evening on the porch, I had been complaining to her that her bookshelves were lacking anything a dummy like me could understand.

"What do you keep all these chemistry textbooks for?"

"For reference," she said, blinking and looking at me perplexed. "You know, for my job?"

"Totally," I said, slurping at the wine in the bottom of my glass and crossing my eyes to look at it.

"Why don't you take my library card and go down there tomorrow? I think they have cheap photocopies, too. You could make a bunch of copies of your resume," she said.

"Totally, totally, sounds good."

The next day I went downtown and experienced The Main Branch for the first time. Lola was right, they did have cheap copies, and for ten cents I made a copy of her library card that I could use at the self-checkout machines. I didn't want to keep bothering her for it, and it might come in handy.

It did, in fact, come in handy, and a couple of months later, when the electronic voice would come over the loudspeaker and startle everybody in the silence, I could be a part of the group that got to leave with something to hold them over through the night of fractured sleep. I would scan the barcode on the fading piece of paper at the self-service kiosk and then tuck it carefully back into my wallet.

❮∿∿∿

The Tenderloin at night was a dark, twisting sea of dirt and noise. There were figures everywhere,

58

nodding out in the shadows or screaming and weeping up at the street lamps and the impossibly dirty windows up above. The brown brick apartment buildings in the neighborhood were thick with soot, and that included any windows or glass doors. During the day, I could only imagine what some of those apartments looked like on the inside. Sometimes, when one of the residents would lean out the window to pull in their laundry or vomit, I would try to get a peek in one from down on the street, but all I ever saw was a black hole and maybe a dead plant on the sill. At night, though, the windows were alive. You still couldn't see all the way inside, but if you looked up while walking on Turk and Hyde, there was no end to the drama. People fought and smoked crack in front of the windows, all operating under the assumption that they were upstairs and as long as no one looked up, they were completely hidden.

In the weeks that had unfolded since I saw Caleb last, I had hardly spoken to anyone with the exception of Ray at the liquor store or telling the occasional tweaker to get away from my sleeping spot. I had begun to retreat and spiral into my own little world and being able to bring some books back to be read by the light of Caleb and Knut's laundry room window or the streetlight right above the traffic island was a bright spot. While it was depressing and horrific to go to The Tenderloin and watch people rob each other and scream in each other's faces and live as brutally as they were forced to live, I had to admit that I found a small bit of comfort in the fact that I wasn't quite there yet. There was still quite a long way to fall and I could still turn things around. I had seventy-five dollars and my sleeping spots hadn't been discovered or destroyed yet, so I had a few things going for me. Many of the people who used the library during the day used it to sleep for as long as they could until a security guard caught them because the spots they had staked out for the nighttime so many years before had long been found or renovated or built over. In that way, I wasn't quite homeless yet, I just didn't have a home that was indoors. So each night I would squirrel away a book in my backpack and carefully carry it to one of my homes, where I would bundle up in my brown army blanket and squint to try to read in the soft yellow light, thankful for the few things I did have.

There was a definite hierarchy and a certain amount of etiquette that was required to get by when spending the day at The Main Branch. There was a time limit in the bathroom and it was heavily enforced by a security guard who was unlucky enough to have been scheduled for the post. They were always the cruelest and the most likely to kick you out for any perceived slight. I understood the reasoning for the enforcement but I once spilled bourbon all over myself while trying to pour some in my coffee in the privacy of the stall because the guard had decided my time was up and banged on the door, startling me. I couldn't imagine how hard it must be trying to shoot up or discreetly smoke a little bit of crack under such high-pressure conditions.

There was also the constant, divisive issue of seating. Sitting on the floor seems like a fine idea until you do it for six hours and chairs are a hot commodity. Elderly people and those with crutches or walkers got first dibs, but after that, it was the Wild West. Some of the seats were claimed in perpetuity; a fact I learned when I first started coming to The Main Branch and mistakenly sat in Wild Bill's favorite wooden chair on the third floor. I had just sat down when a man in a greasy brown coat with darting eyes got off the elevator. He walked up to me and exhaled, exasperated.

"You're in my chair," he said.

"They just opened," I said, "how can it be yours?"

He grabbed the back of it and tilted it forward, tipping me off and flipping it upside down. On the bottom of it, scratched in what was either red pen or blood, were the words "WILD BILL'S CHAIR." I took another look at him, confirmed that the name probably checked out, and went to find a spot on the floor.

The elevator was another point of contention and drama and if you had the appearance of being able-bodied enough to use the stairs, you were expected to. One day, though, my feet were just too battered and swollen to climb up to the third floor and I boarded the elevator along with a small group of seniors and dirty men with canes and walkers. The doors had barely shut when one of them began sniffing the air.

"Oh my god, what is that smell?" he said.

I sniffed too but didn't smell anything.

"It smells like B.O. in here," whined an old woman.

"Well, it's making me sick," said the first man.

I kept smelling to no avail, but as we passed the second floor on our way to the third, I noticed a man with stringy hair and crutches next to me motioning to the first man. He was nodding his head toward me and mouthing something. That was when it hit me. In this elevator, in the public library downtown, in one of the grimiest neighborhoods in the country, I was the one who smelled bad.

I tumbled out of the elevator on the third floor and tried to hide the fact that I was blushing. I kept going back to the way he said I was making him sick as I crossed the rows of tables and went straight to the stairs and through the lobby and out the door and onto the street.

"It's making me sick."

I started walking up Hyde Street back toward The Mission, smelling the armpits of my shirt but still not coming up with anything. The inside of my nose must have been worn down from smelling myself twenty-four hours a day. I had gotten extremely adept at avoiding catching a glimpse of my reflection on any surface since I was too scared of what I might see, but walking along the mirrored glass of an office building, I couldn't help myself. I stood in the middle of the sidewalk, staring. It seemed that my gray hairs had tripled and I was beet red from the sun. I looked like a moldy tomato wearing a faded shirt with a hole over the nipple.

I had quickly crossed over from simply being down on my luck to just being a regular old bum. As I thought it to myself, I realized that every single one of those people in the library had at one point had a moment just like this one. Every one of them had just hit a rough patch and every one of them had a first day of being on the other side of the threshold where I was standing, right there in the middle of Hyde Street with people trying not to touch me as they went around, angry. It was a secret moment that only those of us from the library knew and understood.

I kept walking down Hyde, then turned quickly onto Market, ignoring the dull, deep pain in my feet. I could feel The Tenderloin behind me. Long, dark hands slipped out from the shadows and tried to pull me back, but I kept walking quickly to the spot under the stairs at Caleb and Knut's house. I didn't have anything to read that night but I was just happy to get away. I may have been a bum, but I wanted to be a bum where the sun shined and there was grass to sleep on. Once you were in The Tenderloin, it was too late, and I wasn't ready to say that it was too late.

The electronic bell on the door rang when I stepped into Ray's store and the sunlight streamed in through the dusty windows above the shelves. It must have been a weekend because there was a line of young professionals buying champagne and orange juice to take to the park and leave behind when they were done. I got in line behind a young man in loafers and plaid shorts. He tried to look at me without turning around and I saw him sniff the air a couple of times. No one else came in after me and when I got up to the counter, it was just Ray and me in the store.

"Ray," I said, "how do I smell?"

He didn't even have to lean forward. In fact, he leaned back.

"Not great," he said.

"A pint of Ancient Age, please."

Outside on the sidewalk, I squinted into the sun and tried to ignore any stares I was getting as I cracked the plastic ring on the bottle and brought it to my lips. It was hard and sharp-tasting, and I fought past my throat's urge to reject it, swallowing about a third of the bottle in one gulp.

The last few weeks suddenly felt like a bad dream in another world. I felt foolish and panicked at the thought of having wasted so much time in the library, at giving up so quickly, at only having money going out and none coming in for so long. I stuck the bottle in my back pocket and took out my wallet. After the

Ancient Age, I was now down to sixty-two dollars. I groaned with dread out loud and pulled the bottle back out of my pocket and back up to my lips, bumping into a man on the sidewalk as I tilted my head back and finished the first half of it.

"Hey, come on," he said.

I spun around unsteadily to face him.

"Real nice," he said, gesturing to the bottle. "It's not even noon."

"I'm on vacation," I said. I had no idea why, and it surprised me coming out. It just seemed to be the only lie that might explain everything. He looked me up and down.

"For how long now?"

I turned back around and went to the park. Sitting on the hill, I finished off the rest of the bottle in less than a half-hour. I considered going back to Ray's to get another one but I didn't want to have to lie to him and say I had spilled the first one. He would see through that anyway. It was also getting harder and harder for me to sit up in the grass, so I assumed that walking would soon be out of the question. I watched as all the colors and figures in the park slowly started to blur together like a painting doused in turpentine and I passed out in the sun again, just like I had so many times before.

Chapter Five

The guy at Mission Pawn and Loan was starting to get pretty pissed off. His white ponytail and small, gold-rimmed glasses screamed aging hippie but he was definitely not chill or laid back and he wanted me out of the store. He peered over the spectacles at me while he helped other customers and shook his head every time I picked up one of the three cheap guitars that I had narrowed my search down to. I was on the last $55 of my roll and what hurt more than anything else was that on the wall behind the old hippie was the guitar I had sold to get the roll in the first place. It had a big "NOT FOR SALE" sign on it, but it was absolutely on the wall as a coming attraction. There couldn't have been more than a couple of weeks left on the pawn loan but I was too afraid to take the slip out of my wallet to check. The old hippie knew as well as I did that I was never getting it back, as was evidenced by the fact that I was there trying to buy another one for under fifty bucks. I had bought the guitar on the wall many years prior to that, after receiving a small inheritance from my grandfather, and it had been on tour with me dozens of times. I carried it with me on Greyhound buses and slept with it cradled in my arms in those bus stations. It tore my heart in half to see it up there, being primed to go home with someone else who would never know the pain and joy it had been through. I shook the thought away and went back to looking at the three options I had in front of me. If I thought about my old guitar anymore, I would start crying, and then the old hippie would definitely kick me out.

As it stood, I had no way of making any money and no hope of finding a way to make some. My shower schedule was inconsistent at best and my shirts and pants had so many holes they barely counted as clothes anymore. I was 100 percent unemployable. My only hope to make enough to eat was to busk playing music on the street. I was no stranger to this and had often busked when I was on tour and there was no show scheduled in order to eat or put more gas in the van when I had one. I figured that I could at least put food in my stomach that way and San Francisco was full of train stations and tourist areas where people would be quick to part with their spare change. It wasn't ideal, but if I could get a cheap guitar, I had a loud, clear voice, and could sing Hank Williams songs to entertain a few folks from the Midwest well enough that they might throw me a few quarters so I could buy some ramen noodles.

I had, at the very least, figured out the source of my uneasiness with my situation, aside from the obvious discomforts of poverty. The problem was that if I was living so close to the edge and just existing like that, I was a bum, but if I was playing music, I was at least giving something. I was giving out a part of myself that was good and had long been neglected with my old guitar held hostage and strung up like some red-light district window display. As long as I was playing music, the best part of me was still alive.

I remembered a conversation that Caleb and I had once when we were on tour as a two-piece band. We had pulled his beat-to-shit truck over at Whiskeytown Lake in Northern California on our way to play a show in Portland the next night and got an RV campsite, which ended up being just a parking space in an otherwise empty lot. We spread out our sleeping bags on the cement and cracked open tall cans while the summer stars turned above us. I was sure that I was the happiest I had ever been at that moment. I was doing the one thing that fed my heart and I had it all open in front of me, unattached to anything. We weren't getting paid. We saved up for months at our dishwashing jobs to be able to go on tour and if the job wouldn't give us the time off it was fine because we could just quit. There were always more dishwashing jobs and in the meantime, all I wanted to do was play music and drink warm beer with my best friend in places we had never been before.

"We should just do this," I said, opening another tall can. "Fuck work."

"You can do whatever you want," said Caleb, "as long as you're playing music."

"Yeah."

"No, I mean it," he said, sitting up and finishing his beer and throwing it into the empty parking lot with a clang. "You can do whatever the fuck you want as long as you keep playing music. Drink, do drugs, do heroin, who cares? As long as you're playing music it's worth it."

I thought about Caleb as I sat in the pawnshop. That version of him was long gone, and that specific memory had a jarring effect after spending so much time with the Caleb who was now living and stressing in San Francisco. Even though it had only been a few years, everything had turned upside down and it could only be righted by the one thing that I had ever really believed in.

The first of the three guitar options I had in front

of me was a big jumbo 12-string with a hole in the top near the bridge and rusted strings ready to cut into my fingers and add tetanus into the already toxic mixture in my blood. The second was a standard-issue nylon-string classical guitar that played well but just didn't have the volume that I knew I would need on the street with all the buses and screaming and the drunks joining in. The third was the one that intrigued me the most. It was small. Maybe even a little bit less than three-quarter scale, which is usually the size for kids. When I picked it up to play it, though, it was incredibly loud. It twanged and vibrated with the bass that came out and its small size made me think that it would shake apart at any moment. Its major selling point, though, was the fact that it came with a case. I tried to picture myself carrying around the big -string, holding onto the neck with it slung over my shoulder and the image brought up too much of the Great Depression hobo riding the rails for me to be comfortable with. Since I couldn't afford a case, it was going to have to be the tiny guitar, even though it looked comically small with me holding it and I worried that it would make me look even more insane. I brought it up to the old hippie at the counter, and he rolled his eyes.

"Are you all set?"

"Yeah, how much is that one gonna be," I said, pointing to my old guitar on the wall.

"A lot more than this one," he said.

He went to the cash register and started ringing up the tiny guitar. I looked at my old one on the wall with the sign stuck in the strings over the soundhole. I remembered sleeping on the gray and white tile of the Seattle bus station with my head resting on the case while that guitar was nestled safely inside. Every now and then I would open it up and smell the inside of the case. It had a familiar and cozy smell. I could imagine myself being in there, too, warm and safe like my guitar instead of on a tile bench in a bus station at three in the morning.

"Fifty-two ninety," the old hippie said, his hand already outstretched.

I gave him the entirety of my roll and he came back with the change. Three dollars and ten cents. That was all that was left. No more safety net. No more comfort.

I left with the tiny guitar zipped up into the soft backpack case, and didn't turn around to look at my old one strung up on the wall. I could only hope that someone else would open up the case when they bought it, and smell exactly what I had.

I started on my way to Haight Street as soon as I hit the sidewalk. It was a Tuesday afternoon, which I only knew because of the siren that howls every Tuesday at noon in San Francisco as a part of an air raid test. I had long given up on charging my cell phone and had taken to almost completely relying on the position of the sun for the time and the occurrence of the siren for the day of the week. It was all one big, half-drunk stretch. There was no point in keeping track of time when there was no end in sight.

I walked across the park, then climbed the hill that separated The Mission from Upper Haight, and was suddenly in the kaleidoscope of murals and overpriced psychedelia that makes up the Haight-Ashbury. Tourists in tie-dye shirts wandered down the sidewalks with ice cream from the multi-million dollar "hippie" ice cream shop on the corner, and I could almost smell their money. They wanted to get rid of it. They had brought it in order to spend it, and I would be more than happy to take it for a smile and a song. As I got settled in a spot in a small doorway, I unzipped the case and spread it out in front of me, tossing the two dollar bills and the dime in there as bait, hoping that no one would snag it as they walked by. I held the guitar in my arms since it was so small that I didn't need a strap to hold it up, and I began to play a song by The Grateful Dead. It was the only one by them I knew because I hated the Grateful Dead, but it seemed like an appropriate song and if it was going to go over well anywhere it would be here. I closed my eyes and began to play.

Set out running but I take my time, a friend of the devil is a friend of mine.

As I sang, I realized that it had been months since I had even listened to music let alone played it. Suddenly, my blood felt thick and rich and I could feel my heart start to beat and swell with rhythm again. I hadn't just missed music, I had been starved of it. In fact, I had not seen any beauty or any light in my life for what felt like a very long time, though I had no way of knowing how long for sure.

First one says she's got my child, but it don't look like me.

Without stopping, and without opening my eyes, I continued to sing, and tears started to stream down my cheeks. I had completely forgotten how it felt to be connected and present in the moment. For so long I had only wanted to escape, but while playing that song by a band I couldn't stand, I felt at home. When I opened my eyes, there was a smattering of ones and fives which had been dropped in the case and amounted to about twenty dollars. I called it a day and went to get drunk in the park and sing and play some more, this time just for me.

<hr>

The next couple of weeks were a blur of different sidewalks and street corners. I learned how to project my voice and to make the little guitar as loud as I possibly could. Musicians who walked past would often stop and give me a surprised look, always pointing at the little guitar as if to say, "There is no fucking way that sound is coming out of that toy guitar."

But it was. At night, I would hold on to it as I slept under the stairs and every now and then I would unzip the case and stick my nose in, happy to know that I could still hold on to something good. Haight Street was easily the biggest cash cow, but it was hard to find a good spot, and after getting shooed away more than a few times by the counterculture capitalists who owned the stores on the street, I decided not to go back. After that, I stuck to the BART stations. BART trains ran from the city to different parts of the East Bay and beyond, and its riders were generally local, well-off commuters. They were generous with their change and the people who worked in the stations usually didn't chase me off. The first time I headed down the steps of the 16th and Mission station with my tiny guitar case, I decided to ask the woman in the bullet-proof glass information booth if she wouldn't mind if I set up and played. She set down her book and pressed the button on the microphone.

"Are you good?"

I eyed her for a moment, having not anticipated the question.

"I'm very good."

She took her hand off the button and raised her eyebrows, then motioned out to the lobby of the station and folded her arms. I set up the open case with a few dollar bills worth of bait, then closed my eyes and began to play.

Hear that lonesome whippoorwill. He sounds too blue to fly.

I peeked one eye over to her and saw that she was still sitting with her arms crossed and looking at me. A man in a suit passed by and threw in a dollar.

The midnight train is whining low. I'm so lonesome I could cry.

I tried to put as much of a Hank Williams yodel into the vocal delivery as I could and another man in a suit threw in the change from buying his ticket.

When I was done, I let the last note echo out into the station and off the tile walls, then opened my eyes and looked over at the woman in the booth. She still had her arms crossed and when our eyes met, I gave her a shrug. She lifted her hand and held it flat in the air, then wiggled it back and forth to tell me that it was so-so. We laughed, and she went back to her book and left me alone.

For a couple more weeks, I sang and played at bus stops, train stations, the wharf, the park, wherever I thought there might be someone who would part with a buck or two and not yell at me for blocking their doorway. I didn't make much, but I also didn't need to buy that much, and I had gotten the roll back up to a respectable, if not slightly ominous, $333. One Saturday night, I was in The Mission, wandering Valencia and pushing past the crowds of drunk people accidentally burning each other with cigarettes out on the sidewalk. I normally avoided playing in the neighborhood since there were plenty of entertainment options, and for the most part, the weekend drunks had already spent their money and were only interested in asking to play my guitar, or yelling Freebird as they stumbled up to me. I always agreed, but not before reminding them that the song was 14 minutes long and contained many solos, all of which I would be performing through whistling, and that I expected them to watch the whole thing. Without fail, they would sway back and forth and tell me to shut the fuck up or just walk away. I never once had to play it. On that Saturday night, though, I set up on the steps of a bank on the corner of 20th and Valencia, took a swig from a small bottle of Ancient Age in my back pocket, and began to play. I hadn't gotten more than two chords in when I felt someone poking at my shoulder. It was dark, but I could see that there were two men standing on the steps with me. The one poking me was tall and spindly, with long, greasy blonde hair and a ripped-apart smile. The other was a short, stocky man who didn't talk but giggled at everything the first one did.

"Hey man," he said, "this is our corner."

He pointed to the violin case he was holding, and the silent one shook a small tambourine at me and giggled.

"I've never seen you guys here," I said.

"We've never seen you, either."

We stood there looking at each other before I finally spoke.

"Fine, that's cool, I'm gonna get out of here."

I put the guitar in the case and they didn't move. When I slung it over my shoulder, they didn't get out of my way. I pulled out the bottle of Ancient Age.

"You guys want a drink?"

The greasy one snatched the bottle out of my hand and took two big gulps, then handed it to the silent one, who finished it off and handed it back to me.

"Thanks," I said.

"I'm Fast Eddie," the greasy one said, then he pointed at the silent one. "He's from Schenectady."

"Cool," I said, trying to get around them and head up the street. "I'm just a bum but you guys are real hobos, that's awesome."

That was when Fast Eddie pulled out a knife.

There is a moment when someone pulls out a knife in the middle of a busy street and holds it to your stomach, where you think that there is no way this is going to fly. Surely, someone is going to walk by and see what's happening and they are going to stop it. They are going to know that this is not right, and they are going to help you. As I learned on that corner, though, they never show up, and even if they did, they would probably be too drunk to notice or they would think these people were just kidding around and then they would move on with their evening. I know this because that is exactly what happened with Fast Eddie and the silent man from Schenectady that night. The knife pressed up against my ribs and I watched as row after row of drunk tech workers and art students stumbled past. Some glanced over and possibly saw the flash of the steel in the streetlights, but most had their eyes forward, focused on whatever they had come out that night to get their hands on. Fast Eddie's eyes were intense and dark and locked into mine. His dreadful breath went up my nose and came out through my eyes as they watered and dripped onto the sidewalk.

"Fuck," I said. "What do you want?"

"You tell me," he said, exhaling his rot up my nose. "I'm the one with the knife."

The statement didn't make sense, but I knew what he meant, and he reached into my pocket and pulled out the roll.

"Come on, Eddie."

"Fast Eddie," he said, correcting me and putting the roll in his pocket. "You can keep your toy guitar."

He pushed me back and I tripped on the step behind me, falling on my ass and almost smashing the guitar which had once again become my only possession aside from my backpack full of reeking dirty clothes. Fast Eddie put the knife back in his pocket with my roll and went down the steps, vanishing into the flow of people on Valencia. The silent man from Schenectady shook the tambourine and giggled at me one more time, then followed Fast Eddie into the anonymous hoard walking down the sidewalk. A man in a shiny silk shirt and ironed black jeans came running up to me, his face determined and focused. I looked into his eyes and held out my hand, grateful that someone at least saw what happened.

"Hey, can you play Freebird!?"

⌁

I walked to the traffic island in Noe Valley. I didn't want to be anywhere near The Mission that night or maybe ever again. It was packed with people and every time someone bumped up against me or happened to get too close while I waited for a crosswalk light to change, I turned around with my fists clenched and teeth bared. I needed to get away before I killed someone in imagined self-defense, or got stabbed by another one of the Fast Eddies of the world.

As I crossed the boundaries of the neighborhoods, the crowds on the streets started to thin and I found that I could start to relax my shoulders and let my hands unroll from the white-knuckled fists they had been in since parting company with the murderous hobos. As soon as I was able to turn a corner and get onto an abandoned street, I started shaking. Tremors of fear and anxiety tore through me and I felt that even my chest, the very center and core of my body, was quaking and teetering on the edge of full collapse. The strings of the little guitar in the case on my back played an atonal song as they vibrated along with me. The only thing I could think of was to try to get as drunk as possible but quickly remembered that there was no way to do that. The roll was gone, and while Ray would probably stand me a pint of Ancient Age, he had been too kind already and that was just another step further down than I wanted to go just yet. I was going to actually have to feel this one. There was not going to be any escape.

I came up to the traffic island and went through my usual checks for syringes and broken glass. Finding none, I plopped down in the dirt, put my head in my hands, and started to cry. This was different from the hopeless feeling I was familiar with. This was a crushing weight that came with knowing that as long as I was trying to live outside the boundaries, there were going to be others who had their own rules as well, and they were always going to be better at it than me. I was a tourist in the underground and Fast Eddie was around every corner. I let the tears come and soon my face was slick with fear and years' worth of frightful hangovers and anxious nights as my sobs fell thick and heavy out on the street. I unzipped the little guitar from the case as I shook and wept, and the first thing that came to mind was a song that my mother used to sing to me when I was scared or sad as a kid, which was often. I took deep breaths and tried to steady my hands enough to form the simple chords. Through a wavering voice choked with tears, I sang.

You are my sunshine. My only sunshine. You make me happy when skies are gray. You'll never know dear how much I love you. Please don't take my sunshine away.

When the song was finished, I could breathe in and out without catching my lungs on more sobs. My mind was clearer and an idea made its way in through the vibrations from the last notes on the guitar. It wasn't perfect but it might get me out of the traffic island and away from the knife that waited for me in Fast Eddie's hand.

Chapter Six

I took the stairs to the top floor of the library where the computers were. I didn't dare use the elevator, knowing that I hadn't showered since I said goodbye to Caleb and let him move on into a world without me or my ghastly smells. It was going to be bad enough for whoever had to sit next to me. I didn't want anyone to be stuck in a small box with me on the way up.

It was still early. I had woken up on the traffic island with my face stuck in the guitar case and my arms wrapped around myself, as a garbage truck wailed and crashed next to my head, and the shaky walk to the library had taken me a long time. I moved slowly and carefully, still tensed up and remembering the point of the knife as Fast Eddie pushed it into my stomach. His rotten face blended in with everyone I passed on the street and the closer I got to The Main Branch, the more everyone started to look like him. My nerves were crackling and shooting through my limbs and face and I could feel a twitch starting above my right eye. The little guitar felt heavy on my shoulder and for a second I thought about ditching it; throwing it in the middle of Market and letting a streetcar run it over as it splintered and snapped and played its final death chord. It was the last thing that could be taken away and I thought I might as well just go ahead and get it over with, but I couldn't bear the loss of anything else for the time being. I continued on, avoiding the mirrored windows on Hyde Street, terrified at the possibility of seeing Fast Eddie's grinning face bobbing up and down on top of my own stooped shoulders.

When I got upstairs at The Main Branch, there was one computer open and I shuffled and clanged my way into the seat, bumping a man with a caterpillar mustache who was sitting next to me with the little guitar case. I started a countdown, and right as I got to "one," he logged off and stood up quickly, hurrying away from the nervous energy and the smell of old socks that spread around me in a wide radius. The other man next to me stayed put, but he didn't smell much better, and we nodded at each other in recognition and let our collective stench be our own security system. I never let go of the strap of the guitar case, or my rapidly deteriorating backpack, and operated the computer with one hand. There are times to be relaxed and let one's guard down and there are times when it is imperative to keep all of your wits about you and to treat every person who comes near you as a threat. I had a feeling that it would be a long time before the former came around again.

⟵〰〰〰

The Craigslist gigs section is a list of one-off jobs usually posted by someone desperate enough to let a stranger from the internet come and do some terrible task like cleaning up a construction site or moving furniture. I was certainly familiar with it and had often used it in the past to make a few bucks here and there without having to commit to anything or make any promises to anyone. That was the deal.

I thought back to the last time I used it. I had needed a hundred bucks to pay my rent on the basement in Seattle and answered an ad looking for someone to "help on a moving truck." It paid $150, so I was even going to have some left over for a few months' worth of rice and beans. When I met the man who had posted the gig in the fishy mist of the next morning, it was immediately obvious why he needed the help. He was driving a lurching box truck and when it pulled up in front of the spot where we had agreed to meet, a step stool came down and hit the ground as the door opened. He was a man of about fifty who was certainly less than five feet tall and looked like a real-life version of one of the Super Mario Brothers. His mustache and small, curly afro were weighed down by the wet air as he shook my hand.

"I'm Parker, thanks for meeting me. You're not gonna rob me are you?"

"Rob you of what?" I thought.

"No," I said.

We spent the day driving around Seattle and picking up furniture and other "valuables" that Parker would then supposedly refurbish and sell. He passed the time in the truck by telling me about his various sexual escapades and I fought back the urge to ask him how it was physically possible for him to engage in those activities with a regular-sized woman. By the time the afternoon rolled around, it was pouring rain and both of our moods had soured significantly. We argued and snapped at each other as we hauled couches down from tenth and twentieth-floor apartments in the Central Business District and I was sure he dropped an armoire on my foot on purpose, even though he freaked out and screamed at me as it tipped over and smashed on the sidewalk. He looked even more like a cartoon character as he jumped up and down and balled up his fists and when I couldn't help but laugh, he got angrier. At the end of the twelve-hour day, he dropped me off back downtown and handed me a hundred-dollar bill.

"Hey man, this was supposed to be one-fifty," I said, my heart dropping because I had known this was how it was going to end.

"Yeah, but you know, that armoire was gonna go for at least two hundred so you're lucky you don't owe me money."

I looked at the bill in his hand and shook my head, knowing, as I snatched it and put it in my pocket, that it was all he had brought and all he had ever intended on paying.

That was more or less a typical experience with the gigs section. However, this time I was not looking for any physical labor. I wasn't even sure I was capable of it. I was almost completely made up of peanut butter sandwiches, ramen noodles, and whiskey, and considering how heavy the little guitar felt on my back, trying to lift an armoire would be suicide and I wasn't quite there yet.

⟵〜〜〜

I stepped out of an elevator and shambled up to a glass desk where a woman about my age was sitting in a starched and crisp white shirt and black slacks. When she looked up from the computer her face dropped and one of her hands shot to the phone, which I assumed had security on the other end, so I started talking before she could pick it up.

"I'm here for the beer market study. From Craigslist. I spoke to Dan yesterday."

Her face relaxed into a smile and after she handed me a clipboard with all the necessary forms, I watched her pull some hand sanitizer from her purse and squirt it into her palm. I had heard about studies like this that needed subjects and paid for them, and with a little bit of guesswork as to the demographic they were looking for, I had managed to lie my way into this one for an hour's worth of watching beer commercials and fifty bucks.

A man who I assumed was Dan, the person I spoke to on my dying cell phone in the library the day before, came out and looked around the waiting room. He pointed at me.

"Matthew? Come on back."

I picked up the little guitar case and my backpack and started to follow him.

"You can leave your stuff here with Tanya," he said.

I looked back at the woman at the desk and she gave me a friendly eyebrow raise.

"I'd really rather not," I said, clutching my things to my chest.

Dan shrugged and we headed back to a conference room.

For the next hour, I watched six or seven commercials for a local beer that I would never drink because I could never afford it and filled out a small questionnaire about each one while Dan asked me a few questions. He was maybe five years older than me but his blinding smile and expensive haircut gave the impression of someone who had known what he wanted at an early age and went for it. It felt amazing to have someone like him speak to me like my opinions mattered and be genuinely interested in what I had to say, even if it was only for the sake of the market study. I had to fight the urge to crawl into his lap and ask him to tell me it was going to be okay. When the session was over, he shook my hand and led me back out to the waiting room, where Tanya handed me a brand new fifty-dollar bill and it was all I could do to not call her an angel and tell her I never wanted to leave.

I immediately ran back to the library and emailed as many of the different studies as I could, trying my best to gauge the demographic they were looking for. I kept my phone charging in the corner of the library and it buzzed and flashed all afternoon as I sent email after email and said yes to every single one that called me back. By the time the voice came over the library loudspeaker and yelled at all of us bums to go back to the holes we had crawled out from, I had lined up at least one study every day for the next two weeks, and by my calculations, it added up to about four hundred dollars. It was more money than I had seen in a long time and the thought of it being on the way made me feel lighter and stronger.

For the next two weeks, I ran back and forth across town, carrying the backpack and guitar case from office building to office building. Most of the studies were focus groups and they are just like they are portrayed in movies and television. A group of people of disparate ethnicities and genders all seated around a big table talking about what they liked and didn't like about a commercial or television show, complete with executives behind one-way glass. The one thing we all had in common was our need for a quick buck and most of the time, the companies knew that and gave us cash. Sometimes, at the end of a study, though, it was revealed that we would be receiving a check, which meant that I would have to go to the Check Mart check cashing place downtown. They took five percent because they didn't require a valid California ID, which I didn't have. I tried to avoid those studies as much as I could and only go for cash, but I still got suckered into a few.

I started to see some of the same people all the time. They were bottom feeders like me but like all the best scum suckers they knew the different tips and tricks for finding the studies.

"You gotta sign up for the mailing list," said George, a man in his seventies who always wore a gray, grease-stained trench coat. "That way you get first dibs."

"The real money is in the medical studies," said Angela, a woman who chain-smoked outside all the buildings beforehand and often got up in the middle of the focus groups to have a cigarette.

I noted this when she said it because it sounded terrifying, but I was in the zone, and by the first week had already gotten my roll up to $250, which I kept in a hidden duct tape pocket on the inside of my pants.

The weeks went on and I signed up for more marketing studies. I started to be able to pick out exactly the kind of person that each study was looking for and lean into it with my answers on their questionnaires to ensure I'd get picked. According to the records of many marketing companies in the city of San Francisco, I am a father of two, I am diabetic, I am Native American, I am a veteran, and I suffer from consistent heartburn. Only one of these was true. No one bothered to check on any of them and I found myself elaborating on the fake stories even though no one asked, since most of the time they were just trying to check a box next to a demographic for their antacid commercial.

"Oh, I'm just coming from dropping Hunter and Tyson off at their mom's house. They've been really good during the divorce," I would say.

They would look at my matted hair and shaking hands, and weigh their options as to whether they should call Child Protective Services and have the state take away my fake kids, or just try to pretend they didn't smell any cheap bourbon on my breath and go about their business.

By the end of the first month, I had a little over six hundred dollars in my duct tape pocket, and at night I would reach my hand down the front of my pants and hold on to it with a tightly rolled fist, figuring that anyone who might come across me sleeping in the traffic island would just assume I had gone in there to do something untoward and leave me alone, not knowing the treasure that I was actually holding. It was more money than I had been making singing on the street, but the way that Angela had talked about the real money being in medical studies echoed in my mind. I wondered if I could keep this ball rolling.

The next day at The Main Branch I came across an ad that said:

SUBJECTS NEEDED FOR EEG STUDY.
MALE. AGES 20-30.
$500.

I didn't even have to lie for this one and they called me a few minutes after I had sent my response. A curt, easily annoyed med student on the phone told me to be at the UCSF Medical Center the next morning at 10 a.m. I didn't even bother looking up what EEG stood for, or ask what the study was about. All I saw was the possibility of having over a thousand dollars in my pocket, and nothing was going to stop me from getting it stuffed into my shredded pants.

⟵〰〰

"I don't know how we're going to get this on here."

Two students in white coats were standing over me, trying to fit a black spider web of mesh over my head and underneath my matted, dirty hair.

"We should have said that you need to wash your hair before we do this, but we just assumed you would," said the first student who was about my age but may as well have been a different species from me. His glasses were an expensive name brand that even I recognized, and he wore a watch that I could tell he needed and used. The second was a woman maybe a couple of years older than me and she stood in the corner of the little office next to a TV on wheels, trying to put on an extra pair of gloves to put even more distance between herself and me.

"We're going to have to use the rods," she said.

"The rods?" I said, turning to look at her.

"Do not move your head please, this is hard

92

enough as it is," said the first student.

When I walked into their office that morning and told them I was there for the study, the first thing the two of them did was look at my hair, which was stringy and greasy, and then at each other as they exchanged pained looks. When they brought out the things they called the rods and started using them on my head, I understood why my dirty hair had been such a problem. They used the plastic hooks, which were about the size and shape of knitting needles, to dig into my scalp and try to clear out a spot where the individual electrodes of the EEG machine could make contact with my head and not the helmet of dirt and sweat that was covering it.

"Ow, shit!" I yelped as the first student twisted the rod.

"Well, I'm sorry but we have to do this."

It took about two hours to get the EEG cap on my head, and by the time it was done, my scalp was raw and burning, and both of the students were angry and sweating.

"Okay," said the second student as she turned out the lights, "now we can finally begin. Here," she said, handing me a small paper cup with a clear liquid in it. "Drink this."

The pain in my head was too distracting to ask questions so I did as I was told. It tasted like saltwater and as I gulped it down and the first student turned on the small TV and lowered the lights, my heart started to race.

They began showing me a series of photographs on the bright television and when I saw a photograph of an animal, I was supposed to press the button on the remote control they had given me. It was easy at first, but as it went on, the photographs went faster and faster and every time I blinked, the first student would yell from behind me.

"Please for the love of God try not to blink so much or we're going to have to end the study."

I couldn't bear the idea of having gone through the whole horrible process and leaving empty-handed, so I strained to keep my eyes open as tears ran down my cheeks. After a while, all the photographs started to blur together and I couldn't tell whether it was on purpose or if my eyes were so dried out they were playing tricks on me. Every time I started to ask a question, they would scold me and tell me if I kept moving it would ruin the study. I fought the urge to rip off the cap and scream and I can't begin to guess how long I sat in that chair, trying not to blink. When it was finally over, they took the cap off and led me out to the front office. I was shaky and dizzy and surprised to see through the big picture windows in the waiting room that it was now dark outside.

The trauma of the experiment and whatever was in the plastic cup had run deep and I felt like all of my nerves were on the outside of my body, pinching and recoiling at the very air that surrounded me. I swayed on my heels as the two students handed me form after form to sign. I didn't read them. I couldn't. My eyes were darting all over the room and the muscles behind them were throbbing and pulsing as more clipboards were put in front of me. I signed and signed, and eventually, the first student took off his glasses, rubbed his eyes, and extended his hand to shake mine in a gesture of solidarity usually reserved for people who have been thrust together and made to go through hell.

"You did pretty well in there. Most people freak out after a while. You must have a pretty high pain tolerance."

As he spoke, I watched his face twist and his mouth started to look like a gaping hole that contracted and expanded with each word and I recoiled from him. His hair was now disheveled and hanging over his eyes and he raised his eyebrows as he looked at me, unsure of what to say next.

"You're good to go."

I started to walk out the door but he stopped me.

"Hey man, you left these."

He was holding the little guitar and my backpack, but my scrambled brain didn't recognize them at first. I felt like he was trying to give me something important but I couldn't quite place it. I took them from his hand in a daze, confident that I would remember what they were at some point. As I started to step out of the room, a thought crept up from somewhere in the back of my shattered mind and I looked at him quizzically.

"Hey wait, where's the money?"

He looked confused.

"Oh, I mean, we can't just give you that much cash, we don't have it lying around. The school will send you a check in about two weeks."

The words were like a hot knife splitting me down the middle. I didn't want to make a scene, but my head was aching and my eyes wouldn't stop twitching and rolling in their sockets. Without thinking, I grabbed him by the front of his shirt.

"After all that. I get nothing?"

"No, we're going to send you a check," he said, trying to twist away.

I quickly caught myself and tried to make it seem like I was giving him a hug, which somehow seemed worse. Without letting go, I whispered to him, unable to stop myself from being weird.

"What address did I give you?"

He got himself out of my grip, looked at one of the forms, and rattled off Caleb's address, which I gratefully recognized and understood.

"Good," I said, "I wanted to make sure it didn't go to my lake house."

He knew it wasn't true but couldn't tell if I was joking or just lying and neither could I, so I quickly turned out of the room and down the hall, leaving him standing there confused and happy that I was gone. That night I stumbled to the stairs under Caleb and Knut's place. The traffic island felt too open and flashing images of big cats and terrifying elephants were going off in my head. I didn't want to add the headlights of cars to the mix. I clutched the small guitar close and dug my nose into the zipper, happy to remember what was mine and what was happening.

For the next couple of weeks, I wandered around The Mission, terrified and trying to get my bearings. Even though I had sworn not to go back there after the Fast Eddie incident, it was familiar, and the dirty, cracked streets absorbed sunshine and felt warm on my feet. Plus, I still wasn't brave enough to go back to the traffic island and I had no sleeping spots elsewhere in the city. It was the closest thing I had to a home. I felt like a piece of my brain had been ripped out in that dark room and it was taking its time to grow back. Each day I felt a little bit better but was still on edge, and the nights were full of terrifying visions of screeching and slashing animals. They were imprinted there and it took a long time for them to finally go away. Once they did, I decided it was time to go over to Caleb's and get my check.

I rang the bell on the metal cage and Knut opened the door. The last time I had seen him, he was spraying Lysol in my face and screaming. I immediately tensed up and prepared to run but he almost looked like he had been expecting me.

"Caleb's not here," he said. "But I think I know what you want."

He went back into the house and came out with an envelope, passing it to me through the metal grate.

"You're doing medical experiments now?" he said.

"How'd you know?"

"I'm a med student, I've sent out tons of these checks. What did you do?"

"Something with an EEG."

He nodded his head and squinted his eyes.

"How did you like the barbiturates they gave you?"

"Is that what that was?" I said. "I didn't like it at all. It fucked me up."

"Yeah don't do those too much. That stuff's bad for you."

"I don't plan on it."

He didn't immediately go back into the house, and I looked at the envelope, then back at him.

"Knut, I'm sorry about what happened between us. I'm sorry I maybe took advantage of you guys."

He answered quickly like he had been waiting.

"Thank you."

I started to walk away but turned around.

"And I've been sleeping underneath those stairs around the corner."

He exhaled some air out of his nose and crossed his arms.

"I know. You snore like a drunk animal."

I froze where I was standing on the sidewalk.

"I actually started to worry when I wouldn't see you," he said. "I'm sorry I acted that way, too."

"It's cool," I said. "I get it."

We smiled at each other through the cage and I tapped the envelope on my forehead.

"Well, you don't have to worry about me anymore. I think I'm gonna be an inside cat from now on."

Chapter Seven

It was July and the streets and sidewalks of The Mission were gluey with spat-out gum that had hardened over the winter and mixed in with the cement until the sunshine warmed it up and brought it back to sticky life. Everything in The Mission in summertime felt slow and bogged down. The birds took longer to take off and preferred to sit on top of the tan and burnt orange buildings, waiting for anything to fall discarded onto the street. The people who had lived in the neighborhood all their lives hung out of windows, watching the new money roll in and take over shockingly expensive, renovated floors of what used to be single-family homes. The new batch lived packed together, eight or nine at a time, MacBooks and fixed-gear bicycles cluttering the space that was once reserved for family meals or listening to baseball on the radio. They littered in the park and drunkenly dropped bottles of champagne on the ground under windows where single plants baked and wilted in the sun. During the week, they went to jobs downtown or in the SOMA district, where big tech companies were starting to sprout up like strangling weeds. Their meals were provided there and that gave them reason enough to never go home to The Mission until the weekend when they could blow off steam in one of the brand new bars where you weren't allowed to wear a hat. The rest of us stayed behind in the hidden places in what had become the playground of the new, new rich. They lived there in order to borrow a piece of what made it so special and endearing and somewhat untouched, but they held on too tight and it was starting to die.

I didn't grow up in The Mission, or San Francisco at all, so I could not claim to not be a part of the problem, but I certainly wasn't one of them. My carbon footprint in the neighborhood was low and I wandered around like a tourist who had never left, trying my best to hunker down and keep my shoulders around my neck to protect it from being slashed. I walked down Mission Street from 14th to

Cesar Chavez in the morning, staying on the shady side and elbowing my way around the people coming out of bakeries with sea shell-shaped, pink-dusted pastries, shielding my eyes when I walked past Mission Pawn and Loan, terrified of seeing my old guitar hanging up in the window. Though it was early, the heat was already starting to come off the street in waves and I was dripping bourbon-laced sweat down my temples. When I got to Cesar Chavez, I crossed the street and turned around, walking back on the side of the street that pulsed and flickered with sunlight and heat. There was, of course, a half-full pint of Ancient Age in my back pocket and I took gulps of it in every alley and hidden corridor I came across. In The Mission, there are plenty of places to hide, and I was thankful since the last thing I needed was an open container ticket from some cop who couldn't think of anything better to do with his time. As I walked, I kept my eyes pointed upward at the apartments and the fire escapes that clung to their walls like old Christmas tree ornaments. I had to find somewhere to live. I could not spend another night on the street.

The buildings in The Mission are not exceptionally tall. They are, at most, four stories and offer no shade like the skyscrapers downtown or the blocked-off project buildings in The Fillmore. The Mission had its own microclimate where the sun could shine directly and as I gazed up at the apartments and multi-unit houses, I could feel my eyes glazing over and starting to tear up. After cashing the check at the Money-Mart downtown, I was left with a grand total of $1,118 rolled up tight next to my thigh, give or take a few quarters that I kept in the actual pocket of the pants. While it was still the most money I had held in my possession in many years and possibly even in my life, I knew that there was no way I was going to be able to find a real, stable place to live with it. It simply wasn't enough. I might be able to pay the security deposit and the first month's rent on a room with some itinerant tech workers, but the next month would come quickly and then I would be right back where I started, sleeping in a hidden traffic island or under Knut and Caleb's stairs. Before I even got to that point there was the inevitable roommate interview, where all five or six of the other occupants would sit me down in the kitchen and find out if I was "going to be a good fit." I was not going to be a good fit. I didn't even have an answer for what was surely going to be the first, and most softball question of the interrogation. "So what do you do?" What was I going to tell them? That I play music on the street and sometimes get medical experiments done on me? Even that depended on whether or not they let me in the house in the first place based on my appearance. If the smell didn't disqualify me first, my life certainly would.

I had so quickly gone from feeling optimistic and light in the warm, early morning sun, to terribly depressed and utterly hopeless. I ducked into another alleyway and took a big swig from the Ancient Age bottle. Then I looked up and saw a sign hanging above a window.

ROOMS FOR RENT $150/WK

My heart started beating quickly and I could feel flashes of light behind my eyes. The path was suddenly so clear. Of course, there were places where people like me could come in from the cold when they hit a little bit of good luck. Images flashed of payphones in hallways and sad, sullen men arguing with tough landlords. I took another big gulp of whiskey and started running as fast as my torn-up shoes would take me to The Main Branch.

<—∼∼∼∼

When I got back to The Mission later that afternoon, I had written out a list of six Craigslist posts complete with names and addresses. At the top of the list, in capital letters, I had printed out "SROs." SRO stood for single room occupancy and was basically a cheap hotel that rented out rooms by the week. Thinking about it brought up images of Edgar Allen Poe and any number of sickly people in the throes of alcoholic dementia crying out in the night. They were perfect for me. Most importantly, I could afford it and would have somewhere to sleep indoors for a while. The prospect of sleeping in a bed filled me with something like survivor's guilt. I felt as though I were leaving whoever I had been before to sleep in the dirt and fight off the rats while I drifted off peacefully in a palace of light and warmth. I shook the thought away and made my way to the first place on the list.

The Kettlebridge sat on top of a taqueria on 16th Street between Valencia and Mission and when I rang the bell mounted to the front of its black metal door, a buzzer sounded and the latch unhitched with a chunky click. Before I even got to the top of the stairs I was sweating and trying to catch my breath but the only available air inside was thick with the cooking smells from downstairs. A man met me at the top and looked me up and down with a face frozen in a frown.

"What do you want?" he said.

"This is a hotel right?"

He waved around his face, swatting at a bug.

"Kind of. What do you want?"

I didn't know what he wanted to hear.

"A room, I guess."

"No vacancy right now, but I'll show you anyway."

I didn't understand what he meant, but I followed him and we turned the corner into a hallway with huge stains on the walls, even though they were painted dark brown. He put a key in a door and knocked as he opened it.

"Bert," he yelled, "I'm just showing the room."

I peeked my head around the corner and saw a room that was perhaps eighty square feet, with a floor covered in trash and an old man lying on a cot in the middle of it. He lifted his head slightly and then let it fall back down, exhausted.

"Okay," I said, "I'm good, thank you."

He shut the door and turned to me.

"Bert's very sick, so maybe come back in a week or two. You can have his room."

The next SRO on the list was called The Donaghy Hotel, just a few blocks down Mission Street. The manager there was equally off-putting, but there was no restaurant below it and he said that he had some vacancies. As far as I could tell, these vacancies weren't contingent on the current occupant's death, so I followed as he swung a gigantic ring of keys in his fist. The room he showed me looked normal at first. It was much like the other one with a cot pushed up against the wall and linoleum floors. However, when I looked up, I noticed that the walls only went up about three-quarters of the way. The rest of the space was sectioned off by chicken wire and as soon as I noticed it, someone in the room next door let out a fart that almost vibrated my chest. The manager banged on the wall.

"Hey come on, I'm showing the place here."

The only answer was a shorter, higher-pitched fart, so I thanked him and told him I would come back later.

←⌇⌇⌇

Back out on the street, I pulled the bottle of Ancient Age out and took a gulp without running into an alley or ducking into a doorway. I had promised myself that I would not be sleeping on the street that night and the way things were going, the only way that was going to happen was going to be in the drunk tank. As had been my luck, though, no cops pulled up to the curb in front of me and I was left with no other option but to go straight to the third place on my list.

The Armstrong Hotel was on Valencia between 17th and 18th Street. It was painted pink on the outside and had a large, arched alcove where the front door was. There was no metal cage, just a bell. I rang it and a buzz unlocked the door, letting me in. The steps were carpeted, and no foul smells greeted me on my way up, just a faint hint of Nag Champa incense and at the top, a smiling middle-aged woman standing behind a counter.

"Can I help you?" she said.

It was all so friendly and normal-seeming that I almost cried. It had been so long since someone had asked me that and meant it. She didn't even look me up and down or sniff the air when I got close. I actually took some time to think about her question.

"Can you help me?" I wanted to ask. *"You can help me in so many ways. You can tell me that I am a good person. You can tell me that I just make a lot of mistakes. You can tell me that it is not too late."*

Instead, I just stared at her for a moment.

"I'm looking for a room. Do you have any right now?"

Her face lit up.

"Absolutely, let me show you."

She grabbed her key ring and I followed her down the hall. There were no bloodstains anywhere and so far nothing that looked like a crime scene. She opened a door onto a much larger room than the ones I had seen earlier that afternoon. It was all white and had big windows that looked out onto Valencia and a fire escape just like the ones I had been looking up at from the sidewalk that morning. I couldn't have been standing there for more than five or six seconds before I turned to her.

"I'll take it."

The woman, who I eventually learned was named Mrs. Seif, raised her eyebrows.

"You want to know how much?"

I caught myself.

"Just tell me, has anyone died in here recently? Like very recently?"

She answered quickly as if it had for sure been asked before.

"No. It's one hundred and fifty a week."

"That is just fine, thank you."

I quickly filled out some paperwork, too excited to pay attention to what I was signing, and paid her in cash after extracting the money from down the front of my pants.

"Sorry," I said as I handed it to her, slightly damp.

She grimaced with her eyes but kept her smile, and handed me the key.

Walking into room 206 and shutting the door behind me, I felt a silence that I could fall into. It crushed me and I felt the weight of it on my chest and the vacuum sucking at my ears like a pressurized airplane. It had been months since I had been somewhere that quiet and I could tell that it was going to take a long time for the adjustment to set in. What should have been a moment of joy and relief was disappointingly terrifying. I wasn't sure how I was going to get used to life inside. I set down the little guitar and my backpack in the corner of the room and unzipped it, pulling out the brown army blanket and spreading it on the small, spring-loaded cot before sitting down. The room was painted thick with layers upon layers upon layers of what was presumably lead paint. The linoleum on the floor was bowed and uneven and gave a disconcerting, wavy feeling if I focused on it too much. There was nowhere else to look, though, so I sat and tried to acclimate to the silence.

In the corner, there was a small sink and a closet with no doors, and it suddenly dawned on me that this was, of course, a single room. The only bathroom was the one down the hall. I eyed the sink and knew right away that I was going to be using it as more than just a sink. The windows looked out over Valencia, and to my delight, there was a fire escape right out front. It was almost like having a balcony. I opened the window and breathed in deep, happily letting the noise from down on the street stream up and fill the empty, vacuous space. Morbid curiosity led me to venture down the hall, where there was a payphone and the door to the bathroom, which I opened and was met with a screaming and banging from someone sitting on the toilet.

"The god damn lock's broken," the voice said, and I ran back to my room and slammed the door, my heart pounding.

It was starting to cross over into nighttime and the setting sun used the blank canvas of white in the room to paint an orange hue on everything. I went into my bag and got out a fresh bottle of Ancient Age, which I brought over to the window to sit down on the ledge and drink while watching what was going on down on Valencia. The hoards moved in and started to take big bites out of Saturday night. The sign for the pizza place downstairs buzzed on and blared straight into my room, vomiting blue and pink all over the linoleum and walls. Big gulps of whiskey went down until I was too drunk to sit on the window ledge without falling off, and as soon as I stumbled over to the cot and my head hit the soft surface, I was deep in a drunken, involuntary sleep.

⟵〰〰〰

I woke up to thunder and lightning. I felt like there was cotton stuffed into my mouth and I was sure that I had been hit by a car. It took almost a full minute of confusion and panic to realize where I was and how much I had drunk. I had left the lights on in the room and they were dimming and flashing with a roaring sound that thundered through the white space and shook into my skull behind my eyes. Sitting up on the cot, fully clothed and on top of the brown army blanket, I realized that I was sweating and almost blind. The sun was screaming into the room. The windows facing out onto Valencia also directly faced the rising sun, and it was shooting like a hot laser right into my room. This did not explain the dimming lights and the roar, however. Standing up shakily, I only made it one step before stumbling to the corner

111

and vomiting into the sink. The roar revved up again and the lights flickered and fizzed above me. The sound of voices out in the hallway brought the whole situation into focus. I was sharing a wall with the communal bathroom, and whenever someone flushed the toilet, inexplicably, the lights flickered. I could hardly be called an electrician but I knew that just wasn't right.

Opening the door and stepping out into the hallway, I was met with a line of people waiting for the bathroom and I took my place at the back. It was all people in their late forties or early fifties, almost exclusively men, and everyone avoided eye contact as they stood in their stained sweatpants and torn bathrobes. After a few minutes of pretending not to hear each person's bathroom noises, it was my turn and I shut the door and sat on the toilet with my pants around my ankles. Putting my head in my hands, I closed my eyes and tried to drown the headache. After a few seconds, though, I heard a noise and looked up to see a man of about fifty standing inside the bathroom with the door open, looking at me.

"Hey man, get the fuck out of here," I said, waving my arms at him.

He didn't move. He just smiled and leaned back against the wall.

"Hey, what are you doing? Come on." I tried to wave my arms even harder, perhaps hoping that he could be coaxed out by the strong breeze.

He still didn't move, though, and looked at me like he couldn't hear me.

"Jesus Christ, get out of here!"

This commotion got the attention of the next couple of people in line, and soon, three or four other middle-aged men were poking their heads in, trying to see what was the matter. Before long, the door was all the way open and the entire line had a direct view of me sitting on the toilet. Finally, a bald man with a thin mustache grabbed the man's arm and led him out, apologizing to me and shutting the door on his way out. I put my head back in my hands and waited a few minutes before accepting that all of my muscles had tightened up, and there was no point in sitting there anymore.

Back in the room, I could feel the white paint crawling into my lungs and the endless roar of the toilet and the corresponding flashes of light started making me sick. Soon I was pacing like a zoo animal. My hands were tingling and as I began hyperventilating, I grabbed my key, threw open the door to the waiting bathroom line, and slammed it shut, running past them and avoiding eye contact that wasn't being offered in the first place. The hallway felt never-ending. Like it was narrowing the further down it I got, but as I sped past Mrs. Seif standing at the counter, I saw the stairs, took them two at a time down to the door, and was out on the blinding street, gasping for air and holding my chest. There were a couple of other residents out front smoking cigarettes who I recognized from the morning's peep show. I pretended to be late going somewhere and ran down Valencia.

At Ray's, I bought a six-pack of a brand of beer that I had done a research study for and took it to the park where people were already gathering to soak up the late morning sun. I sat down on the grass and chugged two of them in immediate succession, placing the empties right back in their slots in the six-pack. I felt the thick beer fill my stomach and fortify it against the previous evening's whiskey and the morning's deep, primal panic. It soothed the tingling in my arms and my breath slowed and became automatic again instead of forced and difficult. It felt good to be outside. My natural habitat. The indoors felt violating and unnatural. There were people stacked on top of me and underneath me and I could feel them moving and twisting in every direction. The thought of the small room with the angry white walls made me open another beer and take it down in three big gulps. They were going to be there when I went back and I didn't want to face them sober and alone. I had wanted to be an inside cat but apparently, it wasn't going to happen overnight.

The beer was now pumping through every part of my body and I finally felt normal and steady, so I popped one more, drinking it all down in about ten seconds. I put the empty back in the cardboard case and took out the two full ones, slamming them down in the grass with my fists and digging them about a half-inch into the dirt. Someone would find them and maybe they could help with their panic attack, too. I got up and started toward Mission Street.

The shops on Mission were busy and the street was packed with people. I was no longer just a tourist. I was nesting. Settling. I passed by Thrift Town and thought about going in to tell the Christian woman who worked there that I had found a place to live. That I was going to be okay. Maybe if I told her that, I would start to believe it. I passed by Muddy Waters and saw the girl working at the counter and briefly considered going in and telling her the same. They wouldn't have remembered me or cared, but I was glad to tell them in my head. I hadn't grabbed my phone when I left The Armstrong, but I also considered calling my mother and telling her that I was alright and that I had found a place to live. I knew she would ask questions though, and I knew that I would feel unable to tell her anything but the truth, and possibly the story about being walked in on while trying to shit, and I knew that would only make her worry more.

As I passed a shop with piñatas of bootleg superheroes hanging from the awning, I stopped and looked in the window. Sitting on the ledge was a row of Venus flytraps. I had only ever seen them in cartoons, and they were small and almost cute and had a handwritten sign that said "Ten Dollars." I bought one and went back to The Armstrong, where there was no more line in the hallway, and even Mrs. Seif wasn't at the front counter. Everyone seemed to have gone about their business for the day and I went to my room and locked the door behind me, thankful that the lights had stopped flashing and the toilet had stopped flushing. I set the plant on the windowsill and stared at its pointy outcroppings that looked like teeth sitting on its almost translucent green leaves. I admired its evolution and the fact that it had taken all of this time to become something perfect, something that was suited exactly for its function. I loved that it had come home with me and that it was sitting in my window, doing what needed to be done.

Chapter Eight

The days passed in a hot haze and I felt slow and lumbering in the heavy air. I would run out of breath just going down the stairs of The Armstrong every morning with my little guitar on my back, and sneaking onto the bus without a transfer became easier as the summer got deeper and the bus drivers decided it was too hot to care. The BART stations were like a sauna and singing in them became torturous. No one felt like it was worth it to reach into their pocket and throw me a quarter. No one wanted to sweat and linger for a moment while they listened to me play "Don't Think Twice It's Alright" before getting on a hot, carpeted train to go to a hot, carpeted office. They just wanted the day to be over and there was no time to stop. I couldn't blame them. I didn't really want to be there anymore either. Sometimes I would stand facing the wall of the station and let my face rest on the cool, white subway tiles while people walked past and stared. Once, while I was doing that, someone dropped a dollar in my guitar case, assuming I was some kind of living statue art piece, perhaps entitled, "Giving Up."

I didn't want to be going out and singing for change anymore but I didn't know what else to do. It was too hot to stay in my room at The Armstrong and I was still not entirely comfortable there. All day, people were coming in and out of the bathroom and the whooshing and dimming of the lights had no rhythm to it. It was maddening. About a week in, I decided it was time to brave a shower. I would have been worried about some kind of foot fungus, but I had been walking around with holes in my shoes in The Mission and The Tenderloin for so long that I was sure I had built up a super immunity. If anything, the fungus should have been worried about getting on me. When I turned on the shower, the lights in the bathroom dimmed and flickered. It seemed like all the electricity in the hotel was connected to the plumbing. The shower was quick and worrisome, with the thought of being electrocuted constantly in the back of my mind.

I thought a lot about the other residents of The Armstrong. They kept to themselves but it was not uncommon to hear soft weeping in the middle of the night coming down from one of the rooms sharing the fire escape up above. The place was full of people who had long been forgotten and most of them seemed to like it that way. I could feel myself being sucked up into their vortex and it would have been incredibly easy to let the days turn into years and slowly fall backward into nothing, so every morning I got up, strapped the little guitar to my back, and left.

At night, though, I had to go back and that was when it was the darkest. The pink light from the restaurant's neon sign punched its way into the windows as soon as the sun went down and gave a hellish glow to the whole room. I would always end up coming back from a day of singing and sweating in the Powell Street BART station with a pint of Ancient Age, vowing to make it last through the whole night, having to stop myself from gulping the whole thing down as soon as I walked in the door. Because I usually spent the majority of the money made during the day on cheap bourbon in plastic bottles, dinner always consisted of dry ramen noodles. The recipe was simple. Poke a small hole in the plastic bag to let a little bit of air out and crush it up with your fist. Then, dump the flavor packet filled with toxic salt inside and shake it up. Make sure that you wash it down with cheap liquor so it expands in your stomach and makes you feel like you actually ate something and didn't just trick your mind into believing that it wasn't rotting away from a lack of vitamins. I had been eating the concoction and nothing else for weeks, even before moving into The Armstrong, and my esophagus was always full of burning acid that tried to escape from the foul bubbles of salted whiskey down in my stomach.

After dinner, I would lie down on the cot with my guitar and alternate between taking swigs of bourbon and singing songs to myself at a low volume. It was the only thing that kept me from shaking and twisting with nerves. I felt more exposed inside the room than I ever had outside on the traffic island. Every time I heard something out in the hallway, or a rat ran up the pipes, I would feel a shock go up my spinal cord and there was nowhere to run. So, to drown it out and fill the silence, I sang and played. I would press my ear up against the body of the little guitar and strum a chord loud enough to make it shake and vibrate, in tune only with itself. I would feel the vibration in my skull and let it scatter throughout the rest of my body. As long as I was strumming along, nothing scary could get in. So I would stay like that all night until the bourbon ran out and I would fall asleep cradling the little wooden dream machine.

Late one night, I had all the lights off and was bathing in the pink bolts of neon, strumming away and swigging at a bottle. Each chord rattled my vision, and with every sip, the movement got slower and sloppier. I strummed and pressed my ear hard against the top, trying to hear it sustain for as long as I could, trying to soak up every last bit of noise before strumming again, and letting the sound waves ripple into my eyes until they disintegrated back into nothing. After a few particularly hard strums, I heard a knock at the door. It took a second to figure out what was going on and at first, I looked at the guitar, convinced and horrified that I had heard something knocking inside it, trying to get out. When the second knock came harder, I sat up on the cot and waited while the rest of the world spun around me. The bottle of bourbon on the floor was almost empty and I had no idea how long I had been lying there, strumming and straining to hear. Opening the door, I had to screw up my eyes to make out that there was only one man there. The bourbon had made me see two at first. This man, I later learned, was Mr. Seif.

"You can't do this anymore, do you understand?"

He didn't even leave me an option to argue or ask what he meant.

"Every night with the guitar playing and the crying."

"What?"

"Every night. It has to stop."

I thought back to some of the mornings I had woken up with my face in a wet puddle on the army blanket. Apparently, I had taken to crying in my sleep and it had been loud enough to wake up the whole hotel. I did my best to speak without slurring.

"Okay, you got it. No crying."

He looked at me, tight-mouthed and squinting.

"I'm going to be watching you," he said.

"Okay, sounds good."

I shut the door while he was still standing there and as soon as I did, my stomach flipped over and landed with a thud in my throat. I started to sweat and could feel the vomit coming up before I knew what to do. I couldn't go out to the bathroom in the hallway with Mr. Seif still standing there. When he said he was going to be watching me, I assumed that meant counting how many times I ran to the bathroom to vomit. It happened so fast, that I only thought to grab my torn and threadbare sweatshirt off the floor and let loose inside it, putting the final wet nail in its coffin. As I emptied it into the sink, which I realized I should have just vomited into in the first place, I noticed the dark spots of blood that flecked the porcelain as I tried to wash it down the drain. I was no doctor, but I knew that the dry ramen noodles and whiskey were going to kill me sooner rather than later.

Conserving what was left of my medical study money wasn't going to do me any favors if my insides were rotting. There was no point in stressing about the money if there was a putrid hole burning in my stomach. Besides, my only sweatshirt was now completely covered in puke on top of essentially being a rag. It was unavoidable. I needed some new stuff. I needed to spend a little bit of money. I needed to live a little bit better.

The next morning, I peeled a hundred-dollar bill off the roll, stuck it in my pocket, and headed out of The Armstrong. It was as if all the thrift stores knew I was coming. Everything I was looking for was right in the front window of everywhere I went. I found a black hooded sweatshirt for three dollars, three plain black T-shirts for two dollars each, and a George Foreman grill for five. I had to take a few trips back and forth to the hotel to drop things off. It was the closest I had ever come to going on a shopping spree, and I fell for it hard. If I couldn't fill my life with anything else, I was going to fill my room with stuff. As I was leaving Community Thrift with a few more T-shirts, something caught my eye in the electronics section. It was a relic. Something that felt ancient and familiar. It was a small TV/VCR combo with a big pink slip of paper taped to it that said: "Working, tested." My heart started fluttering. This was the silence filler. This was the answer.

"Hey, how much is that?" I asked a guy in a trucker hat at the counter, pointing to it.

"Twenty bucks," he said.

"And it works?"

"That's what it says."

"You guys got VHS tapes?"

"Over there for a buck."

He pointed to a wall lined with colorful boxes. They had names on them like *Speed*, *Top Gun*, *Days of Thunder*, and *Air Force One*. Movies that had enough explosions that I would never have to be alone in room 206 again. I would always have Tom Cruise and Keanu to keep me company.

That night, I turned everything on as soon as the sun went down. I had set the television on top of the counter and plugged it in as far away from the sink as I could. Seeing as how the plumbing and the electricity were so inexplicably intertwined at The Armstrong, it seemed wise to keep them separate. I had folded the new-to-me clothes nicely and put them in the doorless closet. Seeing them in there, clean and ready for a new day, gave me a small charge. I kept looking up at the T-shirts and the new hoodie, beaming with pride. I flipped on the television and popped in a VHS cassette of *Groundhog Day* as the machine buzzed and hummed, engaging its complex series of obsolete motors and gears. I smiled and sighed at the high-pitched whine that came out of the old tube television, then cracked open a light beer and sat on the cot. Right there, I finally felt like I could relax. There was finally more than just the sound of my own beating heart and the vibrations of the guitar strings bouncing off the white walls.

There was no refrigerator in the room, and even

if there had been, it wouldn't have surprised me if it was somehow connected to the payphone in the hallway, so the beer came out of a styrofoam cooler I found at the Mexican market. Along with the ice and beer, it was full of a few cheap steaks, some pre-cut bell peppers, and tortillas; all things that could be cooked nicely on the George Foreman Grill. I got up and watered my Venus flytrap with some of the cheap beer as the sound from the movie behind me filled the room with noise that I didn't have to make or pay too much attention to. The next day, I was going to cook up the steaks and eat my first real meal in what felt like months. At the moment though, I was content to finish all the beers and give my stomach a rest from the acid sting of the cheap whiskey.

I started eating real food all the time. The thought of the sharp and twisted ramen noodles scratching their way down my throat brought up visions of more blood spurting from my mouth. I cooked vegetables every night, bought from the market down the street, and ate them with plastic forks on paper plates. There was nothing in the room for me to set the George Foreman Grill on, so it sat on the white linoleum floor along with the cooler and the stacks of paper plates and napkins. It looked like I was having an indoor tailgate party. When the ice in the cooler started to melt, I dumped it in the toilet, which would make a tremendous splash before being flushed into the building's wiring. After a few days of eating something besides dry, salted noodles, I felt light and powerful. My insides didn't feel like they were bubbling with fear and sodium anymore, and the extra hydration I was getting from switching exclusively to beer had done wonders for my mood. I happily got in line for the bathroom with the other residents every morning and tried to look in their eyes and make conversation, which was always quickly shot down. As long as I tried to connect, though, I felt like I wasn't slipping into their lonely world.

One night, I was cooking up some chicken breast filets on the grill and watching *Twister* when there was a loud knock on the door. It startled me and I knocked over the beer I had set on the floor next to the cot.

"Hold on," I said, trying to mop up the beer with a couple of dirty socks.

Before I could stand up all the way, the doorknob was turning and Mr. Seif blasted into the room.

"Hey man," I said. "Come on."

"What do you think you're doing!?"

He was furious and shaking his head as if trying to come to his senses or wake up from a bad dream.

"I'm making dinner, and trying to clean this up, you scared me."

"You can not do this here. There is no cooking here. Get rid of this right now!"

"What do you mean?" I asked. "It's just a George Foreman Grill."

"I don't care what it is! This building was built in 1907, everything is a fire hazard. Get rid of it or you are out of here."

The thought of having to leave The Armstrong after finally getting settled in grabbed me by the throat. I couldn't bear to do it all over again. I reached over and unplugged the grill, and the sizzling stopped after a few seconds.

"You can not do this here."

"Okay!" I said, and I threw my hands up and sat on the cot, red-faced and staring into space, as if getting scolded by a teacher.

He eyed me for a moment and shook his head again, then left the room, slamming the door behind him. *Twister* played loud and piercing in the new silence, so I switched it off and laid down to go to bed.

The next morning, the first thing I saw was the crate of individually wrapped instant noodles sitting next to the television. I bought it when I first moved in and had mercifully not thought about it in the few days since the grill had entered my life. That morning, though, I knew I was going to have to choke one down eventually and the thought filled me with dread. All the optimism of the last week drained away and I felt like an empty shell again. Knowing I couldn't cook and eat like a normal person reinforced the hard fact that there was a cap on my existence and I would always be clinging to the margins. Surviving, but never living. The George Foreman Grill sat with the half-cooked chicken still crushed between the dual heating surfaces of the machine. I was going to leave it there for a while. Sometimes I liked to see how bad things could get.

I left The Armstrong and went straight to Ray's. He was just opening, and when I asked for a pint of Ancient Age, he looked at me, surprised.

"You were looking pretty good, Matty. I was thinking maybe you got a little bit cleaned up. But I can see that's not the case."

He rang up the bottle and I gave him the money.

"What's a kid like you doing with nothing going on on a Tuesday morning? You know, your life is going to slip past you. You're going to wake up and be fifty tomorrow. If you're lucky."

He pointed to the bourbon.

"You know, my brother died from a bleeding ulcer from alcohol when he was thirty. That's not too much older than you, is it? It was horrible, man. He was bleeding out his nose, his mouth, his asshole, it was crazy. They just couldn't stop it. He had to wear a diaper until he died and it would be full of blood and shit."

I had picked up the bottle and it was still suspended in mid-air as I gawked at Ray with my mouth open wide.

"What the fuck, Ray?" I said.

"I'm sorry man, you have a good day."

"What? How?" I said.

"I'm sorry man, really. I don't judge or anything. I just worry."

"Well, I appreciate that," I said.

And I did.

I went to the park and sat on the hill as my stomach growled. I pulled the whiskey and a packet of ramen noodles out of my backpack. Harsh, burning acid bubbled up into my throat just looking at them. There were two girls to my right who were cutting something wrapped in tin foil in half. As they split it apart, I caught a glimpse of the cross-section. It was the most beautifully constructed burrito I had ever seen. The colors of the rice, meat, and beans were all perfectly separated, like a flag or layers of the Earth. I was renewed. Nourished only by the thought of it. I rushed up to the two girls and they all but screamed as I stumbled to a halt above them.

"Excuse me," I said, panting. "But where did you guys get that burrito? It looks amazing."

"Oh," one of them said, "Taqueria Compadre. It's on 19th and Mission."

I hadn't even stuck around to hear the last couple of words. I thanked them and ran off, leaving the whiskey behind and feeling incredibly stupid for not having thought of this before.

Taqueria Compadre was brightly lit and painted in a rainforest motif. There were yellow booths crammed up against one wall and pillars along which people were lined up. It smelled of grilled meat, sweat, and stale beer that was spilled and mopped up and spilled and mopped up in an endless cycle. It was breathtaking. I got in line, and when it was my turn, I ordered a super steak burrito. I loved the sound of it. Super steak. It was like something a rich person would order. Something that everyday people couldn't get their hands on. I paid, and when they called my number, I took the yellow basket with the tin foil tube and sat down in one of the booths, which were scratched with tags and burned with old joints discretely smoked year after year. I ripped off the top of the tin foil and bit into it like a shark. Then again, and again. I ate half the burrito in less than a minute, before finally setting it down to actually chew. Everything went from black and white to color. Everything was starting to work again.

I stared at the wall of Taqueria Compadre while I chewed. There was a mural of some people on a river, gathering water and passing it back and forth in a fire line to each other. Where the water was going was anyone's guess, but they were making it happen either way. The most important thing, though, was that they were smiling. All of them were locked in this motion forever. They were suspended on this wall and doomed to repeat the same moves as long as the building was standing. But I imagined that they were happy. They were doing something. They had a reason to exist. Just as I was fixating on the smile of one particular person in the mural, there was a crash in the open kitchen and I turned to see the dishwasher in his rubber apron, standing with broken glass at his feet. Everyone in the kitchen clapped, and most of the people in the booths did as well. The dishwasher stood, blushing for a moment, then went and got a broom. I had been so lost and twisted up and backward, but everything was so simple now. I needed to put on some of my new clothes and I needed to go to every restaurant in town and ask if they needed a dishwasher. Someone was going to need one and I was going to be happy to fill the position. I wasn't going to beg for change anymore for a song. I was going to scrub some pots, try not to break anything, and I was going to smile the whole time.

Chapter Nine

The trollies that run along The Embarcadero on the way to Pier 39 are old steel boxes painted in bold, mid-century modern colors. They were built for tiny people and they sway along on malformed wheels, sparking and grinding against metal rails. The seats are hard, wooden benches that rattle on the uneven ground. It is not much more comfortable than being tied to the back of the thing and getting dragged along the concrete. The polyurethane varnish that covers the wood of the benches was tacky and sticking to my new black T-shirt in the early morning heat. I imagined that they had to refinish them every once in a while to cover up the vomit and other atrocities that were committed on them by tourists going back to their hotels in Union Square after a night at Fisherman's Wharf gulping blue drinks at the Bubba Gump Shrimp Company. The thick coating covered up years of reeking sins. I sat on one of these trollies at 8 a.m. on a Tuesday, dressed in my new clothes, with my hair combed as much as I could hope to comb it. I had only been able to spend a few precious moments in the bathroom getting ready while the line of men waited in the hallway. The result was a slicked-back style that sort of made me look like a freshly-shaven ex-con who had found Jesus.

I carried a stack of resumes with me that were essentially just pieces of paper held together by an intricate web of lies. I had paid a wino with a credit card double at The Main Branch to print them out for me. I couldn't remember a lot of the restaurants I had worked at. Most of them weren't even in business anymore and the ones that were had long ago had a complete staff turnover. Some of my old managers were dead. Many of the old chefs I had worked for were in jail. My only hope was that none of that would matter.

Pier 39 is lined with bars and restaurants serving seafood, barbecue, and the ubiquitous clam chowder in a sourdough bread bowl, which is something only tourists eat. As the trolly came to a stop in front of the aquarium, I straightened out my shirt and picked off a piece of lint that had fallen on my shoulder. I was putting faith in the idea that I would stumble onto a place so in need of someone in the dish pit that they would hire me on the spot. It had happened before, and if it was going to happen anywhere again, it would be here. Tourist restaurants are in constant flux and I felt like my odds were good that at least one of the places on the pier had a busboy or dishwasher who had thrown down his apron and stormed out the night before.

There was a group of guys squatting on milk crates, smoking and eating behind a restaurant on Beach Street. Morning shifts in kitchens start early, so it was their lunch break. I walked up and waited politely for a lull in their conversation, but it never came, so I spoke up loudly.

"Hey, where's the chef? Donde jefe?" I asked.

The group stopped talking and they all looked at the ground, not interested in dealing with whatever I was bringing to the table, adding to their already strenuous workload. Finally, a kid of about seventeen stood up, finishing his plate. He wore a short-sleeved, white polyester shirt with metal snaps and looked at me suspiciously.

"I'll get him, come on."

I followed him to the back door of the kitchen, which was screaming with noise. Music, pots and pans banging together, people yelling. I stayed in the doorway and a few seconds later, a three-hundred-pound man with red hair and sunken, yellow eyes came around the corner. He was eating a piece of baguette.

"What's up?" he said, wiping his hands.

I stuck my resume out.

"I just wanted to see if you needed any help right now. Like a dishwasher."

He looked at the piece of paper in my hand and took a bite out of the chunk of bread.

"Not fuckin' really," he said.

His mouth was full, but I still understood.

"It's a bad time right now," he said. "Bad economy. There's no tourists this year."

He swallowed the giant ball of dough and I watched it go all the way down his throat through his double chin. He waved away the resume I had put out and went back into the kitchen.

There were more restaurant crews on the pier having their lunch break. I interrupted them all and asked to see the chef. Each one, one after the other, told me the same thing about the economy. About how this was the slowest summer they had ever had in twenty-five years on the pier. How they just had to let someone go because there wasn't enough money. How they just had to cut everyone's hours. No one took one of my expensive resumes. I went to every single restaurant on the pier and did my best to cut them off at the pass by telling them how many different types of places I had worked at, which was sort of true, and that I could even help with prep work, which was probably true. By the time I got to the Bubba Gump Shrimp Company at the very end of the pier, the collective kitchen crew break was over and everyone had gone back inside to prepare for the supposedly nonexistent lunch rush. The resumes were now sweaty and crumpled in my fist and the one on the outside of the stack had a big dirty thumbprint on it. The afternoon sun was starting to coax sweat from my shoulders.

I came across a diner on North Point Street with no one in it at noon. That wasn't a good sign, but I went in anyway. There was a squat old man with a mustache sitting at a table by a television, playing solitaire. He had a wide array of pill bottles spread out on the table and looked like he had been there at least all morning and more than likely for years. A woman who looked to be about his same age with a crooked beehive hairdo came out from the kitchen. She was obviously his wife only in that way that couples often start to look like each other after being married for a long time.

"Can I get you a menu?" she said, looking out over her red-rimmed glasses.

"No, thank you. I was just wondering if you guys were looking for any help. I don't know if you need a dishwasher or anything."

I handed her a resume and mercifully, she took it. She pushed her glasses up her nose and studied it for a moment.

"Otto!" she yelled over to the table. "Otto!"

She screamed his name a couple more times until he looked up. I had a feeling he could hear her just fine.

"Otto, you wanna talk to this guy? He's a dishwasher."

Otto shook his head and went back to solitaire.

"Come on," she said. "I'll talk to you outside."

We went out front to some empty patio tables and she motioned for me to sit down. Then she went to a blue BMW parked in front of the restaurant and got a pack of cigarettes from the front seat. She sat down with me and lit one up, then studied my resume some more.

"So, why do you think you would be a good fit here?" she said.

"Oh, well," I thought for a moment but didn't want to leave any silence for fear that the chance could slip out of my grasp.

"I don't really know anything about you guys but this seems like a nice place and I can tell that it's family-owned. I know something about pulling yourself out of nothing and I understand how hard it is to run a business and if you can get it going then um, that's a really precious thing, you know, not to be too um, you know, precious about it."

She took a drag off her cigarette and nodded her head, so I continued.

"And I think that I'm a hard worker, and I've been a dishwasher at a bunch of different places, and um, I can do prep work, and uh let's see what else..."

I was trying to fill the silence, but she just smoked away at her cigarette and stared. When I finally couldn't think of any more buzzwords to say, I stopped and she stubbed the cigarette out in an ashtray on the table.

"Well, I gotta say," she said. "You're saying all the right things."

My heart started beating. It was going to work. I would have a real job to go to instead of singing for money in the street.

"Thing is though," she continued, "the economy's real bad right now. There's barely been a tourist season. Maybe come see me around Christmas time."

She got up and handed me the resume back.

"I don't need this," she said.

She went back into the restaurant and left me sitting on the patio. Christmas was months away. For all I knew I would be dead by then. I considered keying her BMW for getting my meager hopes up as I left, but only for a moment, and went down to the edge of the pier to look at the sea lions instead.

On the far end of Pier 39, there is a stretch of wooden balcony that looks out over The Bay. There are some floating docks right underneath it, upon which one can find dozens of sea lions lying about and begging for food. The tourists often oblige despite all the signs that line the pier saying not to feed them. I sidled up to a spot on the railing and looked over at them. They were slick and shiny from the sea and some of them were sleeping on their backs, the high noon sun glistening off them and making them look oily to the touch. I watched as a kid took an entire corn dog off its stick and waved it at the sea lions, taunting them. A few took notice and shimmied over close to the edge of their floating dock to get right underneath it. The kid waved the corn dog for a while, checking to see that his parents weren't looking. I was the only one who noticed what he was doing. I watched as he thought about it, and I saw the determination in his eyes when he decided to drop it. The corn dog swirled and rotated in mid-air, then landed on the dock right in the middle of three sea lions. Chaos broke out. They fought and gnashed at each other. One of them was pushed violently off the dock, while two others wrestled for the fallen corn dog. The tourists looked on, horrified, and the kid who threw it disappeared into the crowd. I turned around and decided to head back to The Mission. At least I still had the stack of resumes. No one had taken any so they were still good to use tomorrow.

I walked down The Embarcadero and passed by a big dumpster with its front locking gate swung open wide. Sitting, leaning up against the trash, was a laptop computer with the power cable wrapped around it. I stopped and looked around. There didn't seem to be anyone nearby. It wasn't like someone had opened up the gate to empty some trash and would be right back. If they had, they had long forgotten. I bent down and picked up the computer. It didn't have any liquids on it. It didn't appear to have any structural damage. I opened it up and tried to turn it on. Nothing happened, but I thought it might just have a dead battery. At the very least, I could sell it on Craigslist for a few bucks. There had to be somebody who would want it for the screen or the battery. I had seen some pretty shabby things listed there. This would be a sure sale, and considering how the day had gone, forty bucks could get me a long way. I stood up and, trying not to look sketchy, walked down The Embarcadero with the laptop tucked under my arm.

I took the trolly back to Market Street and walked the rest of the way to The Main Branch. Along Market, there were batches of street performers and people who could write your name on a grain of rice. I stalked through them, trying to keep the laptop as secure under my arm as I could. I needed the money but it was safe to assume that there would be someone else walking along Market who needed it more. They wouldn't hesitate to swipe it out from under my arm and take off into the traffic and mayhem of downtown. I passed by the famous cable car turnaround on Powell Street. Downtown San

Francisco is always colder than the rest of the city. The tall buildings block out the sun, and the red brick sidewalks emit cool air as the wind off The Bay whips through the streets. I stopped to look and laugh at the vacationers who were waiting for their turn to ride. All of them were wearing shorts and T-shirts, shivering in the frigid wind as they watched a man dressed as a train conductor from the nineteenth century guide the cable car safely around in a U-turn. The sweat from my morning in the sun of Fisherman's Wharf had soaked into the T-shirt, and as the wind picked up, it chilled the moisture and made me shiver. I hadn't planned any better than the visitors had.

When I got to The Main Branch, I immediately set the laptop down on one of the tables and plugged it in. There was nothing. It didn't power on right away and it didn't power on after a few minutes so I figured it was toast. That ended any hope I had to get a price in the triple digits for it. I didn't know anything about computers. I had never been able to afford one of my own, so I never bothered to learn anything about them beyond how to use them in a basic capacity. However, I had to assume that the parts in the laptop were worth something to someone. I headed over to one of the library computers and pulled up Craigslist to post a listing for it:

**FOR SALE - WINDOWS LAPTOP
FOR PARTS ONLY. DOES NOT POWER ON. $40.**

I included my cell phone number at the bottom of the ad and headed back to The Mission. The laptop and resumes were starting to feel heavy in my hands and I realized I hadn't eaten all day, so I stopped for a corn dog at a liquor store and ate it as I walked. The sun started to set and fall down below Market Street and I tried not to think about the next day. The rejection that I was going to face. I started to think that maybe I would take the next day off. I would have to go back to eating dry ramen, but the forty bucks from the laptop would be enough to tide me over for a little bit.

I had charged my phone while I posted the ad. It hadn't been turned on in over two weeks. There was never any good news on the other end. Whenever I did turn it on there were voicemails from collection agencies and former landlords from long ago threatening to sue me. No one was ever leaving me a message letting me know that I was getting some money. It was always the other way around, so I took to leaving the battery dead. There was a consistent moment of anxiety while it booted up. I dreaded what was on the other end. When I turned it on while leaving the library though, a text from my mother popped up right away.

JUST CHECKING TO MAKE SURE UR OKAY

This was an easy one to dodge and I saw an

opportunity to set a marker and buy myself some time.

ALL GOOD JUST BUSY. CALL SOON.

The response was vague enough that I could stretch it out before she got really worried. I was in a sweet spot of not letting my parents know how bad things really were and also not lying. I had been very busy lately. I immediately got another text from a number I didn't recognize.

HEY. I WANNA BUY THE LAPTOP. CAN U MEET DOWNTOWN?

It was too perfect. Here I was. This was going to be the easiest forty bucks I had ever made. I was made for this. I was a survivor. I texted back, asking if they wanted to meet at Civic Center in 10 minutes.

SURE. I'M WEARING A RED BULL HAT.

I spotted him right away as I walked up to the Civic Center BART Station, leaning against a railing and smoking a blunt. When he saw me carrying the laptop he put the thick weed cigar out on the bottom of his shoe and stuck it behind his ear. He was wearing Oakley wrap-around sunglasses and the promised Red Bull hat. His tracksuit was stained and he wasn't wearing a shirt underneath it. Pube-like hairs stuck out of the zipper, and he danced to some imaginary music.

"Hey hey, is that for me?" he said, pulling a wad of money out of his pocket and smiling wide.

He licked his fingers and separated two twenties, handing them to me still damp.

"Yeah, here."

He took the laptop and let the charger hang down and scrape on the street.

"All good, all good. Good deal, thanks."

He walked off. I watched for a minute while he tried to light the blunt, carry the computer, and walk at the same time. I thought maybe I should help him, but our interaction had been so brief, the money so easily made, that I didn't want to risk tainting the perfection of it. Eventually, he got it lit, and he shuffled down toward 6th Street with the charger dragging behind him through the spit and vomit all over the sidewalk. As he crossed Market, he dropped the computer in the crosswalk and screamed at the car waiting at the red light while he picked it up and tried to smoke at the same time. I turned around and started walking back to The Armstrong.

I was at the intersection at Market and Mission Street when I heard a noise coming from my pocket. I so rarely had the phone turned on and actually on my person that it startled me. Apparently, I hadn't noticed the first few texts. The text ringtone on the little gray flip phone was quiet and I couldn't hear it over the roar and grind of Market Street. When it rang though, I heard it on the last one and pulled it out just as it went to voicemail. I opened up the text messages and saw a barrage of misspelled hate from the guy in the Red Bull hat.

HEY FUK U THIS THING DOESN'T WORK

YOU FUKKIN RIPED ME OFF!

THIS SHIT BRKEN

I weighed the pros and cons of writing back to him. I thought about how I might explain that I had said in the ad that it didn't work. I had, in fact, stated it twice in order to avoid this very situation. Not to mention, it was only forty dollars. In what universe is a working laptop of any variety going to sell for only forty dollars? Apparently, we had both walked away from the exchange thinking that we had gotten the better deal. Both of us had gone about our merry way down the street, unable to believe our luck while everyone else had bad days around us. Only he had been disappointed. I thought about explaining it to him, then I listened to the message he left me. He sounded like he had gotten drunk quickly. He was angry. He threatened to kill me. He said if he ever saw me again he would cut my throat no questions asked. He told me to watch my back.

It was then that I decided not to try to reason with him. I would just have to do what he said and watch my back like I had been doing for months now. If he thought that I was going to live my life any differently just because he told me that he would slice my jugular open in broad daylight over a forty-dollar misunderstanding, he was mistaken about more than just the content of the ad on Craigslist. Whether or not he was going to knife me when I least expected it was irrelevant. I was going to add him to my pile of worries. I was going to be paranoid anyway. Maybe forever. My phone kept dinging and ringing all the way back to The Armstrong. He wasn't giving up. The texts got more and more graphic and threatening. It was escalating and I could tell he was getting drunker by the misspellings. By the time I got back to the hotel, he had resorted to calling over and over again. I went up to my room and listened to the phone buzz and buzz from the middle of the cot where I left it.

I was trapped again. I was forty dollars richer and someone was out to kill me for it. It seemed like such a small amount to get murdered for. When he finally did cut my stomach open and let my organs spill out onto the cobblestone sidewalks of downtown, the story would for sure say that it had all been over forty dollars. This guy seemed like he would tell everyone what the beef was about. I could picture him screaming in the courtroom as they took him away.

"I want my forty dollars back!"

People would look at that and they would shake their heads and they would talk about what a shame it was over nothing, and the people who saw it happen would say how gruesome the crime scene was. They would tell their friends what it was like as the guy jabbed at me wildly with the knife. They would talk about the look of horror on my face and how my eyes never closed as my intestines spilled out onto the street. I remembered something my father said to me when I was a kid, refusing to wear a helmet when I rode my skateboard. He said that I would fall and hit my head and I would die. Then, people would walk past my grave and they would say what a shame that little boy didn't wear his helmet, and now he's dead. I didn't like the idea of people talking about me after I was dead then any more than I did now, so I cracked open another beer, swallowed it down in four big gulps, and put on *Top Gun*.

It didn't matter. The next day I was going to get up and keep looking for a job. This nickel-and-dime stuff was going to get me killed. I needed a paycheck again. I thought about the few times in my life that I had steady money coming in, no matter for how short a period of time. Those brief moments were good, and if I could get something steady going, I could stop getting involved in shady deals and medical experiments. I could stop getting drugged and robbed and having my life threatened. This wasn't what people did. People like the owners of the restaurant I had interviewed at got up every day at the same time and they went to the same place every day. They had a routine and a BMW. The resumes sat on the counter by the sink. I got up and put them on the shelf so they wouldn't get any water on them. I was going to need them. I opened another beer and watched as Tom Cruise sang The Righteous Brothers, and fell asleep wondering if I could have made it as a fighter pilot.

Chapter Ten

I sat in the baby-shit brown office, sweating and fidgeting in the cloth chair. I could smell years worth of asses wafting up from the cushion and I watched as Kevin looked at my resume and dabbed his forehead with a greasy napkin from his lunch. He looked up at me and raised his eyebrows when our eyes met.

"I'm fuckin' hot. Are you hot? It's hot in here."

I met Kevin at the Civic Center BART station. I had been headed downtown to pass out some resumes at the mall and then walk along The Embarcadero drinking a beer to try and tamp down the awful idea of working at the mall. Before I got the chance though, a man bumped into me on the stairs leading up to the street. He was easily three hundred and fifty pounds but had been sprinting up the steps. He knocked all the resumes out of my hand as he passed and stopped on a dime as if whatever he was in such a rush to get to didn't seem all that important anymore. Before I could yell, he was apologizing over and over again, helping me pick them up. He talked fast and I could barely understand him. He had short-cropped blonde hair and a midwestern accent and sweat was dripping off his chin and earlobes. When he saw what he had knocked out of my hand, he stopped apologizing.

"Are you looking for a job?" he said, "Because I need workers."

I stopped picking up the resumes and a couple of people pushed past us on the stairs, giving us dirty looks and barely squeezing past Kevin who didn't even acknowledge them.

"I...yes," I stammered.

"Okay great, come with me," he said, and he started power-walking up the stairs.

I stooped down to pick up the rest of the resumes, but he turned around and waved the one in his hand at me.

"Just leave those, you're fine, I've got this one."

I dropped the rest of them on the steps and

followed Kevin up the stairs. He took them two at a time and didn't look back to see if I was keeping up.

I learned that Kevin was the Head Usher of the Market Street Theater, which was a large live theater that hosted touring Broadway shows and big-name, family-oriented acts. The season was in full swing and he was pressed for ushers to work the shows.

"People just stop showing up all the time," he said. "I'm pretty flexible, but come on."

Due to the seasonal nature of the theater's schedule, ushering was usually a second job or something for a retiree to keep busy with. He set my resume down on his desk and took his tie off.

"I work in HR during the day," he said, "I'm spending my break with you before work tonight." He closed his eyes and for a moment I thought I saw him fall asleep as a bead of sweat formed on the tip of his nose and dripped onto his stomach. Then, he snapped them back open and jumped up out of the chair.

"Let me show you around and we'll see if this is something you think you can do," he said.

My entire job search up until that point had felt like fishing in a wild and raging river. Impossible and overwhelming. This was the first time it actually seemed like I had a chance. Every other manager or supervisor I had given my crumpled resume to immediately looked me up and down. Kevin had barely even glanced at me. He certainly hadn't noticed that my hair was stringy and greasy. Showering at The

Armstrong had become more and more unsettling to me. Every time I got in, all I could picture was the lights dimming as water seeped under the water-proof membrane and electricity shot out of the shower head, cooking me to a shriveled, smoking ball. It felt safer to wash my ass and armpits in the sink in my room. If that sink could talk, it would tell only of the horrible things that I put it through. If Kevin was the one person who was going to give me a chance to get out of The Armstrong and out of the BART stations, I wanted to at least try to impress him.

We stepped out into the lobby and walked up the large, middle staircase. Everything was painted, carpeted, or upholstered in either the poop brown of Kevin's office or dark, dated burgundy. Accents of gold kissed the ornamental tapestries that lined the inside of the theater and as we stepped in, they gleamed in the dim, pre-show light. Kevin explained that the theater had been built in 1912 and that The Three Stooges and Rin Tin Tin had all performed there. I wanted to ask what exactly Rin Tin Tin's act had been, seeing as he was a dog, but he moved on before I could.

We walked up the stairs and he pointed out each of the sections to me. The mezzanine, the balcony, the loge. I burned the names into my mind and tried to be as present as I could. I didn't want to be caught off guard if he was going to surprise me with a quiz at the end. We got to the top of the balcony and looked down at the stage. It felt dizzying. It was as if a small breeze was all it would take for me to fall forward and sail into the orchestra pit below.

"Basically, you stand here at the door and the people give you their tickets, then you show them to their seat," said Kevin. "What do you think? Something you can handle?"

My immediate reaction was to be offended. Describing such a simple task and asking if I could handle it seemed sarcastic until I looked at him. His eyes were wide and he was smiling, genuinely wondering.

"Oh," I said. "Oh yeah. Definitely, no problem."

"Hey, that's great," he said. "You can start tonight."

He slapped me on the back happily and I had to grab the back of one of the seats to keep myself from tumbling into the black hole down below.

The shift started in two hours. Kevin asked if I could find a white shirt, a tie, a pair of dress pants, and a pair of dress shoes by then. I assured him I could and immediately counted my roll in a panic as I left. It was going to be close. I went to the first place I saw, which was a nameless, dingy-looking store on Market with the word "Apparel" printed above the door. When I walked in, a bell rang and the smells of food curled up my nose as a man and a woman looked up, startled, with their mouths full of whatever they had cooked in the back. To my surprise, they had everything I needed, and to my relief, it seemed to be around what I could afford. By the time they finally rang me up and I walked out, their food had gone cold and I had three dollars and fifteen cents to my name after taking out the next few weeks of rent at The Armstrong. I was already aching for payday.

I got to the theater right on time, dressed in a blindingly white button-up shirt and crisp slacks that were a little too big in the ass, and gave me a bubble butt. I walked through the front doors of The Market Street Theater into the lobby and ran into a group of people dressed just like me, but with burgundy blazers that matched the seats inside. Kevin was talking to one man in a blazer who appeared to be at least ninety years old. He put his hand on the old man's shoulder and nodded to him as he walked away. The old man, who I later learned was named Larry and was, in fact, ninety-one years old, kept talking quietly to himself.

"Hey, lookin' sharp," said Kevin, handing me a key. "Go downstairs and grab a jacket, they're on a rack."

The door to the basement men's locker room was already open, and there was another man, perhaps in his seventies, in there getting ready. He was tall and lanky. He looked like Paul Lynde and had a snaggletooth up front. He introduced himself as Dennis and I introduced myself as Matthew. It was on my resume, so that's what Kevin called me. That was who I would be there. Matty lived at the hotel. Matthew worked at the theater.

"Well, Matthew, isn't it interesting? We don't know each other at all," he said, buttoning the gold buttons on his blazer. "I could be a famous novelist or a millionaire or a murderer."

I was suddenly aware of how dark the basement was and how it was only us down there.

"We'd better get up to the meeting," he said, and he bounded out the door and up the stairs. I grabbed a blazer from off the rack, put it on, and followed him, keeping him in my eye-line.

At the meeting, I got a good look at the people I would be working with. It looked like a scene out of The Addams Family. Most of the other ushers were quite elderly, and more than one of them had a walker. Others were obvious tweakers, sweating and twitching in their starched collars. Still others looked like they simply didn't belong anywhere else. Everyone had something off-putting about them. A birthmark or a cast or a long cocaine fingernail. I relaxed as I watched them mill about and laugh with each other. I was ready to have somewhere to fit in.

The show that night was a Rodgers and Hammerstein musical from the late forties. Kevin passed around a clipboard with a map of the theater and everyone's name marked where they were to be positioned. I was next to the door that led into the balcony. After everyone had initialed beside their name, I started to walk upstairs to get in my position before the doors opened and the patrons came pouring in. Kevin grabbed me by the shoulder as I passed.

"It's a pretty light night so I put you in the balcony with David and Levant. They'll show you the ropes."

When I got to the top of the stairs where the balcony door was, the first thing I saw was a little man in his sixties or seventies with dyed, jet-black hair rushing toward me in a burgundy blazer.

"Are you Matthew? Are you Matthew?"

His voice sounded like he had just drunk a big glass of milk. Like Kermit the Frog. He had little jowls that swayed as he came toward me. He didn't walk along the brown carpet, he glided.

"You, are you Matthew?" he said once more as he came to stop in front of me.

"I am," I said.

"Well come on, come on, Jesus Christ let's go, they're gonna let them in any minute."

He grabbed my arm and led me through the doors and into the theater. Below us, the black hole was lit up with a colorful set with a seaside backdrop and the orchestra was tuning up in the pit. The deadened, dissonant music reminded me of my first night in The Armstrong. It was the focused sound of a perfect vacuum. I hesitated for a moment as I let my stomach settle and get used to the height. David grabbed my arm again.

"Come on, here, take these."

He handed me a stack of Playbills.

"Where's your flashlight?"

My heart started racing.

"I...Kevin didn't say anything..."

David rolled his eyes.

"Well, how the hell are you gonna read the tickets? It's darker than shit in here."

He reached into his pocket and handed me a small silver flashlight.

"Don't be without it again," he said.

As he finished rolling his eyes for the last time, another man in a burgundy blazer walked through the door. His hair was slicked back and he was incredibly pale. He almost glowed in the dark.

"There you are, Jesus come on, come on," David said to him.

I was relieved to find out that his impatience didn't only extend to me.

"Thirty years I've been working with this fuckin' guy and he's been late every day."

"Yeah, yeah, come on just give me the books," said the pale man, who I assumed was Levant.

When he spoke, I got a glimpse of the inside of his mouth. It appeared that his teeth were filed down to points in the front, and when the words came out, they sloshed and slurred.

"Levant's gonna go up top, you stay down here,"

said David. I had to pry my eyes off Levant's sharpened mouth as David hissed at me.

"I'll take their tickets and if they're seated down here I'll send 'em to you. If they're up there, they'll go to him and you guys take them directly to their seats, got it?"

I nodded and Levant went up to the very top of the balcony. David nudged me.

"He thinks he's a vampire. He's a fuckin' weirdo."

Then David took a pair of scissors and a small mirror out of his pocket and started trimming his dyed bangs, letting the clippings fall on the brown carpet.

I had a minute or so before the doors opened and people started pouring in through the balcony doors. I went along the aisles with the flashlight and looked at the numbers stamped onto metal tags on the seats, trying desperately to memorize them. They were all out of order and seemed to skip several numbers where the aisles broke the row of seats. As I was trying to figure out how it all worked, I heard a loud whistle from behind me over at the balcony doors. David was holding some Playbills in his hand and waving them at me as a woman in her eighties and her husband, who was perhaps even older, waited beside him. More people were lining up behind them and Levant the vampire was already leading a couple to their seats up above. He moved gracefully and waved his hand toward the seat like a butler as he led them to their row. Another whistle broke through the soundproofed air and I ran over to David and the old couple. He handed me the Playbills and I took their tickets and walked with them down the aisle. Luckily, their seats were in an easy section, and I found them quickly. As I started to walk away. I heard the woman make a cartoonish, "ahem" sound that stopped me cold. I turned around.

"Aren't those for us?" she said, pointing to the Playbills in my hand.

"Of course," I said.

I handed them to her.

"Sorry about tha..."

Another sharp whistle cut me off, and I ran over to David who was waving more Playbills and shoving another elderly couple at me.

The seating went on for another 45 minutes. For every single one of those minutes aside from that first couple with the easy seats, I was a confused mess. I sat people in the wrong place. I couldn't find seat 26 because the only thing next to 24 on the even-numbered side was a metal pole. Every time I tried to ask David a question, he would make a loud clucking sound and roll his eyes before shouting the answer at me and nudging the patrons waiting to be shown to their seats.

It had been a long time since I had worked. I forgot how humiliating it was. A quarter of the way through the seating, I was pouring sweat. Big drops fell down off my hair and the grease stung my eyes. David kept whistling, and the mostly elderly crowd got more and more impatient. It was hard enough for them to get up the stairs all the way to the balcony and once they got there, they had to deal with an angry Muppet, a confused man who reeked of bourbon sweat, and a vampire.

By the time the seating was almost over, it got easier to narrow down where people were supposed to be simply by the process of elimination. When the show actually started and David and I closed the doors and took our seats in the lobby, I was drenched with sweat and my heart was pounding. The seating felt like it took hours and my feet were killing me from running up and down the steps. I looked over at David to see if he was seething with hatred at me for my poor, sweaty performance, but he had taken out a ball of yarn and some needles and was happily knitting on a bench in the lobby.

When the show was over, David and I opened up the big doors that led from the theater out to the balcony lobby and stood at them, waiting to say goodnight to the patrons. Smells of perfume and light sweat wafted out of the theater and filled the lobby before the people did. Once they came out, they all came out smiling. Some of them were old enough for the show to have been a part of their youth and others were just happy to have seen some people singing and dancing for a while. Some of them seemed to know

David, and many of them handed me back the crumpled and greasy Playbills that they had been clutching all night. I watched as they all milled around in the lobby and eventually filtered out and into the street.

We closed the doors and went downstairs where the ushers were waiting to be released to go home. As soon as we got down, David rushed ahead of me and glided over to Kevin who was sweating and scanning the lobby for any lost patrons. My heart sank and I turned red. David grabbed him and began talking in a low voice into Kevin's ear. I knew he was telling him how much he had to yell at me and how I had seated people in the wrong seats and how I was an embarrassment and that even a vampire could figure it out and he was possibly hundreds of years old.

I started sweating again as Kevin whistled and gathered everyone around. I had been fired before. It wasn't going to be a big deal. I was a veteran. I hoped that the meeting would be short so I wouldn't have to wait a long time for Kevin to dismiss everyone and then call my name and ask to see me in his brown office. Then, he would tell me that it just didn't work out and that unfortunately, we wouldn't be able to move forward. I thought about my new clothes and the last of my money spent on them. I hoped that the white shirt would be warm enough when I was back sleeping on the street.

"Hey, can I have everyone's attention please?"

Kevin said.

A few of the older ushers kept talking and when he repeated himself they continued.

"Guys," he said. "Can you listen up real quick?"

They kept talking.

"Guys. Guys."

The oldest of them nudged another, who was leaning on a cane. They all turned, looking annoyed.

"Thank you," said Kevin. "Hey, I just want to take a quick moment to talk about Matthew over here."

My heart started pounding and sweat pooled on my back in the tucked-in shirt. Was he really going to fire me in front of everyone?

"It was Matthew's first night tonight, and frankly..."

I closed my eyes. If no one could see me, maybe I would disappear.

"Well," Kevin continued. "He did a great job."

My eyes snapped open and my heart slowed.

"David told me that he had the balcony figured out only halfway through the seating tonight, so just a quick round of applause."

There were some murmurs and some impressed nodding of heads and applause slowly rippled through the gathered crowd.

"Alright, everybody, see you tomorrow night," Kevin said. "Matthew, same time tomorrow for the meeting."

I pointed at him and nodded, smiling, as the

other ushers slowly dispersed to hang up their burgundy blazers and go out into the downtown night.

When I stepped out of the theater, the air was cold and my white shirt clung to my back with sweat. I felt it turn to slick ice above my butt crack. Cabs were firing up and down Taylor Street and on every corner there was someone with an empty Carl's Jr. cup or a hat, shaking it and yelling for change. A group of people leaned up against the wall of the theater and puffed yellow clouds of crack smoke out over the heads of the pedestrians walking past. I could smell the plastic-y, melting smoke as I went by and turned into the first liquor store on the corner.

I bought a tall boy of Olde English with one of my last balled-up dollar bills and headed down Market Street, shivering from the cold sweat that wouldn't dry. I hadn't brought my hoodie. I had only planned to come downtown and apply at the discounted clothing store everyone stole from on 4th and Market. I had seen employees sleeping in the racks and smoking weed by ducking underneath the cash register so I was reasonably certain they might take me on. Running into Kevin had changed everything. The theater was full of weirdos and people frustrated with having to live in the world. No one fit in, so everyone fit in. I didn't mind being yelled at by David. He was funny and it didn't make me mad to see him get angry with me. Clearly, he was like that with everyone.

Every job I had previous to this made me feel like an outsider. Like I was intruding on someone else's space and inconveniencing them. There, among the ancient vampires and secret meth heads, I could finally blend in. It was the first time I ever felt like I could possibly be good at a job. As simple as it was, it was my first win in a long time and I didn't quite know what to do with it.

I took long gulps of the malt liquor and the ice running down my back finally melted as my face started to flush. My feet hurt like they did the first night on the traffic island. The new shoes were killing me, so I stopped and sat down in an empty brick doorway to change them. I sat there for a while on Market Street watching people walk past and drinking my beer. I took my shoes off and stuffed them in my backpack, waiting a moment before putting my other shoes back on. I sipped at the beer and laughed as people eyed me up and down as they went by. I was in a white shirt and tie, slacks, no shoes, chugging malt liquor in a doorway. Sometimes it was worth it just to make people wonder. The world felt much more familiar down there than it did just a few moments prior when I was feeling like a successful professional. When it dawned on me that a patron from the theater or, God forbid, Kevin, could walk past, I put my other shoes on, took another sip of the beer, and got up to walk home to The Armstrong. Once there, I fell face-first on the cot and fell asleep with the lights on.

Chapter Eleven

There were shows at the theater every day but Monday and two on Sunday and I worked all of them. I got to know the seats better than my own room at The Armstrong. I laughed with the old men down in the basement locker room and I helped some of them with their ties when they couldn't stop their hands from shaking. I worked regularly up in the balcony with David and Levant. We were strange ghosts lurking way up high. A burnout always on the brink of homelessness, an eccentric ex-hairdresser, and a vampire, haunting the old rafters.

Aside from David and Levant, there was Larry, who was by far the oldest of the entire crew. He was 91 and he looked every second of it. Larry could only work down in the orchestra since he couldn't get up the stairs and often the elderly patrons, who would normally need the most help, were younger and much more agile than he was. Then there was Paula, a tall, spindly woman with thinning hair who smoked Marlboro Red 100s down to the filter in the alley outside the cast door. She was either formerly or currently a meth user judging by her physicality and mannerisms but she sprinted around the place like a gazelle and ran up the stairs in big, high-stepping hops. She acted as Kevin's de facto assistant and had the privilege of getting a walkie-talkie so the two of them could communicate. Before the audience was let in, Kevin would radio her up in the balcony to make sure all the ushers were in place.

"Let's rock and roll," she would always say.

One thing that you had to be careful about with Paula was how you started a conversation. If you casually asked her something like "how's it going?" she was going to tell you. She was not going to give a canned answer like "fine" or "good." She was going to lay it all out on the line. She was always looking for someone to vent to and I had spent so much time by myself over the last few months that I was happy for the one-sided conversation. It took all the pressure off me and there was no danger of an awkward silence.

She lived in the swank Russian Hill neighborhood with her 97-year-old grandmother and always had a gripe about it.

"Ninth-generation San Franciscan," she said one day, "and the state can't even help with a nurse. I'm the one that has to do it all. Cooking, cleaning, doing laundry, wiping her ass. You ever wipe an old lady's ass before?"

We were eating slices of pizza in the lobby before a show and I had just taken a big bite as she asked me.

"Only once," I said, my mouth full, "but just for fun."

She laughed and wiped her hand on her burgundy blazer.

"You joke, but it's a mess down there. Everything's the same color as these walls," she said, pointing around the lobby.

Not every usher was hiding their struggles as well. Some were already at rock bottom and this was the only place that would scoop them back up. People like John. John was middle-aged and persistently drenched in sweat. He carried a handkerchief with him at all times, but I made sure not to use any burgundy blazers that he had worn. The collars always ended up yellowed and stiff. He wore his hair in a big, drooping pompadour and I caught a glimpse of it one morning while walking past The Voltaire Lounge on Valencia. John was sitting at the bar with two shot glasses and two pints in front of him and his head cradled in his arms. When I would see him having an imaginary argument with himself down in The Mezzanine as great streams of perspiration fell down his face, I wouldn't interrupt. I knew where he was coming from.

For the most part, I immediately loved all of the weirdos at the theater. They each had their own set of problems and they were dealing with them in their own ways. We were all one and the same. Most of them were concerned mainly with themselves and I enjoyed listening to their trials and tribulations. I never shared any of my own. I took on a sort of voice of reason role there, in the way that people sometimes get typecast in new social situations, and I enjoyed feeling like I came from some position of authority.

Mostly, everyone was much older than me with the exception of Austin. Austin was tall and gangly with a bushy red beard that almost matched the blazers. He was loud and talked with a Southern accent. He openly commented on the performances during the intermission and I had heard that he once jumped on stage and sang with the chorus during South Pacific and no one noticed except for a few ushers. He was friendly with everyone and the old ladies loved him. He would speak to them in his low drawl and hold their arm as they walked down the aisle.

"Shit," he told me. "They love that. You would not believe the things they try to give me as a tip. I only keep the pills, though."

We became friendly immediately, recognizing each other as kindred spirits lost on the path. Most people our age were getting married, having kids, getting promotions, and buying houses. We were helping Larry tuck his shirt in and get up the steps in time for the pre-show meeting. We both considered small victories to be major wins. We never talked about life outside of work, but when you are lost, you can easily spot someone else who is searching for their way. When the shows would let out, he would often invite me to go have a drink at The Trophy Room just down the street. I would always decline on the grounds that I had a long walk. I didn't want to let my guard down and let anyone in on how I lived and how bad it was. I didn't want to lose my new status as the voice of reason.

Every night I thought about joining him and I would hesitate a little bit more every time before finally relenting and saying I should probably just head home. After one particularly brutal night at the theater, he didn't invite me, and instead, as we left the front doors, he followed me, talking the whole time about a man in the mezzanine who had a heart attack during Phantom of the Opera. I had seen some sort of commotion down there from the balcony but was anxious to hear what happened. He talked as we walked down Market.

"I looked over, and he was just lying on the

fuckin floor man it was crazy. Right during 'The Music of the Night.'"

"So what did you do?" I asked.

"I called fuckin 911 dude," he said, "and they had to carry the guy down the steps. I don't think he's gonna live."

"Crazy," I said.

"So crazy."

We were stopped in front of the liquor store I went to every night on my way home.

"Well, I gotta get some stuff in here," I said.

"Cool," he said, "me too, sounds good."

I didn't know what to say. I expected him to head off or keep going but he followed me in and we both bought six packs of malt liquor tall cans and opened a couple of them as soon as we were out the door. We kept walking and I thought that maybe he was also going to The Mission so we talked more about work. About David. About Levant. About Kevin. We finished our beers and when I got to the door of The Armstrong I stopped again.

"Were you headed somewhere?" I asked, trying not to let on that this was where I lived. The guys were out front smoking and none of them gave me away because they didn't seem to like me and never said hello.

"What do you mean?" Austin said. "I thought we were hanging out. I bought so much beer."

He held up the two six-packs of Olde English tall

cans.

"Come on, let's go," he said. "Is this where you live?"

I couldn't think of an excuse fast enough, so I held my breath and motioned for him to follow me.

We went up the stairs and ran straight into Mr. Seif who was sitting up front. As we started to walk past him, his voice boomed from behind the counter.

"Excuse me," he said. We stopped and turned to look at him. "You must sign in."

"What?" I said.

"All guests must sign in. Did you read your rental agreement? Can you read?"

"Yes," I said, just trying to get through the interaction as Austin signed his name and looked back and forth at Mr. Seif and me. Mr. Seif stared at the two six-packs of malt liquor Austin had set on the counter that were sweating all over the sign-in sheet. I had never noticed it before and since I didn't have any friends, the sheet had never come up. He finished signing his name and picked up the beer as we headed back down the hall. Austin kept looking back as we walked, but I kept staring straight ahead, trying to get to my door and out from under his hot, accusatory gaze.

When I opened the door to my room and let him in, it was as if I was walking into someone else's place. I was looking at it objectively for the first time, seeing it through Austin's eyes. There were beer bottles all over the floor. I had taken to just setting them in one corner of the room and gathering them all up to distribute evenly around The Mission late at night when the pile got too big. I would set them on top of trash cans neatly, making them easy to gather and throw in a shopping cart. It was my good deed. I had to sneak the clinking and clanking garbage bags down the stairs past Mr. and Mrs. Seif's door. On this particular night, it had been quite a while since I had made one of my late-night trash fairy runs. The pile was large and sprawling out of its corner and all over the floor. There were clothes thrown everywhere and random packages of ramen noodles peppered every available surface. VHS tapes sat out of their sleeves, and one empty sleeve for *Lake Placid* was sitting on the floor in a shallow puddle of beer, slowly disintegrating.

'Damn, Matty, don't clean up on my behalf," said Austin.

Before I could reply he walked over to the window leading out to the fire escape and opened it. He took a deep breath.

"Smells like Saturday night, my friend," he said.

He stepped up and out onto the fire escape and lit a cigarette. I joined him, stopping only briefly to think about how I had never been out there before. I wasn't sure about its weight limit. Austin saw me hesitate and started laughing and jumping up and down, his feet sending a big boom down the length of the steel.

"It's solid as hell, man," he said.

We sat on the fire escape and drank the Olde English. As soon as I started talking, I couldn't stop. The stories poured out of me from the last few months. Austin listened and drank the beer, lighting cigarette after cigarette and throwing the butts out into the middle of Valencia, watching them spark as they hit the ground. Now and then he would laugh or whisper "Shit" or "Jesus," but he let me get it all out. I hadn't told anyone any of this and as the night wore on I realized I hadn't told anyone anything in a long time. So much time spent alone under a street light or in this electrified white room, looking for something and finding nothing. I was so thankful to let it all out. To tell the story of Fast Eddie and to describe Lola and try as hard as I could to remember everything about her. Her face and voice were starting to fade now, just like the basement in Seattle and Knut's face screaming at me in the hallway. Now that they were out in the open, they finally belonged to someone else. Austin could help me keep those memories safe.

We sat out on the fire escape for many hours. I watched as the traffic and crowds of people out on Valencia got thinner and thinner. Then, the bars closed and waves of people poured from them while I told Austin about trying to buy a stolen van. They all stumbled home with each other or alone and we opened more cans of Olde English. When I was done, I slumped back against the wrought iron, exhausted and spent. As soon as I was finished, he lit another cigarette and began talking.

He had finished grad school and received his MFA in industrial design six months prior. When he was done, he didn't know what to do with himself. He had put so much effort into finishing school that he never once thought about what he would do once he did. So, he sat around his apartment drinking whiskey until his girlfriend kicked him out. She had just finished law school and his existential crisis wasn't in the plan. He was living in his truck in The Tenderloin around the corner from the theater. I could see that he had also been anxious to tell someone all of this because that is the thing that no one tells you about poverty: it is so lonely.

He finished talking and had the same look I did of a huge weight off his back. He lit the last cigarette in his pack and leaned his face against the window sill.

"I just feel like I don't care about anything sometimes," he said, taking a drag. "I think as long as I'm playing music I'm happy. I can kind of do anything as long as I can do that."

I sat up straight and tried to focus my malt liquor vision to look at him.

"You play music?"

He started to answer but then I heard the handle on the room door jiggle through the open window. Austin stopped talking and let the cigarette dangle out of his mouth as we tried to make sense out of the noise. Then, the door swung open and Mr. Seif shouldered his way in. He took a big, sweeping glance of the room. He saw the empty beer bottles and the mess. He saw us out on the fire escape and his eyes settled on Austin. Before I could say anything, he charged over to the open window and stuck his head out with us. It felt violating.

"What is this?" He screamed. His voice echoed down the empty street and a light in the room upstairs turned on.

"This is not allowed," he said. "None of this. No visitors after eleven. No smoking. No fire escape. No nothing."

As he listed the violations, the blood rushed to his face and it got purple and bloated as he leaned down to yell at me.

"Get in from there, get off there," he said.

I kept my head down. I had not read anything in the agreement I signed. I had no idea there were no visitors allowed after eleven. I hadn't even known they were supposed to sign in. After Mr. Seif pulled his gigantic purple face back out of the window, we got up and each crawled through it and into the room. I couldn't bear to look at Austin. There was something about it that felt like getting yelled at by someone else's dad. The smallness and shame that had been lifted in the past few weeks at the theater suddenly came rushing back into my body. My shoulders drooped, my eyes burned and my hands started to tingle. I could feel my breath getting shorter and I was starting to take in big gulping gasps as Mr. Seif continued to yell at us. He looked around the room and started kicking over beer bottles and picking things up and waving them at me, angry.

I couldn't say how long Austin and I stood there in the middle of the room while Mr. Seif screamed at us. He seemed to get angrier the quieter we were. I went to sit down on the cot while he yelled something about rules and how the people in the hotel never wanted to follow any rules and that was why they had to live there instead of in their own house with a family. I had put my head in my hands, so I didn't notice right away when another voice joined him in the chorus. When I looked up, I saw that Austin had his finger in Mr. Seif's face, whose eyes were widened with surprise. It was the look of someone being mauled by an animal they had beaten. Unable to comprehend how it was possible that something they had broken so thoroughly had any strength left to fight back.

"Listen here, you little weenie," Austin said. Mr. Seif brought his hand to his chest like a shocked old lady. "My friend here is a paying customer. Do you understand me?"

Mr. Seif didn't say anything, waiting for the next part of what he thought was a hypothetical question.

"I'm talking to you, do you understand me?" Austin said, screaming now. Mr. Seif cowered back.

"Yeah."

"Good," Austin said. "He's a paying customer and you're gonna treat him like one. With some god damn respect."

Mr. Seif started to say something and Austin cut him off, talking quietly and slowly inching closer to his face.

"And if I hear anything from my friend there," he pointed to me, "about you talking to him like that again, I'm gonna walk over here and I'm gonna burn down this fucking hotel."

Mr. Seif's face drained. The purple gave way to red, which gave way to pink, and finally a pale, ghostly white.

"Because," Austin said. "I have nothing to lose. Do you?"

<www

The next morning, I woke up to the toilet flushing and the quiet, sad murmurs of the people in the hall. As soon as my eyes opened, a low, wild moan drained from my mouth and into the pillow. I could only half remember the night before. As the seconds passed, images started to flash. Mr. Seif's purple face, the look of fear as Austin threatened him. The way he just stayed in the middle of the room when Austin said goodbye to me and then left. He finally shook his head, then turned to me.

"Please clean this up and don't use the fire escape unless you have to...you know...escape a...well..."

With that, he left the room and I passed out. I was certain that there would be some sort of eviction notice on my door in the morning. There was no way the rules allowed you to threaten to burn down the hotel. Even though I hadn't been the one to say it, I knew Mr. Seif could only see me when he thought about it. I put my shoes on and pressed my ear to the door. I thought I could hear him out there, talking to someone in line. I couldn't bear to look at him. I figured that if I avoided him altogether, I wouldn't have to face the consequences. If there was an eviction notice on my door, would it count if I never saw it? I stepped to the window and looked at the fire escape. If it was meant to escape fires, then surely it would work for escaping awkward situations.

I stepped out onto the steel and felt the hot sun stab into my eyes. It took a long while to adjust and I didn't dare start climbing down until I could see. Once I got used to the bright, burning sun, I found the metal latch that held up the ladder and undid it. The ladder slowly lowered to the ground below on a set of springs and I climbed down to the sidewalk, pushing it back up, where it latched in place. The men out front smoking watched me as I avoided their gaze and ran down Valencia. Running away again. I spent the day in the park drinking beers and a half-pint of Ancient

Age. By the time the sun was high in the sky, my hangover was gone and had been replaced with a sleepy, full-body drunk. I got up and staggered up the hill.

I hadn't been to the traffic island in over a month. There was trash in the clearing and a broken bottle. Someone else had found it, it seemed, and they hadn't taken nearly as good care of it as I had. I pushed everything out of the way with my foot and fell on the ground, pushing my ear into the cold dirt. I wanted to lay there for years. I wanted to fuse with the ground and feed the tree, leaving Mr. Seif to clean out my room and wonder what happened to me until he figured I had died somewhere out on the street and eventually forgot.

◆◇◇◇◆

I woke up a couple of hours later with my eyelids glued shut. I was gasping for air and had slept on my arm which was now completely numb. Dehydrated and sunburned, my eyes were crusted over and I had to pry them open with a dirty fingernail. My back hurt and as I turned over I came face to face with a hypodermic needle that I hadn't seen when I laid down. Something was different under the oily tree in the traffic island. I couldn't come back here, that was for sure. My body rejected being outside now. It had

179

gotten a taste for a blanket and a cot and a roof above it. As much as I thought I was immune to the comforts that most people looked for, I couldn't deny that shelter was a little more than just a comfort. I started to get up slowly. Every bone creaked and snapped and as the blood rushed out of my head, the headache started just as I knew it would. Like it or not, I would have to go back to The Armstrong.

The sun was just starting to set and the wind was picking up, carrying with it some blasts of cold that had caught rides in from the ocean. I brushed the dirt and leaves off my back and headed down the hill. Mr. Seif would be waiting at the front desk for me. Waiting to hand me my eviction notice. I had seen them before. I could picture the font. I got to the front door and started slowly up the stairs, trying to savor my last housed moments. All I could think about was how quiet Mr. Seif had gotten when Austin yelled at him. It was the silent resignation of someone who has decided not to worry about something because soon it will be gone. When I got to the top, I turned the corner and he was sitting there, reading the newspaper and drinking a cup of tea. He had just raised it to his mouth when I walked in and he stopped, letting it sit there in mid-air. My heart pounded as he looked at me.

"Good evening," he said. Then he took a sip of tea and went back to reading the paper.

My eyes were wide and unblinking but I slipped

past him, almost breaking into a run to see if he had perhaps nailed the notice to my door. There was nothing. Surely he had just slipped it under the crack and it would be laying in a puddle of beer on the floor. I whipped open the door. There was nothing. I started laughing to myself and backed out of the room and down the hall. Mr. Seif was in mid-sip at the front counter.

"Good evening," I said back to him.

He turned and studied me for a moment, then lifted his mug in a greeting and went back to the paper. I laughed again, all the way down the hall, before shutting the door behind me and cracking open a warm can of malt liquor left over from the night before.

Chapter Twelve

By the time I woke up the next day, the bathroom line at The Armstrong had already run its course. The whooshing and flashing and sad murmuring was over for the morning. My eyes tried to adjust to the glaring white walls as I turned over on my side and knocked over a few beer cans that were left by the cot. One rolled across the linoleum and bumped against the door. As I watched it, I saw that it had rolled over a piece of paper sitting on the floor. I frowned and scrambled over to pick it up, knocking over more cans and bottles in the process.

The paper was actually a few pieces stapled together and it had The Armstrong's logo in the top right corner. My eyes were crossed and trying to shrivel back into my skull from the light. I had to close one of them to be able to read it. Then I had to read it six or seven more times to fully understand what it said. The words were plainly typed but I couldn't grasp them. They seemed to fall apart like wet tissue paper draped over my brain. My lease at The Armstrong was up. I had to move out the next day. I could read that. I just didn't understand. Lease? How long had I been living there? It had felt like weeks but was it possible that I had been living there for over a year? Had the theater and the middle-aged ghosts that lined up outside my door every morning sucked so much life out of me? Had I completely replaced my spirit with malt liquor?

I read the paper over quite a few more times. I had been living at The Armstrong for six weeks. In the state of California, you can't live somewhere for more than six weeks without signing some sort of paperwork and having proof of income and all those things that I had always figured the people living at The Armstrong didn't have. I had just assumed that I could stay like they did. As Mr. Seif had pointed out, I had not read the agreement. As I sat down to read it that morning, I saw that I could stay long-term by putting down a deposit and signing a lease. Otherwise,

I had to be out in twenty-four hours. There was no way I was going to be able to get all the documents and identification I needed in time.

I sat for several minutes on the cot, breathless at my own stupidity. If I had read the agreement, if I had done what I was supposed to do, the most basic, simple thing, I could have gotten everything together. It was far too late now. It was a Monday and the theater was closed. I couldn't get proof of employment. I didn't have two forms of ID. I barely had one. My expired Washington driver's license was starting to crack and fall apart. Clouds moved over the sun that was streaming in through the window and it got dark in the white room in The Armstrong Hotel. I sat with the eviction notice in my hand and looked around for an unopened beer.

I was too afraid to leave my room for the rest of the morning. The idea of running into Mr. or Mrs. Seif in the hall was too much. Mr. Seif would gloat and raise his god damned mug at me. Mrs. Seif would smile sweetly, feeling bad but not bad enough to let me stay. Both of the options were too much to handle. Picturing them made me cringe and dig into the palms of my hands with my fingernails. I found a couple of unopened tall boys of malt liquor among the pile of cans and bottles in the corner, which had been getting bigger and bigger. Moving out of this room would mean cleaning that up. It would mean being held accountable for it. I may even have to end up counting how many were there. I just didn't think I could handle the number I was sure to come up with.

I looked around the room. Aside from the trash corner and the general filth, I had settled in there so well. The TV was set up on some big waxed boxes I had found behind the Duc Loi grocery store. I covered them with a piece of hippie-patterned cloth I bought at Mission Thrift and they made a nice, sturdy TV stand. All my action movies were stacked up next to the makeshift entertainment center in alphabetical order. My clothes were folded in the closet and clean from the laundromat. My Venus flytrap was smiling on the windowsill at the sun behind the clouds. I couldn't bear to leave this place. It was the only home I had known for so long.

After three more tall boys of malt liquor, my eyes were fuzzy and adjusting to the shadows passing over the white linoleum. I knew exactly what I was going to do. The next morning, instead of moving out, I was going to beg. I would tell Mr. and Mrs. Seif everything. Things I hadn't told anyone. I would tell them how much I needed this place. I would tell them that I had a job and that if they could just give me a little more time I could get everything I needed to stay. I would stay up all night and think of the best way to say it. There were perfect words somewhere out there that would convince them. I knew that. All I had to do was find them before the next morning.

I stuck my head out the door and checked that

the hallway was clear. I didn't want to risk getting caught taking the fire escape down. I crept down the hall and silently checked to see if anyone was at the front counter. When I saw it was empty, I ran through the hall, down the stairs, and out the door. 30 minutes later, I did the same stealth moves, making it back into my room without seeing anyone. I dumped my provisions onto the cot: A pen and notebook, a fifth of Ancient Age, some energy drinks, and blue hair dye. Things got bleak quickly, so I was going to have to go all out.

The rest of the items were self-explanatory, but the hair dye was a last-minute decision. I saw it on a shelf in the dollar store next to the piñatas and candles with The Virgin Mary on them. It was a glossy box with a man on it who looked like Mario Lopez with a dog collar and blue hair. It would have to do. My logic was that I needed to be new. I needed a change. Something that would put me in another reality. Let me wear a mask while I begged for mercy. The box was almost completely in Chinese and upon closer inspection, I realized that it actually was Mario Lopez's face Photoshopped onto someone else's body and head. I briefly considered going to The Main Branch and writing him an email to see if he was aware. There might be a reward for reporting this kind of identity fraud. Instead, I decided to focus on the task at hand. It was 4 p.m.

I cracked open the glass bottle of Ancient Age and

set it on the counter next to the sink. Filling my plain, black mug from Thrift Town, I started to pull words from the air. Even just beginning to think about what I was going to say was making me sweat. I drained the mug and slammed it down on the counter, filling it again and draining it and filling it and draining it. I opened the dye box and let all the contents spill out into the sink. I couldn't remember if I had rinsed it since the last time I pissed in it. There was a small packet of bleach, which I immediately opened and began pouring on my head and working in with the flimsy plastic gloves that were provided. The smell curled down and singed my eyelashes. It was cheap and industrial and I immediately felt a tingling on my head. In broken English, the instructions said to let it sit for 30 minutes. I filled and drained the mug several times while sitting on the cot with a burning scalp, talking out loud to myself, running and revising my potential speech over and over again.

When the half-hour was up, the bleach on my head was burning and itching. I waited it out as long as I could, then I got up to run to the communal bathroom to wash it off in the shower. To my horror, though, when I opened the door, I was hit with a line for the bathroom. I had no shirt on, a towel around my shoulders, and hair almost smoking with bleach that needed to come out. Some of the people in line turned and looked, but no one said anything as I hopped up and down and tried not to scratch at the acid burning through my hair and into my brain.

By the time I was next in line, I was jumping back and forth, trying to scratch my scalp by moving my eyebrows when Mr. Seif turned the corner. He was holding his mug of tea and I saw his eyes jump when they landed on me. I watched as he remembered what was going to happen the next day and his face relaxed, then he lifted his mug at me in a greeting.

"Come on, go," someone said.

The door to the bathroom was wide open in front of me and Mr. Seif nodded toward it and sauntered off toward the counter, sipping at his mug. I ran into the shower and turned the water on, dousing my flaming skull with the cold, electric water.

Once the bleach was out of my hair, I could see straight again. Looking in the mirror back in my room, the blonde made my face look even redder and puffier. I looked worse than I ever had. The beer had been easier on my stomach, but not so much on my face. It made me glad I had gotten the bourbon for the day instead. I was already making better decisions. I figured that once the hair was blue, it would even out, so I dumped the vinyl packet of dye onto my head and worked it in with the second pair of plastic gloves. Then I brought the bottle with me onto the cot, poured another mugful of bourbon, and drained it. I took out the notebook and started writing down words like "trustworthy" and "responsible." I poured another mugful of bourbon and drained it again, writing the words "I am here." The letters started to blur and slip down from the lines as I contemplated them and drained the mug. My speech to the Seifs was starting to crawl off the page and down onto the brown army blanket and quickly, before I could catch myself, I fell asleep. It was 6:30 p.m.

I woke up with a headache shooting down the middle of my face that was only slightly covered up by the itching on my scalp. I scratched the top of my head and when I looked at my fingers, I almost screamed. Black and blue gunk pulled away with my fingers and it took me a moment to remember that I had fallen asleep with the hair dye still in. It was all over the army blanket and the cot, too. I checked the time. It was 7:30 a.m. Panic. Icy panic. I was expected to be out by 8 a.m. when the Seifs opened the front counter. I immediately ran to the quarter-full fifth of bourbon still sitting on the cot, poured a mug to appease the headache, and started pacing back and forth while sipping at it. I scratched at my head and drank from the mug as the seconds slipped away.

At 8 a.m., I was standing at the front counter when Mrs. Seif came around the corner. The look on her face should have told me it was over. Clumps of dye were stuck in my hair and I was sweating great blue streaks down my temples and neck. I was wild-eyed, volatile, and hungover.

"Yes?"

"Mrs. Seif," I swallowed hard. "Please. Please.

Please."

For a second, I was terrified that this was all that was going to come out. Then, Mr. Seif came around the corner with his tea. His shoulders dropped when he saw me and his face scrunched up to examine whatever was going on with my head.

"Please, you guys. I know that maybe we didn't get off on the right foot but I would really love to stay here."

They looked at each other.

"Please, look, I have a job."

I pulled out a crumpled pay stub from the theater and put it on the counter, trying to iron out the wrinkles with my hands, smearing it with hair dye.

"I can work on getting the other stuff, I just need more time, please. Please. Please."

They looked at me and didn't say anything. It got to be too long, so I broke the silence.

"Please, I'll have to go back out there," I said, pointing to the stairs leading out to Valencia Street. "I've gotten too soft here. I think maybe I was always soft. I thought I was tough. I thought I could deal but..."

I took a deep, stuttering breath.

"The idea of having to go back out there is scaring the shit out of me because I don't know if I'll ever get back in."

They looked back at each other.

"Guys," I said. "I'm begging you here, just give me

a little more time."

Mrs. Seif broke her gaze from her husband and turned to me. She placed her hand on the counter, looked at the pay stub, then picked up a pencil. My heart jumped. It seemed like some paperwork was going to be filled out. Then, with the eraser end of the pencil, she pushed the crumpled pay stub back toward me, unwilling to touch it herself.

"I'm sorry, no," she said.

As Mrs. Seif pushed the pay stub back to me, I wouldn't take it. If I took it, that meant I was accepting her answer. She kept pushing it and pushing it toward the edge of the counter and I just stared. She pushed until it fell off the edge and landed limply on the floor.

"Please," I sputtered out. "Please."

Mr. Seif took a sip from his mug and smiled, shrugging his shoulders. Mrs. Seif smiled like she meant it and reached up to grab the strap and pull down the rolling security shutter. They had just opened, she wasn't closing. She was trying to get something between us.

"Please, please."

She started pulling it down.

"Please."

"Please be out by noon," she said. "I'll give you a few extra hours."

"No, come on I'll get everything."

She pulled the shutter down further and I bent

down to keep talking as it got closer to shutting all the way.

"I'll do anything, please don't make me go back out there."

I tilted my head to get a last look at Mr. Seif's grin as the shutter hit the counter and I was left out in the silent hallway.

I kicked the crumpled-up pay stub out of the way and could feel everything coming up. The anger boiling over and fizzing out, condensing and producing hot tears that came down fast. They had nowhere else to go. I let them come. I broke loose with deep, ugly sobs. I covered my face and felt the clumps of hair dye mix with the tears to create huge blue-green streaks down my eyelids and cheeks. I screamed. Guttural and monstrous. Something you hear in The Tenderloin late at night when it is quiet. When those of us lucky enough to find somewhere to sleep at night lay and listen to the frustration and furious sadness of those of us who did not. Blue drops fell on the carpet and I turned around to see the line for the bathroom staring at me with tired, blinking eyes. They saw me notice them there. A giant monster crying in cosmic, cerulean anguish. They watched me look at them and they watched me scream. This time toward them. No one moved or left their place in line. My screams went back to sobs and I walked, head down, past them to my room.

Opening the door, I went in and started throwing

my clothes into bags. Everything I touched was smeared with blue. I threw the T.V. off the cardboard boxes and ripped the fabric off them. I began throwing everything into the boxes. Weeping openly and hurling things in with fruitless violence. I left the door open and let the bathroom line move past it. They watched as I cried and spun around the room sweeping beer bottles and VHS tapes into the boxes with my arms. They stood and gawked at the big blue animal, getting ready to be released back into the wild.

Chapter Thirteen

In front of *The Armstrong Hotel*, two men sit on the bike rack, smoking. The morning air in late summer is starting to thin. It parts as you walk through it and cleans the dried-up dust of the summer from your lungs. The two men light new cigarettes and blow smoke in front of them, nodding at passing women who walk by in sweaters that were recently pulled from the bottoms of drawers. They sit, just like they do every other day, and will until the hotel is demolished or they are both just gone. Whichever one comes first. One of the men takes a deep breath and closes his eyes, tilting his head up to the sky and *smiling. A thump breaks the morning quiet, then another. The man opens his eyes and his smile quickly snaps straight. Another thump on the front door of The Armstrong Hotel makes him turn his head just in time to see someone kick it open, rabid-eyed and red in the face, dirty streams of tears coming down his cheeks, and clumps of blue-black dripping down his neck.*

←∿∿∿

The door swung wildly when I kicked it and it slammed against the wall. I was carrying a cardboard box full of empty beer bottles and as the door bounced back, it knocked the box out of my hand. Crashing and splintering echoed down Valencia.

"Fuck," I yelled.

I swept most of the broken glass back into the box with my foot and emptied it into a trash can on the corner. I walked back, swinging the box in the air as the wind caught it and tried to blow it away.

The two guys always smoking in front of the hotel watched me. I followed them with my eyes as I walked past.

"What?" I said. "What is it?"

"You have something dripping down," one of them said, pointing to his head.

"Thank you," I said. "It's my brain. It's leaking."

He nodded and lit another cigarette, then went

back to facing the sky with his eyes closed and a smile on his face.

I went back up to my room, drained what was left in the bottle of bourbon, and threw the empty into the box. As I bent over to clean up the rest of the corner, drops of green and dark blue fell from my head and splattered onto the linoleum floor. I made another trip down and then went to Ray's still holding the box.

The store was empty when I walked in and Ray looked at me startled.

"What the hell is coming out of your head?" he said.

"I thought I already told you. It's my brain. It's leaking," I said. "Fifth of Ancient Age please."

Ray got it down off the shelf.

"What's with the box?"

"I'm moving," I said. "You may not see me for a while. Or maybe you'll see me more, I don't know."

"Cool," he said. "Where are you moving to?"

I slapped a twenty-dollar bill onto the counter.

"What do you think the box is for?" I said.

Back at The Armstrong, the line for the bathroom was still going strong. It had snaked around the corner and people were staring into the open door of my room. I pushed past them with the box and the bottle and did an arm sweep of the empties on the counter. The line kept moving and the audience was replaced with a new one, all lined up to use the bathroom and catch a show on the way. I cracked the seal on the Ancient Age and poured it into the mug, chugging it down in one gulp. Then I threw the mug into the box and took a swig straight from the bottle as the line moved and another few people peeked their heads around the corner.

I went into the closet and found my backpack. It was crumpled on the floor and when I unfolded it a wet, moldy smell burst up around me. I must have spilled something on it at some point and had just crammed it into the back of the closet. I found some T-shirts, socks, and underwear and threw them in the bag, then took another huge swig of Ancient Age. It was too much and it caught in my throat. The burning, twisting liquid stayed in my mouth and when I finally forced it down, I could feel it starting to come back up. That would have been a terrible waste. I was going to need all the help I could get. I closed my mouth and set my jaw until I felt it go all the way down, then I let out a cough and a horrific gag. Drops of blue fell from my head and saliva dripped down out of my mouth as I doubled over. Some of the people in line turned their heads, while others kept watching and still others smiled knowingly to themselves.

"Hey, lemme get a hit of that," someone said from out in the hall.

I passed the bottle to a hand that stuck into the room. It disappeared then jutted back in, handing me the bottle back.

"Welp, there goes ten years sober," the voice said.

Everyone in the hallway laughed and I took another huge swig then threw the bottle into my reeking backpack.

Now that I had everything I knew I would absolutely need, what was I supposed to do with everything else? The VHS tapes, the television that had glowed and flickered while I slept. The extra pair of shoes, the books. The razors, deodorant, toothbrush, and towels I bought at the dollar store. The tiny guitar. The traffic island was only so big and I didn't have much room in the backpack.

I couldn't think that far ahead. The only logical next step was to get everything out of the room. Beyond that, it was in the hands of whatever weird deity was in charge that day. I lined the boxes up and eyed everything in the room. As far as I could tell, I would be able to fit everything into the four boxes I had. Maybe I could call Caleb and Knut and see if they would let me store them in their laundry room. Things seemed to have been left with both of them on a relatively high note. I had a job. I had gotten rid of the Doc Martens. They couldn't fault me there.

I began packing up the VHS tapes in the bottom of the box. They fit perfectly and I found the Tetris-like packing satisfying and hypnotic. It was a deep well of focus that I fell into easily and found that once they were all packed up, I wished there were more. The line for the bathroom had dissipated by now and there was nothing but the quiet hallway on the other side of the threshold. I shut the door silently and went back to packing as the lights hummed and shined on the streaks of blue-green that covered the linoleum. The army blanket was completely ruined. The dye had dried and stuck the wrinkles together and I could see right away that it wasn't going to come out no matter what. I threw it into the garbage box along with a few other bottles and picked it up to dump it in the can out on the sidewalk.

As I came back, carrying the empty box, I waved to one of the guys always out front smoking.

"Hey," I said.

He was still leaning against the bike rack with his eyes closed and his face pointed up toward the sun. He didn't open his eyes.

"Hey uh," I said. "If I brought some boxes out here, would you guys be able to watch them for a bit? Just while I'm upstairs packing and cleaning and stuff?"

"Mmm-hmm," he said.

"Okay, great thanks so much," I said, turning away. I turned back. "I mean, you're gonna open your eyes though, right?"

"Mmm-hmm," he said.

"Okay 'cause that's a big part of it," I said.

He didn't say anything back, so I nodded and went inside.

I spent the next hour trying to clean the hair dye from the linoleum. I didn't have any cleaning products so I used water from the sink and an old towel. Every time I would start wiping at a spot, it would smear and streak. By the time I was done, it wasn't so much cleaned up as it was spread out enough throughout the floor to not be as noticeable. I brought the boxes down and put them in front of the doorway of The Armstrong, stumbling up and down the stairs as I took more pulls from the bottle of Ancient Age that was rapidly dwindling in my backpack.

Each time I left a box, I would wave to the guy leaning on the bike rack, and he would wave back. I managed to get three boxes stacked up on the sidewalk full of the things I had acquired in my time at The Armstrong. On one of the final trips down, I opened the front door to find all three of the boxes spread out on the sidewalk, open, with a few people going through them. I looked down the street and happened to see someone walking away carrying a VHS copy of *Con Air*.

"Hey, hey this is my stuff," I said to a woman digging through the first box.

She looked up, smiled and nodded, then went back to digging through the box. I turned to the guy leaning on the bike rack. He was still facing the sky, eyes closed, smiling and smoking. I lifted my hand and started to say something to him. He had promised. But as I started to call out, a drop of blue dye dripped down my forehead and settled into my eye. It stung and burned and as I clawed at it, I remembered how many promises I had made and broken. Promises didn't mean anything to me before. Why should they mean something now? When I finally got the hair dye out, my eye was red and dripping, and when I turned around, there were more people going through the boxes. Things were strewn all over the sidewalk now. Clothes, books, tapes. People were carrying them off.

"Hey," I said.

A few people turned and looked.

"You guys want more stuff? There's more coming down."

They nodded and went back to rifling through the boxes. I went upstairs and grabbed the TV. Someone took it right out of my hands as I came out to the sidewalk. I didn't bother to see who it was. I could barely see out of my one eye now and more hair dye and sweat was dripping down and under my eyebrows.

I made more trips back and forth. Each time, I replenished the boxes, watching as people ripped at the clothes and tossed things behind them and into the street. Someone picked up the brown army blanket and threw it out in the middle of Valencia. A car ran it over and it flattened, matted and dirty. Every time I went back up to the room, I took another swig from the bottle in the backpack. The booze, combined with the dripping hair dye, had made me almost completely blind and by the time nearly everything was out of the room I was laughing and whooping on the sidewalk as I watched the little life I had built in the last few weeks get ripped apart by strangers. I watched a man pick up a pair of my underwear, hold them up to the light, and then drape them across his shoulders like a cape. He wandered off down Valencia, letting them flap in the breeze behind him.

The next hour was a blur. I twirled and screamed up and down Valencia.

"Free shit!" I yelled. "Come and get it you jackals!"

People stopped and turned around to come dig through the boxes. Eventually, I started just throwing what was left of the trash into them on the off chance someone would haul it away for me. A few guys with shopping carts stopped and knelt down to sort through the empty bottles. Every time I went up to the room it was more and more sparse. I took a big gulp from the fifth each time and watched that quickly empty as well. By the time I got to the last trip, the only things left in the room were my backpack, the bottle with a little bit of backwash swirling in the bottom, the Venus flytrap, and the tiny guitar. I was drunk and stumbling around, bouncing off the walls and trying to catch my balance. I steadied myself and picked up the last couple of remaining things. I looked around the room. It was back to the bare white with just a hint of a blue-green glaze covering everything. I had done my best to clean up the excess hair dye but I couldn't see straight without closing one eye, so it was hard to tell what was clean and what wasn't. I stood for a moment in the doorway holding the Venus flytrap in one hand and the tiny guitar in the other. Next door, the toilet flushed and the lights flickered on and off.

As I walked past Mr. and Mrs. Seif's counter, I saw the metal shade was still drawn. I banged on it hard and yelled into my cupped hand.

"Okay, thanks so much guys! Love you!"

There was no answer, so I put the keys to my room and the front door on the counter, wiped the hair dye out of my eyes, and went down the stairs. Stepping out onto the sidewalk, there were still people digging through the boxes, but there was nothing left but the dregs. Some of my clothes were out in the middle of the street now, and a man was reading through some notebooks I had filled with drunken ramblings and song lyrics that would never see the light of day. He nodded at it, then tossed it back into the box. I couldn't help but feel a little offended.

"Are you giving those away, too?"

A blonde woman of about twenty-five was standing in front of me, pointing at the guitar and Venus flytrap in my hands. As she said it, I felt my stomach twist and flop, and I leaned over and puked into the street. She stepped back a few feet but didn't walk away.

"Sure," I said, and I handed her both the items. "Take care of them. I didn't."

She took them and slung the tiny guitar over her back. It looked much more natural on her smaller frame and she walked away smiling, not having said thank you.

I looked up and down Valencia. For the most part, everything had been picked through. There were a few things hung over the boxes and laying on the ground but anything of any value had been taken. I stood for a while and watched as cars ran over my clothes and my copy of *Top Gun* was crushed under the wheels of a bus. A few people stopped now and then to peek in the boxes, but seeing only trash, they kept walking.

I didn't know where else to go, so I headed toward Ray's. It was the only landmark I could think of. The only home base. When I was about a block away, though, I remembered that I had bought an entire fifth from him just a couple of hours earlier. I stopped into a different store instead. It was fancier and had an actual deli. It seemed more like a grocery store, which was why I had never been in it before. I got in line behind some people buying pickles and champagne and when it got to my turn, I asked for a pint of Ancient Age.

"$13.57," the cashier said.

"Jesus," I said. "That's a lot of money for the worst whiskey ever."

He shrugged and I reached into my back pocket for my wallet. Panic shot through my body. It wasn't there. The pocket was empty. I took off my backpack and rifled through it. People behind me in line shifted uncomfortably.

"Shit," I said. "Shit!"

The cashier shrugged and put the bottle back on the rack behind him.

"Hold on," I said, going through the front pocket of the backpack one more time and emptying the main one out onto the counter. Underwear and two T-shirts fell out but no wallet. A pair of socks fell off the counter and rolled behind me. A woman in line reached down to pick them up. I snatched them away.

"No," I screamed. "You can't have those!"

"Hey man, maybe you should just go," said the cashier. I recognized the tone. The cops would be coming next.

"Fuck," I screamed. "Where the fuck is it?"

"Hey come on, guy."

Someone behind me in line gently shoved at me and I gathered up all the things on the counter and swept them into the bag, then ran back out onto the street.

I knew deep in my drunken heart that I had thrown the wallet with my money into one of the boxes by mistake. I couldn't even see straight and had been so hell-bent on getting everything out of the room that I didn't even notice. I ran back to the boxes, but there was nothing in any of them. One of them had been completely ripped up and thrown down the sidewalk. I started gasping for air and could feel my hands starting to go numb. It had seemed apt and fitting to go back out on the street with almost nothing, but now I was going to starve. I was drifting in the middle of the ocean and had just given away my lifeboat along with all my VHS tapes.

My head started swimming and I could feel all the blood rushing out of my face. I had been sabotaging myself for years but I had never done it as quickly as I had that morning. I had no money, I had nowhere to sleep, and I didn't have the little guitar anymore to make a few bucks. The season had been over at the theater for a few weeks and I had no idea when it would be starting up again. I hadn't even taken the opportunity to use the shower one last time and get the hair dye out of my hair. My head was itching and my eyes wouldn't stop stinging. All the booze was gone. I was about to get hit with a hangover that was going to bring me to my knees or possibly kill me. There was nothing I could do about it, so I screamed. I started raving on the street. I took off my backpack and swung it around, slamming it on the ground and stomping on it. I screamed again and a few people walking down Valencia turned to look. A few more crossed the street to avoid me. More hair dye dripped down as I started to sweat and claw at my eyes, ripping at my hair and trying to pull it out. Tears poured out and mixed with the dye again and I was blinded by the stinging mixture and rage. Someone tapped me on the shoulder. I spun around and screamed in their face, letting out a horrible sound and the smell of rotten, stale bourbon.

"Matty, Matty, Matty what's going on?"

I didn't recognize the voice at first and I couldn't see who it was. I just started babbling.

"These fuckin' people and this fuckin' shit!" I screamed.

"What?"

"Get the fuck away from me!"

I tried to twist away but some hands grabbed my shoulders.

"Matty, come on, what's happening?"

I rubbed my face and blinked, trying to see through one eye. When Austin finally came into slight focus, I could see that he was searching my face, trying to understand what I was saying.

"You look insane, what's going on?"

I tried to answer, but couldn't. I felt very heavy suddenly, and my knees buckled under me. Austin caught me under the crook of my arm and held me up. I started sobbing and hid my face.

"Matty, it's okay man, it's alright," Austin said.

He grabbed me and hugged me hard, keeping me from falling to the dirty ground strewn with my dirty clothes and trash.

"It's okay, it's okay," he said, and I sobbed harder

and harder.

"I came by to see if you wanted to hang out," he said. "I'm glad I did, come on let's get out of here."

I put my arm over his shoulders and he took my backpack. Together, we walked down Valencia as a few people watched and then went over to the boxes to see if there was anything good left in them.

⟵⌁⌁

There were big blocks of time missing from my memory when I woke up in the back of Austin's truck. I remembered standing on the sidewalk while he poured a bottle of water on my head and helped me wash out the hair dye. He used his hands as a squeegee and squeezed the thick, gummy ooze out of every strand as I cried and let snot and slobber fall out of my face onto the sidewalk. He spoke to me in quick, sharp sentences, telling me it was alright and that the stuff would be washed out soon, focusing on the task at hand and letting me purge the day out of my head. He took the reins when all I could do was lash myself with them. I remembered drinking beers in the back of the truck. I remembered feeling like I had a witness. When there is no one to reflect your own image back to you, it's easy to completely lose sight of how you really are. It's easy to not see how bad things have gotten or how much worse they could be. We sat up drinking beer and singing songs until I passed out again, my eyes red-rimmed and watering. He let me use his extra sleeping bag and we spread out under the camper shell in the bed of the truck, which was parked behind the food co-op on the border of the Mission and downtown. He told me that night that we would find a place to live and that I wouldn't have to sleep out in the street anymore. And I believed him.

Chapter Fourteen

ost of the classrooms at St. Mary's High School for Boys were portable trailers back in 1999. They were the kind used at construction sites when no one was expected to stay very long and the bosses needed somewhere to do the hiring and firing. I didn't like the idea of an all-boys Catholic high school in the first place and the fact that my parents were paying for me to go to one that was on wheels seemed like even more of a scam.

"I'm just afraid you'll fall through the cracks at a public school," my mother had said when I told her I had gotten my fill of religious education.

"I'm going to fall through the floor of these trailers," I said.

As soon as I started at St. Mary's, I found that my apprehension about upper-level religious schooling had been valid. The teachers were mostly disinterested, terrified priests who were browbeaten and intimidated by the packs of wild, hormonal animals that sat in their classes, trying to outdo each other in every activity ranging from humiliation to physical violence. There was no God there. I quickly found that the only way to survive was to stay as invisible as possible. To blend in and sit in the furthest back corner where no one would notice me. By the end of my sophomore year, most of the teachers still didn't know my name and I was of no more interest to my fellow students than a lamp or a desk that had been moved into the corner of a trailer to make room for a presentation or a fist fight. I had also spent so much time making myself small and trying to make as little noise as possible that I was barely passing some of my classes, and in others, I wasn't even doing that.

When I was called into the principal's office one afternoon in the late spring, I had been prematurely celebrating my achievement of making it through nearly two anonymous years while not participating and doing as little work as possible. When a piece of paper with my name on it was brought into my third-period math class, I knew the hammer had finally dropped. The teacher, Father Ferguson, didn't recognize my name on the slip at first, and he had to use the process of elimination to finally land on my face and tell me to head down to the office. While I was glad to get out of the trailer, the possibilities of what the summons could be about washed over me as I headed over to the brick, chrome, and glass administrative building, where, I was to find out, the real shaping of young Catholic minds took place.

When I gave the paper to the man behind the front desk, he directed me into an office, where the principal, Mr. Weatherford, was seated behind a massive oak desk with a large, shiny crucifix staring down from the wall behind him. He looked like Teddy Roosevelt and the combination of this American historical icon and the terrifying Catholic imagery behind him made me feel small and sweaty.

"Mr. DeYoung," he said, trying to hide his quick glance down at his notes for my name. "I wanted to have a sit-down with you so we could talk about your progress here."

My mind immediately shot to my grades.

"You know about our service requirements, yes?"

When he said the words, they sounded familiar, but I was certain that if they had been said to me during an orientation or assembly during my freshman year, I would have been too panicked and overwhelmed by the new school's tough, feral student body to really process it.

"Well," he continued, satisfied with my confused silence. "Each student must dedicate a certain number of hours to serving the community before they can advance to the next year. You haven't done any."

He stared at me for a long time after dropping the news, raising his bushy eyebrows over his thin-framed silver glasses.

"What does that mean?" I finally asked, splitting the quiet in the room.

"I'll have to hold you back until you do."

The words hung like a stench in the air. The idea of spending an extra year in this shrieking jungle of teenage testosterone pinned me to my seat. I had to take a second to catch my breath. All because I didn't know I was supposed to be picking up trash or ladling out soup in the name of the lord this entire time.

"I have a solution, though," he said. "You play the guitar, right? I'm sure I've seen you with it."

It was true, I would bring my guitar some days as a security blanket under the guise that I had a lesson after school when really I just needed to hold onto something familiar or possibly use it as a weapon should the need come up. In a school with no music or art programs, I must have stood out to him, even if he didn't know my name.

"The good news," he continued, "is that the convalescent home needs entertainment a few afternoons a week."

I watched as he scribbled an address on a scrap of

paper.

"They're expecting you tomorrow at 3:30."

⟵〰〰〰

The next afternoon, I walked the mile and a half from school to the address Mr. Weatherford had written down. I lugged my guitar case and it banged against my shins the whole way there as I went over the chord sheets I had prepared of various show tunes and old-timey songs like "Five Foot Two, Eyes of Blue" and "Michael, Row the Boat Ashore." The sun pounded on my face and dried the nervous sweat that dripped down like streams of hot oil into my eyes.

When I finally got to the front entrance of the St. Mary's Home for the Infirm, I wanted to turn around right away but was stopped by a motorized wheelchair that pulled up behind me and beeped as the man sitting in it grunted and gestured for me to move forward. Inside the large, clean entryway, a woman with orthopedic shoes and a soft, childlike voice led me from the front desk to a rec room where a group of people were gathered in a half circle with all manner of tubes, wires, and bags hanging off them.

"This is Matthew," the woman screamed, sounding like a screeching cat in contrast with her gentle speaking voice. "He's going to entertain you."

I kept my eyes down as I stepped into the open

space of the circle, got out my guitar, and laid out my chord sheets. The smell of urine and old soup swirled around in the stale air. When I finally looked up, the little crowd was staring at me, gaunt and haunted-looking, waiting for something to happen that might drown out the groans and pained wails that I was suddenly aware were coming faintly from the private rooms down the hall. I swallowed, taking in a little of the sickly taste from the air, and began to play.

<ᴡᴡᴡ

Three times a week, I would take that same walk over to the home, and each time I would pause outside the big automatic doors, just out of reach of the sensor that opened them as if I could hide from the electronic eye. But each time I would be pushed through by someone trying to get inside, or the thought of having to stay an extra year at the school, whichever happened to come first.

For the first few afternoons, when I would finish playing a song, the group gathered in the rec room would stare at me blankly. Some of them just let their eyes roll around in their heads and others would flash me a wide, ancient smile with rotten teeth barely clinging to their gums, pulled tight against their visible skulls. After a couple of weeks, though, they became more animated as they got used to me and started to feel more comfortable. They clapped their hands or moaned in approval after I played something they recognized.

In turn, I also started to feel more relaxed, lifting my eyes from the chord charts now and then to get a look at who was watching on that particular afternoon. Some would nod and, if they were physically able, tap their feet in time to the music. Some would simply close their eyes, which would always make me nervous and I would keep watching until I saw them shift in their chair or move their arm. All of them, though, would put on the same expression when my time was up. I would pack up my guitar and papers and watch as they were wheeled one by one out of the rec room and back to their respective compartments in the depths of the building. Their faces would drop and become blank and static as an orderly grabbed the handles of their wheelchairs and spun them around to take them to the elevator. I had thought the scene in the rec room was pretty grim until I saw how they felt about going back to their own cells.

↞∿∿

The weeks passed and every Monday, Wednesday, and Friday I would walk through those automatic doors, a little easier each time. When I was done playing and the last resident was wheeled away, I would get the woman at the front desk to sign a form confirming that I had done my time, and that would get turned into Mr. Weatherford's office. Each day I went over to the home, I would feel the pull of running away get weaker and weaker. I began to recognize the tortured, pained faces of the residents and could pick them out individually while I strummed chords and played old songs under the flickering fluorescent light instead of seeing only a shaking and twitching mass of people sitting in different wheeled furniture. I even started to like the smell of piss and soup. It meant I was somewhere that I was wanted and seen.

Most of the residents at the home couldn't communicate well but they saw everything. Their eyes whirled around and spun wildly, but I could tell they were focused on my hands and mouth as the songs of their youth poured out and blanketed them in a wash of what once was. When I showed up one day and the front desk lady looked surprised to see me, my heart dropped. Mr. Weatherford had called, she said. My service hours were complete.

I stood there without saying anything for a long time. I could hear faint murmuring and the hum of the lights coming from the rec room. The weight of my guitar case was making my hand go numb but I couldn't seem to set it down. That would feel like a decision and I wasn't ready to make one. Someone came through the automatic glass doors and they swished open with their electronic wheeze as if the building was taking a deep breath. The woman at the desk raised her eyebrows.

"You must be happy to be done," she said. "I'm sure there are a lot of things a kid like you would rather be doing after school."

"Like what?" I asked, genuinely looking for suggestions.

"I don't know," she said. "Playing sports. Chasing girls."

The weight of the guitar case finally became too much and I set it down with a big resonating thud as the vibration strummed a dissonant chord. The front doors opened again as a man with a walker tottered in. I could walk out those doors at any time, I thought. But what would be the point? Sooner or later we all end up here.

"Could I do one more?" I asked.

The woman's eyes widened and her face twisted with surprise.

"I suppose," she said. "If you really want to."

Ten minutes later, I was standing in the rec room looking out at a circle of withered, melting faces, all of them looking at me and waiting for the music to start. The songs seemed to fall out that afternoon. I played them faster and with extra flourishes, even stomping my foot and shimmying around, trying to give them a real show. By the time I got to "If I Didn't Care" by The Ink Spots, I was dripping with sweat and putting my best vibrato on the vocal. I watched their faces intently, making eye contact with everyone and smiling whenever there was a sparkle of recognition or acknowledgment, and simply holding my gaze when there wasn't. I didn't want to explain that this was going to be the last time I was there, I just wanted to give us all something to hold onto.

When I was getting toward the end of my time, a man wheeled up to the front of the group. I had noticed him before, specifically because he looked much younger than the rest of the residents. His hair and beard were still full and dark brown and his face had a youthful structure without any of the hollow, paper-thin qualities I saw in the rest of the crowd. He handed me a note with a single word on it: "Puff." I knew exactly what it meant. I had included "Puff the Magic Dragon" in my chord sheets and played it once or twice but found that it was too slow and put everyone to sleep, some figuratively and some literally. If this man wanted it, though, I was going to play it. I dug out the chart and began to pick at the strings, singing.

"Puff the Magic Dragon, lived by the sea..."

The man didn't go back to his place in the crowd. He stayed right where he was, about two feet from me.

"Little Jackie Papers, loved that rascal Puff..."

When I got to the second verse, I looked down at him. Tears fell down his face, soaking his beard and dripping down into his lap. I kept eye contact, unable to break away, frozen and hypnotized by this man's sadness. With a final guitar section, I finished the song, and a huge, consuming silence filled the room. Orderlies started to grab wheelchairs and take people away as this man and I stood still, his eyes wet and holding onto mine.

When they finally wheeled him away, I watched as his chair turned the corner and the last inch of it disappeared behind the wall. His room was back there somewhere, and I wondered how long it would take before his eyes completely dried or if they ever would. The rec room was empty and echoing and every sound was amplified as I gathered up my things. Walking past the front desk, I saw that it was vacant and the light outside the automatic doors had faded into the deep blue-gray of evening. The darkness swallowed me up as I floated through the sighing doors and into the night air.

⟵⟋⟍⟋⟍

I didn't go straight home. I wandered as the sun disappeared and the moon slowly took over until I found myself standing in front of St. Mary's School for

Boys, looking at the administration building and the towering steel crucifix that sat on top of it just like the one in Mr. Weatherford's office. I let my guitar case dangle lower and lower until I finally set it down while I stood, bewitched by the building. The large sliding glass doors that led into the offices were emblazoned with the school motto: Fine Young Men Leave Here.

As the moon rose higher over the parking lot and cast long, grotesque shadows across the asphalt, I could see a clear picture of myself running through those same doors. Leaving a fine young man and breathing clean new air as everything opened up and the sky and all the years I had ahead spread apart to greet me. I wasn't trapped yet. I wasn't being pulled along deeper into the maze of a building I would never escape from. I was rolling slowly toward the door and soon I was going to walk out. Standing on my feet and heading to the light.

Chapter Fifteen

I had been staying with Austin in his truck for a week when we got the call that a new season was starting at The Market Street Theater and we should report to work the next day. It was merciful. We had been eating dry ramen and bananas from the dumpster of the food co-op and looking around for a new place to live, even though the entire venture felt pointless. We had no money. We were living in a strange fantasy in which we had the ability to do the things that regular people do. It was comforting to browse through the Craigslist posts for roommates and apartments and say things like "Oh yeah, I could definitely live here," when the truth was neither of us could afford to live anywhere.

When Kevin called Austin, we jumped for joy. The season had been over for a month or so, but now we were looking at another few months of work at least. Austin lent me an extra white shirt and tie since mine had been either thrown into the middle of Valencia or used to clean up puke in my room at The Armstrong. He kept his clothes in an Igloo cooler in the corner of the truck bed, neatly folded and sealed off from the elements. We drank 40-ounce bottles of malt liquor in the back of the truck the night he got the call and played some more make-believe. We talked about getting a warehouse space. We talked about getting a loft. Austin wanted a motorcycle. I wanted a new guitar.

"I should get my drums out of storage at my parents' house," he said.

"You should," I slurred. "We should start a band."

"Done. Jolly good, old chap."

We smashed the 40-ouncers together and the foam ran up and over the cone and we laughed at his fake British accent, which sounded extra bizarre filtered through his real southern accent. When the laughter died down, though, we knew we wouldn't be able to afford anything like that. At the theater, we made, at most, eight hundred dollars a month. For most people, it was a second job. Something to make a little extra money. For us, it was all we could get. We would be able to eat that month, but we weren't going to be enjoying the sunset from the balcony of our Pacific Heights penthouse any time soon, or ever. We would have to think outside the box or end up living in it. I didn't say any of this to Austin, though. We were having too good of a time talking about a future that would never exist.

We went back to work at The Market Street Theater. Austin's shirt was too small for me and I didn't have the right shoes but I was there. Kevin saw us walking up to the lobby together and smiled and hugged us to his big, sweaty chest.

"Welcome back boys," he said, his gaze lingering on my blue-green-black hair. "You both look terrible."

The show was an embarrassing jukebox musical featuring the catalog of Billy Joel. They took a bunch of his songs and loosely hung a plot on them, then laughed all the way to the bank. People loved it. I started to get back into some kind of shape by chasing David and Levant around and running up and down the stairs with elderly peoples' walkers and oxygen tanks. Mostly it felt good to think about someone else for a change. Dealing with other peoples' problems was like a vacation. The housing issue was still burning, though. We couldn't sleep in the truck forever. My back was killing me, and one night I woke up from a dead sleep with someone staring into the back window of the truck camper. As soon as I moved, the figure took off, but I knew it was only a matter of time before someone tried to break in thinking they were just going to steal something but ended up murdering us instead.

I asked every one of the ushers if they knew of anything. Paula had a spare room opening up in her grandmother's house, but it was nine hundred a month and we would have to pitch in by changing her now and then. I politely passed. Everyone else just said no. Housing in San Francisco was tough enough as it was. It was even tougher when you only made $9,600 a year. At one point, I found myself searching the theater for a place to sleep. There were so many hidden nooks and crannies, I figured there had to be a good hiding spot. I went out back and looked up and down the building, climbing a fire escape to see if there were any little compartments that I could steal away into and wait for everyone to leave. It seemed like a fairly solid plan until I remembered that Kevin set an alarm every night before leaving. The last thing I needed was to lose the only source of income I had for trying to live in the air ducts.

Every night, Austin and I would walk back to the truck, drink a couple of 40-ouncers, and try to figure out what the hell we were going to do.

"I don't mind the truck," Austin said. "It's just too small for the two of us."

"I know," I said. "That's why I think you should leave."

We howled and smashed the bottles together, then drank deeply and passed out before having to go back to the theater the next afternoon.

Since actual housing zoned for human use was out, I compiled a list of workarounds and ideas. The first one was a treehouse. I saw the ad on Craigslist and my mind blew open. It was perfect. The ad showed a beautiful backyard and had a photo of a treehouse that looked more like an upscale condo than something some kids built. The rent was three hundred a month. I showed Austin and we made an appointment to go look at it. We settled it right away that we would try to put a deposit down right there. We got paid weekly at the theater, so we had about four hundred dollars between us total.

We showed up at the house right on time and a man in bikini briefs opened the door. He was very tan and seemed fairly drunk.

"Oh nice," he said, looking us up and down. "You guys must be the tree boys."

"I guess," Austin said, and we followed him into the dark house.

All the shades were drawn and there were empty boxes of wine littering every flat surface. He led us out back to an ornately designed yard with gravel pathways and a lush garden. It seemed to be the only part of the house that was kept up. As we walked toward the far corner, I heard a noise rustling in one of the bushes and my heart jumped when I saw a giant

Komodo dragon come lumbering into the pathway.

"Oh, that's just Baby. Don't mind her, she's cranky."

The monster hissed at us and flicked its tongue.

"Aren't those things poisonous?" Austin said.

"Oh yeah," he said. "She'll fuck you up."

We stepped around Baby and walked to the base of the tree. Right away, something was wrong. The treehouse in the photo was nowhere to be seen. There was a flat platform resting between two branches and a few planks nailed into the trunk.

"This isn't what was in the ad, man," I said.

"Oh, yeah well that was what it could be. Just think of the potential."

Austin shrugged and started climbing up the makeshift ladder.

"Let's just see, maybe we can figure something out," he said.

I followed him while the drunk tan man stayed on the ground, talking to the Komodo dragon. I got about halfway up the trunk before getting terrified. There was no way I could even climb this sober. I didn't want to think about what could happen on a day-to-day basis.

"Hey, yeah no I can't do this," I said. "It's not gonna work."

I started to climb down but as I did, Baby ran to the base of the tree and started hissing and snapping. The drunk tan man laughed and clapped his hands as I clung to the trunk in fear. It seemed we would have to keep looking.

We spent the next week visiting every garage, parking space, storage unit, and attic space we could find, hoping to come across some sort of wondrous situation where we could throw down our sleeping bags and be undisturbed for less than two hundred dollars a month. Everywhere was a bust, though. The storage units all had cameras, the garages were all attached to someone's house. There was no way to sneak in and out. Every person we spoke to would look us up and down and immediately ask if we were planning on living there. They could smell it on us, literally and figuratively. The desperation was hard to hide and it was even harder to convince someone that either one of us could claim ownership of enough stuff to our name to warrant an entire storage unit. As soon as we walked up in our torn clothes, smelling like gasoline fumes and stale malt liquor, the owners or storage unit managers would shake their heads. They had seen us before. If there was a loophole to housing in San Francisco, there were many people who had thought of it before us.

I got depressed fast. My back was killing me from the rigid metal floor of the truck bed and we were saving as much money as we could but it would never be enough for a real apartment. We went without eating for a few days to see how much we could save. We lived off the warm case of 40-ouncers we had bought at the beginning of the theater season. One night, I fell asleep and dreamt that I was eating a huge bag of chips. When a person hasn't eaten in a while, it's amazing how much the mind will latch on to the idea of food. It becomes all-consuming. Hunger haunts every moment and immediately throws the body into survival mode. I could see these chips and taste them perfectly. I moved in slow motion and with great difficulty to pull each big, glistening potato chip out of the bag. I could hear the crunch and taste each and every one of them. In the dream, I reached into the bag and tried to pull more out, but something was stuck. I pulled harder and harder but some of the chips were anchored to the bottom of the bag. As I pulled in the dream I started to hear a voice that brought me up out of the ether of sleep and through the veil into the real world. I woke up to Austin screaming.

"Ow, shit ow," he said.

I shot up and realized that as I was pulling the chips from the bag in the dream, in real life I had grabbed hold of Austin's hair. When the chips were stuck, I started yanking on it. Once I explained, we cracked open a couple of 40-ouncers and vowed that we would start eating again.

I found the practice space in the "musicians" section of Craigslist. I liked to sometimes look and see if there were any opportunities to join a cover band or wedding band, anything that might make some money. I could sing "September" by Earth Wind and Fire just as well as any other sad white guy in a ruffled tux. It never came to fruition, but in The Main Branch one afternoon, I saw the listing.

SMALL MUSIC REHEARSAL SPACES
$200/MONTH
24-HOUR ACCESS

A shot rang through my head when I saw it. Rehearsal spaces were usually flimsy, hollowed-out warehouses that some burnt-out metal head had put together with their inheritance. They would charge bands a fortune to store their equipment and practice there and usually, multiple bands would go in on one space and split the rent. This was by far the cheapest I had ever seen, especially in San Francisco where space was at such a premium. The thing that really caught my eye, though, was the phrase "24-hour access." This opened up the possibility that it could at least be a place to keep our clothes and cases of 40-ouncers even if we couldn't pull off living there all the time. Almost every practice space I had rented had some weird guy who everyone was fairly certain was living there but couldn't prove it. If I played my cards right, I could be that weird guy. Austin was working, but I knew he would be on board. If we split it, we could have a roof over our heads for a hundred bucks a month each. It was quite possibly the cheapest rent that had ever been achieved in the city and I couldn't wait to hold that distinction. I had exactly four hundred dollars in a new roll in my pocket. Enough for a deposit and the first month's rent. I called the number and was greeted by a woman who introduced herself as Anna. She said she could meet up with me in an hour and gave me the address. When I looked it up on the computer, I saw that it was just a few blocks down from The Main Branch and it would only take a few minutes.

I sat in the wooden chair and blinked my eyes in stunned disbelief. Everything had been going so poorly lately. Every interaction and chance circumstance felt like it was designed to not work out. Like I was crawling up a big hill that seemed to get steeper and steeper until it doubled back on itself. No matter how much I saved my pennies or searched for some place where my friend and I could lay our heads, we kept coming up empty. For the first time in forever, I felt like something was finally starting to come together. For once, an endeavor didn't feel completely doomed from the very beginning. By finding Austin some shelter, I was even helping someone else, and that was something I had not done in a very long time.

I left The Main Branch and started to walk toward the address Anna had given me. I scribbled it down on a piece of scrap paper I pulled from the information desk. It was a pamphlet offering help for mental illness emergencies. I made a note to hang onto it. It might come in handy. As I walked, I noticed that the neighborhood got more and more compact. It started to become more concentrated with people and I soon found myself swerving to miss people who seemed to be stuck in some sort of endless loop of behavior. A man stood by a parked car and leaned on it over and over again, letting his knees buckle, then straightening himself out. A woman with a headwrap spun in a circle in the middle of the sidewalk while people went out of their way to avoid her, trying to anticipate her moves. On every block, there was a small yard sale going on with stolen goods and broken electrical equipment. A car stereo sat on a blanket with other seemingly unsellable merchandise and a man sat on a bucket, scrawny and smoking, eyeing anyone who might dare to steal these things he had been trying to sell for the last few decades. On the next corner, a man whispered to me.

"OCs," he said. "Come on man, OCs."

OCs stood for OxyContins. They were sold openly on the street and if you bought one, the guy would even lick the time-release tab off for you. I was getting deeper and deeper into The Tenderloin. I had denied it at first, but there was no doubt that this practice space was located on what was known as The Four Corners of Death.

Depending on who is talking about it, The Four Corners of Death are set at different intersections in The Tenderloin. The truth is, this would be an appropriate name for many intersections. I always thought of The Four Corners to be at Larkin and O'Farrell and as I approached the address I had written down on the mental illness pamphlet, it was just half a block down from there. The corner is called this because there is death everywhere. People are regularly found stabbed or beaten to mush, drugs are everywhere and there is madness in the eyes of everyone unlucky enough to have to spend a large chunk of time there. It is a sea of human suffering that has been dammed and herded into a one-block radius that creates a shockwave that resonates for blocks. Just a few blocks further north, though, is Nob Hill, one of the richest neighborhoods in town. The difference was striking and as I turned to ring the bell on the door with the address posted above, I took a look around. A man was standing in the middle of the street, nodding on heroin or OCs as his body bent at the waist, and cars and buses honked as they swerved to miss him.

Anna opened the door and quickly stuck her head out onto the street. She was fried bleach blonde with dripping, tired-looking eye makeup. She whipped her head back and forth suspiciously, then settled her eyes on me.

"Are you Matthew?" she said. Her voice came tumbling out like loose gravel.

"Yeah, that's me."

She took another few glances toward each direction, then grabbed me by the arm and pulled me into the building. We walked up a small staircase and at some point I thought she turned back and said something to me but the pounding and scratching of a dozen different bands playing at once was drowning her out.

"What's that?" I said.

"Yeah for sure," she said, not hearing me or caring.

I followed her down a hall lined with doors. The smell of pot smoke and stale beer was flowing out of the crack under each one. Banging and pounding and errant chords were mashing together into an insane symphony and a few metalheads rushed past us pushing a Marshall amplifier cabinet. We got to a door at the end of the hall, right next to an industrial-looking bathroom with cold tile and a powdered soap dispenser.

"Here we are," she screamed, fiddling with a gigantic ring of keys for a long time before opening the door.

I followed her in and she closed the door behind us, sealing us off from the chaos out in the hall. The room was about eight feet by eight feet and had gray carpet on the floor and blood-red carpet on the walls and ceiling. The sound had nowhere to go in there and it felt like a chore just getting my voice to carry. It was completely dead inside. I could relate to that.

"Okay, what do you think?" She said, pulling a cigarette out of her pocket and holding it anxiously in her hand.

"Looks good. Just what I need," I said. "One question, I usually rehearse at night until the early morning, it's when I'm most productive. Is that going to be a problem?"

I was proud of that lie. It was one of the major benefits of this being a rock and roll type of place. No one asked questions about that sort of thing.

"Nope, no problem, you could be here twenty-four hours a day for all I care."

She lifted the cigarette and put it in her mouth, raising her eyebrows.

"You want it?"

I couldn't believe it. I tried to act casual but my bones were jumping out of my skin and my stomach was flipping over and over.

"I'll take it. How much do I owe you now?"

"Two hundred for the first month, one fifty deposit. Leave the rent in that locked mailbox in the hall by the fifth of the month and we'll have no problems."

I peeled $350 off the roll and handed it to her. She stuck it down the front of her shirt and pulled two keys off the ring.

"Front door key, room key," she said, indicating each one.

She handed them to me and took a lighter out of her pocket, then turned around, opening the door to the wave of noise in the hall.

"Nice doing business with you," she said, and with that, she was gone. I never saw her in person again.

Once again, the room was quiet with just a faint, low rumble of a bass guitar in the empty, carpeted room.

I called Austin as soon as I knew the show was over at work. He picked up and I could hear the noise from the street in front of the theater.

"That's fucking amazing," he said. "That will be perfect for you."

"No man," I said, "there's enough room for both of us, you don't have to stay in the truck anymore. This will at least get us out of the cold and we're probably less likely to be murdered here. As long as we don't go outside."

"Oh," he said. "I'm good. I like the truck. I just wanted to help you."

"What do you mean? What about finding an apartment and everything like that?"

"Come on," he said. "That was just fucking around. But you actually did it. You found a place, that's amazing. Is it big enough for my drums? I could go get them from my parents' place."

I looked around the eight-foot square room.

"Definitely," I said.

"Okay great. I gotta get back in for the next show. I'll see you tomorrow?"

"Yeah, of course," I said, and we hung up.

I sat down in the corner. I always knew I would end up alone in a padded room, I just didn't think it would happen so soon. To Austin, this was too fancy. Too much responsibility. He had gone along with me on the dream, but this was where he got off.

I still had fifty dollars in the roll, so I went down to the Goodwill and found a clean-looking sleeping bag and a couple of pillows. On the way back, I grabbed a bottle of Ancient Age and then crept carefully through the hall back to the practice space. I was confident no one saw me sneak the sleeping bag in and when I closed the door behind me and spread it out, I felt like a kid playing hide and seek. I could feel an excitement in my stomach and wanted to turn inward, curling up into a ball where no one could see me. Someone plugged in an amplifier in the space next door and the lights flickered. I chuckled to myself, happy that some things would never change. Some things were inescapable.

I cracked open the bottle of Ancient Age and took the cap off, holding it up to my lips and letting the fumes come slithering out and up my nose. I put the cap back on and set it down, then picked up the phone and dialed Austin's number. The show was starting so I knew he wouldn't pick up, and it went to voicemail.

"Hey, buddy. Listen, when you're done there, why don't you come here and hang out? I got some whiskey. We'll celebrate that you don't have to sleep next to me anymore. I'll wait until you get here to start."

I gave him the address and told him to call when he was downstairs, then I leaned my head against the carpeted wall and waited for the phone to ring, listening to the screeching guitar next door.

Chapter Sixteen

Mornings in the padded room always started with panic. Not being able to tell whether it was night or day sent me into a spiral that was hard to recover from. Starting every day with fresh anxiety was nothing new, but the complete darkness of the windowless practice space added an extra element of fear that could only be assuaged by someone walking past the crack under the door or the thud of a bass drum somewhere in the warehouse complex that would let me know I had not been set adrift in some unknowable void.

I had found a set of three couch cushions at the Goodwill that looked fairly clean and would lay them out on the floor of the room, covered with a fitted sheet and a down comforter. The entire bed had cost me about twenty bucks and I would pull it apart every morning and stack it in the corner to avoid any suspicion that I was living there if anyone came to check on it. I worried about snoring in the middle of the night but I figured I could always explain that away by saying I had just passed out there. I was sure it would not be the first time it had happened. To help sell it even more, Austin had brought his small, three-piece drum set, a tiny practice amplifier, and a battered old electric guitar from his parents' house and we put them in the corner. At a passing glance, the room didn't look anything like a makeshift home.

After stowing the bed away, I would go to the freezing, tiled bathroom and try to wash my face as best as I could. It was always twenty degrees colder in there and most mornings I would have to brace for the impact of the water combined with the rough industrial powdered soap. Now and then, someone would come in and see me scrubbing my eye sockets and give me a sympathetic look, assuming I was just hungover at band practice somewhere in the facility. Then, I would get dressed for work in Austin's spare shirt and tie, lock up, and head out onto the filthy Tenderloin street.

Mornings in The Tenderloin are a piece of theater

all their own. It is a perfect mix of people who are just getting up, people still sleeping between parked cars or under bus shelters, and those who have been up all night. It's hard to distinguish between them all since everyone in the neighborhood is in a constant state of breaking down or passing out. The bright sunlight would reflect off the water that had been sprayed out on the sidewalk by anyone gutsy enough to run a business there, and buses bumped and hissed down the street carrying people on their way to work in North Beach or the Financial District. They pressed their faces up against the glass to look at the human suffering exhibit and I would wave to them in my shirt and tie as they went past, relishing my position as a featured zoo animal.

The sun shone through the tall apartment buildings and SROs and people who were broken and deteriorating day by day looked up and felt it on their faces. It was starting to get cold and stay cold now. Any bit of warmth needed to be savored and held onto, cherished for as long as possible. I stopped and felt it, too. Whatever worked for the people who lived and died and went crazy in The Tenderloin was going to work for me now. I didn't know how long I would be there but with the rent being what it was I could live there for as long as I needed to, provided I didn't get caught sleeping in the practice space. I felt good. I felt like I had a secret and that I had figured something out that was going to keep paying off for once. The only thing I had to do was get used to the new level of chaos.

The Mission and San Francisco in general was no picnic. There was always somebody around every corner who was looking to take something from you. It was hard to step out on the street without spending money. If it wasn't going to be taken from you legitimately by a landlord or a bus driver, it would be stolen or grifted from you somehow. The Tenderloin, though, was something else entirely. People were hungry there. They needed things. They didn't just want things. They needed them and there was no way to get them. Everywhere you looked, there were people who weren't able to get whatever it was they were missing. They ended up lying on the street in puddles of their own piss or shaking in an alleyway, holding a rusty utility knife and looking for the next person who had made the mistake of not paying attention for a split second. After a couple of days, I mastered a look that said "I am not a rube." It was a cold stare that I held as I walked down Hyde toward Market. A slight frown and a focused gaze, locking onto anything that could be perceived as a threat. I didn't shy away from eye contact. When someone was standing on a corner, screaming about God or the Devil with a brick in their hand, I made sure to meet their eyes. I was no different. I was one of them and I could usually show it by not looking away. Someone who had made a wrong turn while walking to their car after a show at The Market Street Theater would try to look anywhere other than at the lunatic waving their arms or screaming in the middle of the sidewalk, but that was because they couldn't possibly understand. I had been there. That had been me. I wasn't scared to look at someone who was having a hard time out on the street. I had been in their torn shoes before and there was a very good chance I would be in them again.

The padded room was only so entertaining. I had convinced Austin to sign up for a library card and photocopied it just like I had with Lola's. I wondered if someone had found the old one in my wallet in one of the boxes and tossed it away, not knowing how valuable it was. Even more so than the money that was in there. Much more so. Without it, I was cut off and would have had to go back to the room and stare at the carpeted wall all night. When there is no money and when you are not welcome to just sit somewhere, every place starts to feel like a prison. This is especially true if you live in a padded cell with no windows. The only place to go was inside your own mind and I didn't want to go too deep in there. I found a battery-powered radio at the Goodwill and would listen to talk shows about aliens and call-in shows about government conspiracies all night. I had a stack of lent-out books and comic books that I would go through in a couple of days, with the cheap plastic earbuds in my ears and the rhythmic thumping of some doom metal band pounding into my back through the wall. The practice space started to take on the feel of a clubhouse. It was like some childhood fantasy. A space all my own after living in borrowed spaces for so long. It was an incredible feeling to finally have somewhere that would most likely not be taken away from me at a moment's notice. A small, dark corner to sit in while the chaos of The Tenderloin hummed and screamed outside. For once, I almost felt safe.

The books and the radio, though, were nothing compared to the guitar and the drums. It had been so long since I had been able to crank something up and play it loud. The beauty of the space being twenty-four hours was not only that I could live there, but it was also that I could play the drums at three in the morning if the mood struck me. And it often did. Sometimes I would wake up in the middle of the night, confused and grasping for something in the dark, and to shake it off I would sit at the drums and bang on them as loud as I could. I wasn't much of a drummer but it didn't matter. I would play until my shirt was soaked and when that wasn't enough I would strip down naked and open a 40-ouncer as I thrashed the drum set and laughed at myself in the middle of the night. It would almost always be enough to drown out the fear of The Tenderloin and the images of suffering I encountered outside that I could never quite shake. The drums always took care of that. Music was always showing up to mend my heart.

Even though the practice space was cheap, I wasn't getting as much work at The Market Street Theatre as I would have liked. Shifts always went to the people who had seniority and it was hard to beat them out when many of the other ushers had been working there for hundreds of years. Austin was barely getting more shifts than me and we begged Kevin for more but he would just shake his head and say that the union would throw a shit fit if he left the old-timers off the roster. Austin and I would go back to the practice space and crank up the little amp and play music instead of working. It was beautiful. We made loud noises and drank 40-ouncers and sat out on the metal balcony that overlooked an alley off Hyde Street, then he would go back to his truck and I would seal myself in the carpeted room for the night.

After a couple of weeks, I got used to the noise and terrifying smells that came from every direction in The Tenderloin and even found things I loved. AnyTime Pizza sold plain cheese slices for a dollar fifty and they never complained when I would open up the shakers of condiments to dress it up with as much Parmesan and Oregano as I could. I would sit on the plastic stools facing the big picture window and watch as people argued and screamed across the street or passed pills back and forth. Every other Saturday there was a farmer's market at The Civic Center BART station. There was a man who sold roasted pistachios in all kinds of flavors for two dollars a pound. I would buy bags of barbecue or garlic and onion flavored nuts and crack them open while sitting at the base of The Pioneer Monument and look at the buses go by or watch terrified tourists get lost and wander into the mess of The Tenderloin.

I found a threadbare suit jacket at the Goodwill and started wearing it every day along with my borrowed white shirt and tie. I looked like a businessman who had been fired from his high-paying job then never went back to his wife and kids. I stopped thinking about The Mission as my home base and started to understand that this was where I belonged. Here, I could step outside and not spend as much money. This was the neighborhood for people like me. This was where we went to be forgotten and I started to feel like I was blending into the red brick walls and stained sidewalks just as much as anyone else. I found a liquor store that gave me a line of credit and would let me put Ancient Age or flats of 40-ouncers on a tab. They would wave and smile when I came in and always looked happy to see me. They did this for everyone who came in, no matter how much they were nodding off or if they were vomiting in the street right before they entered. They knew everyone's name and welcomed them. This was a hard place to be, and they understood that there was no point in making it any harder. No one living there had anyone they could trust or love, and the people who had been there longest knew that just a little bit went a long way.

I started settling into a strange, play-acted routine. I would wake up every morning, hide my bed away, and put on my wrinkled suit. The tie was too short since I had to have Austin tie it for me, and I would just loosen it at night to take it off. I didn't dare untie it. Every day started with a trip down to the liquor store, where I would get a piece of coffee cake and a 24-ounce beer, and pay off some of my tab if I had recently had the good fortune of getting a few shifts at the theater. Then I would walk up to Union Square and sit watching the people bustling to get to work. There was an energy there that I loved and tried to leech off. People were getting things done. Street vendors sold hot dogs and people wheeled suitcases down the street. The St. Francis Hotel had bellhops out front, and they would stand in double-breasted red suits with great brass buttons, whistling at cabs as steam came up out of grates in the street. It felt like I was in a different city. Somewhere things happened and big-time deals were made. It was a break from the humanity of The Tenderloin and The Mission. I would pretend that I had somewhere to be and nod at other businessmen in the street, who would sometimes nod back. After I finished my coffee cake and beer, though, I would always get sick of the scene and rush back to Hyde Street, ashamed that I had tried to be someone else but refreshed from the change in pace.

Austin and I had band practice every night. We wrote songs together about living in the truck and would play them over and over again, laughing and sweating. He was always ready to play and never missed an opportunity to come by and bang on the drums with me. Mornings got easier. The dread of living in The Tenderloin started to fade. I could always take a vacation up to Union Square when things got too intense and bask for a couple of hours in the fantasy that I was somewhere else if I wanted to.

Austin decided to go stay with his parents for a few weeks and asked Kevin to give me a couple of his shifts. I worked them with gusto. It felt good to be doing something other than sitting in the library or wandering around the neighborhood. I needed it badly. I had two hundred dollars set aside for rent that month, but nothing else, and I left the theater on the last night of the run with a check for another three hundred in my pocket. A quick trip to the 24-hour check cashing place and I had $265 in cash. I stopped at a liquor store and bought a pint of Ancient Age to celebrate and walked down Market Street in my suit, sipping from a brown bag and letting the mist coming in off The Embarcadero settle on my face. Everything was lit up with colored lights along Market and I realized that I had missed Thanksgiving. I hardly ever turned on my phone, but I was sure my mother had left me a message or texted me. I made a note to call her back. It had been months.

As I wandered down Market and turned up Hyde Street to go back to the practice space, something felt off. I took another sip off the bottle and realized that there was no one around. Hyde Street was unusually quiet and further down the block I could see a bus driving past with no one on it. As I started to take note of this, I heard footsteps running up behind me. I thought that maybe Austin had come back early and was running to meet me, so I started to turn around. As I did, though, a flash went off in my head as a fist came flying through the darkness and hit me in the ear. Another fist landed on the side of my head and I went down to my knees.

"Whoa," I yelled. "Whoa, whoa, whoa."

Another blow hit the side of my face and I went all the way down. The bottle of Ancient Age went skidding out into the middle of the street and gurgled out its contents into the gutter. My face smashed against the sidewalk and I could smell piss, but I was strangely calm. I was thinking clearly and for a second it felt normal. Expected. Someone kneeled on my back and started going through my pockets.

"We don't want your wallet, your license, none of that," a voice said.

"I don't have any of that," I said.

Then someone else kicked me in the side. There were two of them, and as one kicked me and the other found the roll of cash in my pocket, I sighed with relief. They didn't seem to have a gun or a knife. At least they weren't going to kill me. They had used surprise to their advantage and it worked well. The one who was standing wound up and kicked me in the face. My ears rang and I felt the knee come off my back as they took off and ran down Hyde Street. Blood came down from my eyebrow and dripped into my eye, and I only saw blurred impressions of their backs as they disappeared down the empty street and turned the corner.

I laid there for a long time. A couple of people came by and stepped over me, but for the most part, Hyde Street stayed empty and echoed with the sounds coming from the apartment buildings up above. There was a dark throbbing in my face and I knew as soon as I stood up, it would get worse. I stayed down as long as possible until the blood had dried and it wasn't flowing out of my eyebrow anymore. Getting up, I felt a pinch in my side and it hurt to breathe but other than that I seemed okay. I wasn't dizzy and nothing seemed to be broken. All my money was gone except for the roll I had stashed in the practice space for rent, so that was as good as spent, too. Stumbling back, holding my side, I didn't feel as surprised as I had when Fast Eddie had gotten me. I felt like I had gotten what was coming to me. It was my fault for getting too comfortable. Too soft. Letting my guard down. I was just another tourist in The Tenderloin. When a car hits you because you ran out in the middle of the highway, you can't blame the driver. I must have looked like a prime target and they were simply too fast for me.

As I got to the door of the practice space, I heard a strange sound up at the corner in the mostly empty night. Looking up Hyde, I saw a man standing on the sidewalk with his hand outstretched, jutting into the sky. He was holding something that was emitting a blue light that flashed on and off and made a buzz at intermittent intervals. He was screaming something and waving it around. It went BRAP BRAP BRAP and it took me a second to realize that he was holding a massive stun gun. The kind you see on cop shows. The kind that will put you down in an instant and contract your muscles to exhaust them and render you powerless. He was wielding it and threatening cars that went past, seemingly frustrated that there were no humans to point it at on the empty street. I only had a moment before he turned and saw me shambling up the block, so I got my keys out, which luckily hadn't been taken, and started fumbling with them in the front door padlock of the practice space. As I got them into the keyhole, I felt something wet on the lock itself. When I lifted my hand and smelled it instinctually, it became instantly clear that someone had pissed into the lock. I didn't stop to try and figure out how or why they did it, I just pushed the door open as the stun gun went BRAP BRAP BRAP out on the corner up the block.

In the bathroom, I got a good look at the state I

was in. My eye was starting to swell up, and I had a chipped front canine tooth. There was blood running down my face and all over my suit coat and white shirt. When I lifted the shirt, I could already see some bruising on my side and I worried that maybe I had some internal bleeding, but I would have to wait and see. I was in no mood to go to the hospital. I didn't want anyone touching me, anyone near me. A metalhead with long hair and cutoff sleeves stepped into the bathroom as I was examining myself and I hissed at him like a cornered possum. He stepped back, putting his hands up, scared of this wild thing he had found in the cold tile bathroom.

Back in my padded room, I put the radio on and changed into a clean T-shirt. Everything ached and throbbed and I laid out the cushions and the down comforter and spread out on them as best as I could. Maybe I would just die there. I wondered how long it would take for the smell to reach one of the other rooms. Would they just assume it was a few dead rats in the walls? Or would they immediately think of the guy who had been seen bleeding in the bathroom? I started to wonder if anyone else had ever died in this warehouse. It seemed old and it was a massive complex, so the odds were pretty good. Maybe I would haunt this practice space. People would report hearing shuffling and smelling stale old whiskey and Anna would shiver as they talked about it.

"Oh yes," she would say. "That's Matty. He died

here."

I started to feel tired and wondered if I had a concussion. I had heard that the last thing you wanted to do in that case was fall asleep, but I was so tired. As I started to slip into sleep, I told myself that if I lived through the night, I would never get comfortable living like this again. Walking around and getting beat up and drinking myself to sleep every night wasn't going to work anymore. This wasn't normal. The only thing waiting for me at the end of this was a neighbor complaining about the smell of my rotting corpse. A story came on the radio about the Middle East, and it got quieter and quieter in my head as I tried to savor it, wondering if it would be the last thing I ever heard.

Chapter Seventeen

I was, mercifully or not, still alive the next morning. It took a long time to get the cushions put away as every breath sent a fresh jolt of pain through my ribs. In the bathroom, I jumped back when I saw the swollen eye and the dreamlike horror of a broken tooth in the mirror. Terror gripped me as I remembered the massive bruise on my side and pulled my shirt up. It had spread all the way down to my leg and was a deep purple and black like a filthy swimming pool. I could feel my heart beating faster, trying to pump blood back into my brain as the color rushed out of my face. I had never looked this bad before. My lip was split and huge and I could feel the jagged edge of the chipped tooth scraping against the back of it. I looked like a boxer who had been killed in the ring but was still somehow walking around. The water that came out of the faucet was freezing and stung so much when I splashed it onto my battered face that I screamed out loud.

It only took one night to reach a new low, and it was going to be a long crawl back up to rock bottom. The rent was paid but I was starving. I hadn't had time to get ramen or bread or any of the staples I usually hoarded for occasions like this. There were no dumpsters where someone could find perfectly good food in The Tenderloin. Anything that could be snatched up had already been found by someone much more destitute. I was only going to find used syringes. I had nothing. Looking around the practice space, there wasn't anything I could sell or pawn. Everything of value belonged to Austin. No one wanted my radio or torn T-shirts, and I was too weak to carry things to the pawnshop anyway.

I stepped unsteadily out of the warehouse and into the blaring, lively morning on Hyde Street. It was a different scene than it had been the night before. The winter sun was kissing every possible corner and there were people packed onto the sidewalk. It felt like everyone had come out of their apartments or gutters or bushes to talk and watch as cars passed.

The burning plastic smell of crack smoke blew into my face as I closed the piss-soaked door behind me and stumbled by a group of people leaning on the wall. They all turned to look at me and some of them sucked through their teeth as they caught a glimpse.

"Damn, you got fucked up, huh?" said a guy in a beanie and a windbreaker, lighting a cigarette.

I smiled with my broken tooth on full display. I could taste a little blood.

"Damn, yeah, you did get fucked up."

I looked at him for a moment and wondered if he had been one of the guys from the night before. His tone was familiar and he was laughing. There was no way to tell, though, and I was too tired and empty to care.

I started walking up to Union Square like always but turned down another corner instead. Looking like I did, I would probably be arrested for thinking I could occupy the same space as those people up there. Not that it would have been so bad. Jail had food and a change of clothes. There was blood spattered down the front of my suit and I could feel my eye throbbing in the socket. The sidewalks parted as I walked and more people looked at me with pitying eyes, then turned away. None of them wondered what had happened. It was clear that I was in the wrong place at the wrong time and had continued to stay in that wrong place.

When the human body tries to heal itself, it burns

up calories and energy. I could feel myself starting to get shaky and irritable and it was all I could do to stand up. My head was getting light and my throbbing eye started to swim. Turning a corner that I had never been down before, I spotted a dumpster next to a liquor store, but there was already someone going through it and I didn't have the energy or guts to fight him for it. That was when I noticed a line of people out in front of a church. It spanned the entire block and was made up of people who looked about the same as I did. Thin everywhere but the booze bloat. They shuffled in place and didn't talk. They just passed half-finished cigarettes back and forth. I crossed the street and asked a man in the back of the line what it was for.

"Food," he said. "They open in ten minutes. Damn, you got fucked up, huh?"

I stood in the line for a few minutes and then it started to move. Everyone shuffled and as soon as the movement began, all talk stopped. People stopped passing the cigarettes and any bottles that had been taken out were stowed away in pockets or finished and thrown into the trash can. More people got in line with us and by the time I reached the corner, I could see that we were headed into a church. It was a famous landmark in the city and had huge beautiful stained glass windows and a cavernous space where people congregated daily to sing and pray. I had been in there as a tourist when I was a kid and I remembered thinking how loud it would be in there for the packed, wailing funerals and how much emptier it would seem for the ones no one came to.

The line was not going into the main chapel space, though. It was snaking into a small door that went down some stairs and into a basement. As we made our way in and I stepped down off the last step, I was hit with a wave of smells and sounds that overwhelmed me and brought me to a complete halt until someone pushed into the small of my back and kept me moving through the line. A large man in a ripped sweatshirt handed me a red plastic tray and I moved along down a line of steam tables, behind which a wide variety of people were ladling and handing out different components of a meal, much like a school lunch line. No one asked any questions. No one shook their head or frowned. They just took my tray, put something on it, then handed it back, smiling. I got a large spoonful of rice, then a roll, then a ladle of delicious-smelling stew over the rice. At the end of the line, I stood for a moment, unsure where to go. A woman gently grabbed my shoulders and steered me to another room full of plastic tables and chairs, where I sat down with a few other men with no teeth and hard, sunburned faces. They scooted out of the way so I could sit, and put a plastic cup in front of me, filling it with Kool-Aid from a pitcher. It was the best meal I had ever eaten in my life. When I was done, the man sitting across from me handed me a plastic mug.

"There's coffee over there," he said, nodding to a huge metal urn in the corner of the room.

"You look like you could use it," he said. "You got fucked up."

I went over to the urn, poured a steaming cup of the strong, greasy coffee, and sat back down. I listened as the men at my table spoke to each other, without comprehending anything. It just felt good to sit and listen and be a part of something with some other people. After I was done with my coffee, a large voice boomed from the entrance.

"Time's up," the voice said. "Bus your trays and we'll see you tomorrow."

A commotion of scraping chairs and tables rose up and I joined the crowd, putting the trays in plastic bins and going back up the winding stairs and out into the street again.

⟵〰〰

As it turned out, there were a lot of resources like the one at the church for people like me in the neighborhood. People who were out of options. If you were hungry in The Tenderloin, someone was always around to help out. There were food banks and organizations that came to the Civic Center Plaza and handed out meals. I found that these places always had a sense of safety. It was not the sort of thing that people wanted to take for granted or cause problems with. They might not come back, and that would be bad for everyone.

One of the best food options in this category was a van run by one man and a few volunteers called Curry Without Worry. Every other day, they would show up and pull onto the cobblestone sidewalk of Civic Center Plaza. They put out a big white tent and set up tables, upon which they would put a pot of vegetarian curry and steam trays of basmati rice. The winter was fully assaulting me by that point. Even though it doesn't snow in San Francisco, the wind from The Bay rushes through the downtown buildings and pierces through anything that crosses its path. The hot curry would warm everything. There was never a time when it didn't hit the spot. It was always perfect, and years later I would still think about it. With just my reeking hooded sweatshirt, I would stand around the fountain in the plaza, sometimes hours ahead of time so I could be sure that I would have a place in line. I always let people who were worse off than me go first, though, and there were always plenty. Everyone made room for those in wheelchairs or with crutches and everyone would help them scoop rice into the paper bowls or carry their food to the nearest curb or bench. It was the one place where everyone was on the same level and it was a welcome break from the constant clawing and scraping and hustling that went on in the neighborhood for the other twenty-three hours a day. Even people who are robbing or beating each other in the street need a rest. Somewhere to feel calm and taken care of. We were all there because we needed to eat, and for just a little bit, it was nice to belong.

This went on for several weeks. I was still getting a few shifts here and there at the theater, but it was only going to be enough to pay the rent. I came to love these beautiful, perfect souls who came to feed me more and more. Not only them but the beautiful, imperfect souls I ate with in the cold Tenderloin night. Whether or not any of us felt like we deserved it, we at least had a place to go where something good would happen. For many, it had been a long time since anyone cared enough to make sure they stayed alive.

I depended on these resources exclusively as the work dried up and I got more destitute. I memorized their schedules and would happily get in line at the church or wait around in the plaza, saying hello to the people I recognized and commiserating about the things going on in the neighborhood. It became a social gathering as much as a means to survive. I looked forward to speaking with Patches, a man with wild eyes and hair that stuck out like he had been electrocuted. Or Francis, a blind man who needed help doing everything, but seemed to have no problem tracking women who walked past. I was never fully convinced that he was actually blind, but I didn't mind helping him to the bench or pouring curry over his bowl of rice.

One night, the wind was whipping through the plaza, almost knocking us over as we waited in line. It was freezing, and as we ate and stood around chatting, I noticed some people I had never seen before. Two men and a woman who looked to be around twenty years old were standing around with us, holding a camera. Now and then, the one with the camera would lift it to his eye and snap a photo. As he did, I saw the subjects of the photographs cover their faces or turn away.

"Oh come on," he said. "This is great."

The more photos he took, the more people started dispersing, trying to get away from them. I walked up.

"What are you guys doing?" I asked.

"Oh, we're from the Art Academy," the woman said. "We're working on a photo series called 'Street Poetry,'" she said.

"Yeah, I don't think that's such a good idea," I said. "A lot of these people don't want their picture taken."

"Oh no," she said. "They're happy someone's paying attention to them."

"They're really not."

"Well, we're just trying to shine a light on them."

"These people," I said, "Us. We get enough light here. The last thing we want is some fucking hipster douchebags exploiting us."

As I said it, the man with the camera lifted it to his eye and snapped a picture of me.

"Get the fuck out of here," I said, swiping at the camera, enraged. "Gimme that fuckin' camera. I'll sell it for crack."

He lifted it again and went to take another picture. As he did, I did the first thing that came to mind and I shoved my finger down my throat. I gagged and a stream of saliva came pouring out along with some stomach bile. The look on their faces turned to horror and the cameraman slowly brought it down to his waist.

"Gimme that camera," I said, lurching at him and shoving my hand in my throat. Real vomit came up this time and splashed around their shoes.

"Is that what you want? Come on, take a picture of me. This is what it is. Come on, shine the light on it."

I shoved my finger down one more time and the last bit of vomit came up and trickled out of my mouth as they turned away and started walking toward Market, disgusted and terrified. The crowd started to gather again, safe from the camera, and I ate my curry in the freezing wind.

←〰〰

A few nights later, I was standing in line, sandwiched between Francis and another man in a wheelchair who was screaming and grumbling to himself.

"Chill out," I said to him. "It's almost ready."

We were waiting for a group called Food Not Bombs, which had been around for years. They served salty vegetable soup twice a week in styrofoam cups handed out by hippies with dreadlocks that would droop and dip into the pot when they bent over to give the cups to people waiting in line. It wasn't anyone's favorite, but it was better than sleeping with nothing in our stomachs. We stood and shuffled and folded our arms across our chests, bracing against the offensive cold that swept through the Civic Center Plaza in what was now early December. As they were setting up their table and pulling the pot out from their van, I heard something behind me.

"Matty?"

It had been so long since anyone had used that name. I was Matthew at the theater and no one out here on the street. I didn't recognize it at first.

"Matty, hi."

I turned around and was met with a silhouette backlit by the streetlights. Golden hair whipped around in the wind and Lola's eyes shone out from the middle of her darkened face. I would recognize them in any situation, and all it took was a moment to get my bearings and remember everything. Who she was, who I was, what I was doing here.

"Hi," I said.

She turned slightly and the rest of the street lights flooded her face, which seemed to energize every single thing in The Tenderloin.

"How are you?" she said, not smiling, and not needing an answer.

Her eyes darted around at the pot of soup and the rest of the people waiting in line for it in the middle of winter. Then back at me.

"I'm good, actually," I said. And I was.

There was too much to explain. Too much to apologize for, and it wouldn't have helped. We stood there for a few seconds as she took everything in, relieved that she had gotten off the train before it fully derailed.

I looked up at the sky to avoid her eyes as they narrowed but refused to dim.

"I don't hate myself anymore," I said.

And I didn't.

It was the truest thing I had ever said.

She smiled at me and nodded, then pointed toward Market Street. I nodded back and pointed to the line of people waiting for soup. She put her hands in her pockets and walked off without looking back, away from the plaza and toward the BART station. There was nothing else to say and nowhere to go from there. I was sorry for a lot, but asking for forgiveness is easy and selfish. Living to forgive yourself is much harder and takes a long time. Where I was and what I was doing was enough for her right then. She had been right to let me go, and I had been right to go. She knew that the best thing to do was walk away.

⟵〜〜〜

I went to the church every afternoon and ate with the same group of people. No one ever complained. No one ever got mad when the food was too salty, even though it often was. Sometimes I could feel my hands swelling up from the sodium as I stepped up the wooden staircase and back out onto the street. Everyone accepted what was given. They had all been in everyone else's shoes. They had all taken too much of something or not gotten enough of something else. Whether it was drugs or booze or love from their friends or family. Everyone was there because they had a hole inside of them and no one else was helping to fill it. The church and the people in vans who set up tents and pots could only offer what they had. It was more than many of us had access to, and no one who sat out in the plaza or on the hard plastic picnic tables in the church basement could take it for granted for very long. We all knew, more than most other people, how quickly things could change and how fast they could be taken away. Every moment was a thin edge that was so easy to fall off, down into a void that was inescapable without taking someone else's hand. You would have to be a fool not to grab it.

Whenever I would get a chance to work at the theater, I stopped getting annoyed when elderly patrons needed extra help to get up and down the aisle or to the bathroom. I shined my flashlight for them and let them grab my arm. It was nice to do something for them that they couldn't do themselves. Just like my friends in the soup lines, I knew how hard it was to be helpless and how much it meant when someone came along to make it just a little bit easier.

One night, after the show, Kevin called me into his office. We sat in the brown box and he exhaled and smiled at me.

"How are you?" he asked.

"I'm good, man," I said. "I'm actually really good."

He smiled again.

"You seem good. You're thin, though."

He was right. My white shirt was billowy and puffed out from under the maroon blazer. I had to get a smaller size for the last week, and I was fairly certain it had been John's before he disappeared. He had fallen down into the void and no one had heard from him for months. I tried not to imagine how much of his bourbon sweat was soaked into the fabric of the collar.

"What do you do besides this?"

"What do you mean?"

"I mean what's your other job?"

"I don't have one. This is it."

His smile disappeared and he leaned back in his chair.

"How?" he said. "You're only here a couple of hours a week."

"I make it work."

He looked at me for a long time, rocking back and forth in his chair with his arms folded across his massive chest.

"You've seen some shit, haven't you?"

He didn't say it with any animosity or humor. I considered the question for a moment, stopping my breath like I had been caught in some shameful act. Then I felt the familiar heat of tears starting to come up from the bottom of my stomach and up out of my eyes, silently.

"Yes," I said. "I have."

I felt like Kevin was looking right into me. He seemed like he had seen some shit, too. It was hard not to, working in this neighborhood, and he had been there for a long, long time.

"I have to say I didn't think you would end up staying here for very long. Most people work a couple of shows and then disappear. It's part of the business. It's part-time. People come and go."

"I like it here," I said. "I like you guys."

"We like you, too."

More tears came and he leaned forward.

"You play music, right? I remember Austin telling

me something about that."

"I do," I said. "I love it."

"I was wondering," he said. "Do you need a full-time job?"

My eyebrows shot up and my heart started beating at twice the speed.

"Desperately," I said. "I'm not making it work at all, actually."

"Well," he said. "I have a friend who works at Taylor Junior High in Berkeley. She needs someone to work on the music program there. It doesn't pay much but it's better than here and you don't need a teaching degree or anything. You wouldn't have to eat in the plaza anymore."

He smiled at me again.

"I saw you there the other day," he said. "But that's not why I'm asking you about this. I think you'd be good at it. Is that something you would want to do?"

I stared at him for a moment while the tears dried on my cheeks and others fell to take their place. He stuck out his hand and I grabbed it, shaking it for a long, long time.

Chapter Eighteen

As the train went under the water, I trembled and tried to catch my breath. The light green cloth of the BART car seats was stained and matted and it made me sick to think about it, let alone look at it. The seats had been installed sometime in the early '70s and whoever decided that cloth was a good option clearly had more faith in humanity than I could ever dream of having. At least on the buses and light rail around the city, the seats were hard plastic that could be hosed down at the end of the night. These had seen all manner of vomit, urine, and God knows what else pass through their interwoven fibers. Any sort of liquid that fell on them just seeped into the fabric and down into the crusted cushions below.

Going into the tunnel that crossed The Bay always made me uneasy. There was nothing around the train but concrete and the ocean. If there was an earthquake, the train would be covered in seconds. As I thought about it, my head pounded and I started to sweat through my white shirt and tie. I unbuttoned the top button and squirmed in my seat. A woman sitting across from me with a wire cart full of garbage bags and laundry touched my leg.

"Are you okay?" she asked.

The loud howling of the train in the concrete tunnel drowned her out, but I could read her lips and see the concern on her face.

"I'm fine, I'm fine, I'm fine, thanks," I said.

"Okay, because it kind of looks like you're on something."

I looked around the BART car at the commuters who did this every day. Some were staring at me but most were avoiding my eyes.

"What? I said I'm fine."

"Well whatever it is you're on, I want some," she said.

"You really don't."

I tried to get comfortable in my seat, but I could feel my hands and face getting numb as I started to hyperventilate. I felt like I couldn't get enough air and the whooshing sound that came pumping into the car was crushing me. It was relentless and all I wanted was to get out. I leaned my head back on the stained cloth and tried to catch my breath, focusing on breathing normally and not sucking in the air with my chest. The sweat was pouring down now. Kevin had set up this interview for me. He had tried to lift me up and push me over the wall and I was already panicking on the way there, gasping for air and flopping around in my seat like a fish. If I could just get to the other side of the tunnel, I would feel better. I would have the option to get off at the West Oakland station and start running somewhere. It didn't matter where. As long as it was off this train and away from this horrible morning.

The scream of the train in the tunnel finally subsided, and when I focused my eyes out the window, I saw that we had come out the other side into the port of West Oakland. Below us on one side were rows of houses in various states of decay. Some of them had sagging roofs and splintered support beams like broken bones left to rot and bleach in the saltwater air. On the other side was The Bay with shipping containers, rusted, half-sunk barges, and the towering metal loading cranes that sat like sleeping animals guarding the industrial equipment below. When the train stopped at the West Oakland station, I didn't get off and I didn't run away. I sat bolted to my seat, determined to make it to Berkeley. My legs were like jelly anyway and I wasn't even sure I would make it more than a few feet before collapsing with exhaustion and fear in the doorway of the train car. Instead, I took the big bottle of water out of my torn backpack and gulped three big swallows. People were still staring intermittently, but they had almost completely lost interest. They were mostly just watching to see if I could keep the water down and I hated to admit that I had trouble with it. I could feel it bubbling in my stomach and twisting my insides as it sloshed around.

I couldn't afford to run away. I needed this badly. I also couldn't stand the idea of letting Kevin down. I had let people down most of my life. They either chalked it up to me just being who I was or they walked away. It all depended on the severity of it. Something about Kevin, though, made it impossible for me to disappoint him. I needed to do well at this. If only just to not let him down. I was terrified, though, that it was too late. That I had already blown it. I took another few sips of water, holding the bottle with two shaking hands to steady it, and the train car doors closed as we moved through the East Bay.

The East Bay is an amazing cross-section of different strata of wealth and poverty. As we moved from the water inland, the houses got nicer, the stations got cleaner, and I started to feel more out of place. By the time I got to my stop, I had mustered up enough strength to get up out of my seat and walk, teetering off the train car and up the stairs, into the glaring sun of Berkeley, to try and find the bus that would take me to Taylor Junior High. I had never been more scared in my life.

The previous afternoon had been spent at The Main Branch, sitting at a computer and sweating over a new, more professional resume. What I ended up with was a delicately constructed page of padding, exaggerations, and outright lies. Nothing that would get me in too much trouble or put me in a position where I would endanger anyone, but it was dishonest at best and laughable at worst. It wasn't that I didn't have any work experience, it was that I had too much. So many jobs that had only lasted a few weeks. I had just combined them into one and called it customer service. I had tried to take some of my experience touring in punk bands and drinking my way across the country and turn it into something impressive-sounding. "Working Musician." This was perhaps the most egregious lie on the whole thing. What I had been doing that whole time could hardly be called working. I simply took Greyhound buses and played haphazardly slapped-together shows until the money ran out, which usually wasn't that long. Sometimes I would buy a cheap car and drive it around, playing open mic nights along the way until the wheels came off, then walk to the nearest Greyhound station and buy a ticket to wherever home was at that time. "Working" implied that I had been making a living from it when all I was doing was running away from making a real life.

The jobs that I put under my customer service label had only been for the purpose of financing these trips and I never made much of an effort to keep them past the moment that I made enough to go on one. I made up phone numbers and addresses for them as well as fabricated the names of managers and tried not to dwell on the lies too much. Those weren't the kinds of places I wanted on this resume anyway. The only things I had learned at those jobs that I could impart to some kids was how to steal out of the cash register by ringing people up and not completing the transaction on the computer. Then, whatever was left over at the end of the night was mine to buy cheap malt liquor with and go back to whatever basement I was living in, in whatever state I happened to be residing that month. The things I learned at the kitchen jobs were even worse and I figured it would be best to leave them off of this resume entirely. By the end, I had put together something that seemed about ten percent convincing. I would have to rely on Kevin's reference and my personality during the interview. This was why I thought I might be doomed.

After coercing a terrified-looking college student in the library to use his credit card to print out a few copies of my resume for me, I went home to the practice space to sit and rehearse how the interview might go. I tried to think of how I would answer as many questions as I could possibly think of, as music from a dozen bands blended together and created a loud, deep rumble. Every time I tried to think up an answer for questions like "can you explain this gap in your employment," all that ever came to mind was the truth. I didn't think that telling someone I was having a nervous breakdown while living in a greenhouse in Austin, Texas would be a good answer. It was a decent story, but it wouldn't fly in an interview situation. There were already so many unexplained things on there, confusing them more with the truth would have been an immediate fail.

As I laid on the cushions and stuffed toilet paper into my ears, I started to get more nervous. This had the potential to be a humiliation on a grand scale. I knew how deeply unqualified I was and had to somehow convince the school otherwise. I had tried to start myself on the right track. The way The Tenderloin is situated, between leaving the library and getting to the piss-covered front gate of the practice, I passed four different liquor stores. I knew that a few belts of Ancient Age would settle my stomach and keep my head from spinning in a million different directions, but declined to go in. As I turned the light off in the space to go to bed, I started to regret it. As soon as I was in the dark, visions of failure started dancing in front of me. I tossed and turned on the cushions and the gaps between them started to hurt my back. When I looked at my phone, I saw the time: 11:30 p.m. I had to be up in six hours. I fought with myself as I sat up and turned the lights back on. I fought with myself as I put my shoes on. I fought with myself as I walked down the hall, past the rooms of bands still practicing even at this late hour. I fought with myself as I stepped out onto Hyde Street, which was still buzzing with activity. By the time I got to the door of the liquor store that gave credit, I had stopped fighting and just watched myself from above as I got a pint of Ancient Age and a 40-ouncer of malt liquor and put them on my tab. I knew that this would be the only way I would get any sleep, but also knew the possibility of what could happen the next morning. By that time, though, I was barely even paying attention to myself. I just sat there, in the back of my own mind, as I cracked open the pint on my way back to the practice space and took a deep, long swig.

⟵∿∿∿

I stepped off the bus and onto the sidewalk a block away from Taylor Junior High and immediately vomited. It splashed as it hit the sidewalk and I jumped back, trying to avoid getting it on the pair of black work pants I had washed in the chipped porcelain sink at the practice space. I turned in time to see the people on the bus either pressing their faces to the glass to stare or turning away to recoil as the driver closed the door and lumbered on to the next stop. It was 7:45 in the morning and the sun was still casting a sickly glow in the marine layer of fog that sat heavily above me. Though my stomach felt better, my head was now being crushed in a vice and there was a spike going through the left side, which made my eye twitch. Between the hangover and the panic attack on the BART train, it was hard to know which was the cause, but it didn't really matter. I pulled the bottle of water out of my bag and took a few big gulps. The water landed in the bottom of my stomach and I started salivating. I tried as hard as I could to keep it in there. I bore down and clenched my fists but there are some things that you can't stop your body from doing. There are some things it does on its own and all you can do is white knuckle it and try to hold on as tight as you can. The water came up in a wild firehose formation, all over the sidewalk and a wooden fence cordoning off someone's backyard. I wiped my mouth and walked toward the school.

There were kids playing in the playground when I turned the corner. It was like hiking in the woods and coming across a mama bear and her cubs. I immediately felt that I shouldn't be there. That I had come upon something that I had no business being involved in. They terrified me and I felt my stomach flip over again. There was no way I was going to allow myself to puke in front of these children, so I held on to the chain-link fence and fought it, thankfully managing to keep whatever rotten fluid was left down where it belonged. I wandered through the outdoor cement hallway, marveling at how small everything was, how low the drinking fountains were. Had I once been this small? Keeping a concerned frown on my face to signal that I was actually looking for something and not just prowling, I eventually found the front office where I was supposed to meet with Mrs. Anita Gutierrez, the principal. The door to the office was thick with years of coats of paint, and it stuck as I tried to open it, giving me one last chance to turn around and find somewhere to throw up before taking the bus home and never thinking about this morning again. Instead, I pushed harder and entered a brown and tan carpeted office, dense with electric heat. A man at a desk looked up at me and raised his eyebrows.

"I'm Matthew DeYoung," I said. "I have an appointment with Mrs. Gutierrez at 8 a.m."

There was no turning back now. This was going to happen.

Mrs. Gutierrez sat behind a beige desk littered with papers and an ancient computer. There were things stacked on textbooks and posters on the wall with various celebrities holding books and the words

"READ" emblazoned on the bottom. One of them had Nicolas Cage holding a copy of *Siddhartha* by Herman Hesse and leaning seductively against a wall in a leather jacket. I was staring into his eyes when Mrs. Gutierrez cleared her throat and flipped my resume over. I was sweating and I couldn't hide it. I didn't want to keep wiping my forehead, so I just let it drip down into my eyes and sting them, hoping she wouldn't see. It didn't work. She handed me a tissue and my heart sank.

"This is quite a resume you have here," she said.

"Oh, good," I said. "I try to do a lot of different things."

She looked over the piece of paper at me and set it down on the desk.

"That's good. We like that. We like having people from all walks of life here, Mr. DeYoung."

"You can call me Matthew," I said.

"It's okay, Mr. DeYoung. We go by last names here."

"Okay, Mrs. Gutierrez."

She smiled at this, and the sweat started to dry up on my scalp and temples. I blinked some of it away and out of my eyes.

"The thing is," she said, "we have a lot of kids from different walks of life here too. A lot of them come from places that aren't happy. Do you know what that's like?"

The way she looked at me told me that she knew

the answer, but she wanted me to tell her.

"Yes, ma'am I do."

"And for a lot of them, this is a place where they can let go. Where they're safe and free. Do you know what it's like to have a place like that?"

The question caught me off guard and I tried to think. I tried to come up with a time or a place where I had been able to let my shoulders drop and unclench my broken teeth. The first thing that came to mind was an image of myself standing inside a church, waving a golden incense burner over a small coffin while a family sat and cried in the front row. I could smell the incense and remembered the feeling of being free from my desk and the nuns back in the classroom. I remembered the elation of being there and being alive.

"I think so, yes. I had a place like that."

"Then you know how important it is that a place stays like that. Forever."

"I do."

She handed me another tissue.

"I think right now Mr. DeYoung, you need to find that place for yourself again."

She smelled the air softly and I could tell that I was sweating Ancient Age. I wanted to crawl into my own chest and make myself as small as possible.

"I think that until you do, you can't make that place for anyone else. Would you agree?"

"I would."

"When you find it, sir, I want you to come back and see me. I like who I'm looking at. I need you to like him too. Then, the kids will really like him."

She put my resume in a drawer in her desk and extended her hand for me to shake.

"I'll hang on to that. You hang on to my number, okay?"

"I will Mrs. Gutierrez," I said. "Thank you."

On the bus ride back to the BART station, everything was in black and white. My vision, no longer blurred by the promise of what may or may not be, was blended into one coherent spectrum of dark and light. My stomach was settled, my breath was back to being automatic, and everything else was empty. When there was no more room for the adrenaline and other chemicals that made me sweat and shiver and tremble, all that was left was a big space no longer filled with questions and visions. Just the remainder of time I had left to sit in the small, padded room back in The Tenderloin and wait it out.

I got off the bus and finished the big bottle of water, feeling it drain into my stomach and soak into my veins, finally getting its footing. Then I took the stairs down to the train and got on the SF-bound car when it screamed into the station. It was a repeat of the morning but in reverse. The water stayed down, my hands steadied, and the sweat clung to the surface of my skin, waiting for the next opportunity for it to drip down and soak my face. I took a seat on a huge brown stain in the shape of a landmass on a map and no one stared at me as I put my elbow on the metal ledge of the window and watched Berkeley disappear and turn into Oakland, which turned into West Oakland and then back under the water, where I barely noticed that we were exiting the tunnel and stopping at the Civic Center Station. I got up and made my way back through The Tenderloin to the practice space, the only remnant of the morning being a slight headache that I could hardly feel as I turned my key in the big metal front door and went inside where the drums pounded and guitars screeched and squealed.

<∿∿∿

When I woke up in the practice space, there was none of the usual panic or gasping for air as I tried to make sense of my windowless surroundings. I simply sat up and leaned against the carpeted wall. The last thing I remembered was coming back from the interview, splashing some water on my face in the freezing bathroom, and then stripping off my sweat-stiffened clothes once I was inside the soundless confines of the space. I didn't know how long I had slept, but the headache was completely gone and all traces of the nerves and tingling had left my limbs. I got up and neatly packed away the cushions and blankets, then got dressed in my cleanest-smelling T-shirt and the threadbare hoodie.

Stepping outside onto Hyde Street, it was nighttime. Only the liquor stores were open so I assumed it had to be past midnight. I shoved my hands into my pockets, put the hood up, and headed north up Hyde. I passed the first store where I had a line of credit and peeked in to see who was working. Nick, the owner, was sitting on a stool and reading the paper with the news on a small TV stashed behind a beef jerky display. He didn't look up and I kept walking. I passed the store that had homemade pecan pie and then, further up, passed another one that would sell Ziploc bags with everything you needed to mix a cocktail. These packages contained things like tall Coke cans and two airline-size bottles of Jim Beam, or coconut rum and piña colada mix. I walked past and kept heading up the street. A man stepped out from an alley as I walked and whispered to me.

"OCs. Oxy," he said.

I shook my head and didn't look back as he ducked into the alley. I kept walking until I hit Union Square and found a spot on the cement wall that lined the square. Laying down with my feet dangling over it, I watched the sky as the clouds flew in from the ocean just a half-mile away. I laughed as I realized that the entire time I had been in San Francisco, I had never once gone to the beach. I had seen pictures of it and had certainly walked the Embarcadero, which ran along The Bay, but I hadn't seen sand the whole time. I had landlocked myself in an underground maze and stayed in my lane, only leaving it when forced to, like I had been that morning. People walked by me and sometimes brushed up against my feet. I would catch snippets of their conversations, but they seemed far away and barely comprehensible. I focused on the clouds and watched their slow movement as they found their places for the evening and settled in, where they would remain until the sun came out again and burned them away.

Chapter Nineteen

It would be difficult to accurately say how many days I stayed under the blanket on the three couch cushions in that padded room. Once I laid down, everything went black. Days? Weeks? The lack of windows made each minute fade into the next and blur within themselves. I had turned off my phone and put it in the hole in the front of the drum set's big bass drum, covered up by the pillow that Austin had put in there to help deaden the sound. It wasn't enough that it was turned off. It needed to be completely out of sight. The only way to mark time was to listen to the programs on the radio. Talk shows and call-in shows about political topics I couldn't begin to understand played through its tinny speaker. It was nice to feel like there were people in the room without having to participate. I could lay on the cushions and look up at the spotted carpet on the ceiling, trying to relax my eyes enough to let the dots shift and swirl into a big blur while people chatted on, using incomprehensible words like "deficit" and "constituents." After a while, I lost track of how many of the shows I listened to and what time they were usually on and drifted into one long, flowing, perpetual night.

I knew for sure that I had missed shifts at the theater. Kevin had probably called over and over again looking for me. Or maybe just once and then shrugged and called someone up to replace me on the schedule. Now and then, I would look over at the bass drum and feel like I could see the phone underneath the pillow, pulsing and vibrating, though I knew it was turned off. I started to picture waves emanating out from it and sinking into my skull. The air in the practice space was stale, and when the band next door would start up their rehearsal and hit notes on the bass guitar, dust shook away from the carpeted walls and settled on the blanket and in my hair. I would turn the radio up and try to sleep through it, sweating in the tepid warmth that had built up in the days of keeping the door closed. Leaving the space to go to the bathroom had become a terrifying chore, so I started peeing in the empty 40-ounce bottles and stacking them in the corner. Before that, every time I had gotten up and gone into the cold porcelain bathroom down the hall, I ran into somebody practicing there with their band, and nodding at them or making a quick, two-sentence conversation proved to be far too much to handle. There was failure, anxiety, and the stench of death coming off me at every angle and I knew that everyone could see it and smell it.

The bands practicing in the other rooms started to seem louder. Every song and noise started to blend in together and the screech of feedback and the relentless pounding of bass drums started to pry into my brain. The thumping and wailing scratched against the walls like fingertips, clawing their way in and reaching through the hung carpeting to wrap around me and envelop me completely. Every note was a reminder of the world outside those four carpeted walls. People were out there doing things, following dreams, looking toward the future. I couldn't hear my radio and I was certain that the noise was worse than usual. It was normally something I could push away into the background, but ever since that night before the interview, it started to get into my bloodstream. It was poisoning me from the inside out. I began to feel very small in the room as the ceiling stretched and groaned higher and higher and the noise got bigger and deeper. It laid on top of me, smothering me and sapping all my strength. My limbs felt heavy and breathing became more and more difficult as I sat on the dirty carpeted floor, stuck to it like Velcro. I tried to lift my arms but they were too heavy, so I settled for moving a finger. Once the finger was lifted, I could pivot my hand on my wrist. My heart raced as I tried to slowly move my forearm, desperate to get up and out of the room as minutes crept by like days. Finally, after what seemed like thousands of incremental movements, I was able to get up off the cushions and put on my shoes, stepping out into the hall. Out there, it was even worse. People were milling around outside of their spaces, pushing amps, and hauling drum equipment. I immediately put my hands to my ears and drew looks from a few metalheads taking hits from a bong. I turned and saw the fire escape balcony and rushed to it as fast as my atrophied legs would carry me.

The noise was still crushing and oppressive outside. Then I noticed the ladder. It stretched up the face of the brick building and went all the way up to the roof, where it disappeared into a single point in the sky. The primal part of my mind took hold of my hand, and I grabbed the first rung. Then I grabbed the second and the third and the fourth until I was scaling the building. I didn't dare look up or down, I just climbed the metal ladder, not worried about when it was last serviced or whether or not it was going to pull away from the wall and tumble down under my weight. All I could think about was getting away from the noise. With every step up the ladder, the pounding and squealing diminished slightly until I was just a few feet from the top. At the lip of the roof, I swung my arm over the side of the concrete and pulled myself up. By the time I got to my feet on the tar and gravel rooftop, the noise was gone. There was nothing but the sky and a few taller buildings above me and I was completely, mercifully alone. The breeze from The Bay rushed in through the corridor of concrete structures and lapped at my face as I closed my eyes and let it wash over me, around me, and all the way through me. The only things up there were some pieces of utility equipment and HVAC ducts. Even the noise from the street and the life below didn't make it to the top. It got to about the halfway point and then was whisked away by the wind and the distance, dissipating completely and leaving my ears with nothing but the sound of the vacuous sky.

The silence pushed in on my body. I could feel it working its way into my skin and my bones. The sun was just starting to set below the building to the west and I could almost hear it creaking as it fell, holding on for dear life before it crashed into the ocean below. I went back to the ladder and without looking down, climbed back onto the metal fire escape porch. The band practices lapped at my feet and I could feel the noise cover me from the bottom up as I descended. I went back into the practice space and grabbed two of the couch cushions, then climbed back up the ladder, holding one in my teeth as it rubbed against the sore, broken canine in the front.

I got the two couch cushions and threw them down in the center of the rooftop, then climbed back down and got one more and the blanket. Before leaving the room, I looked at the small plastic radio that was still weakly pumping out a talk show. I brought my foot down on it and it crumpled and splintered with very little effort. The sound from the speaker stopped. I had expected it to slow down and fizzle out like electronics did in cartoons, but it just went away. There wasn't even a crackle as I lifted my foot up and saw it broken on the floor. I tossed the blanket over my shoulder and held the last cushion in one hand, as I carefully and slowly climbed the metal ladder back up the side of the building. I placed the three couch cushions in line and laid the blanket out over them under what had become the night sky and I laid down on top of it. It was cold now. I figured it must have been the middle of December or at least somewhere around there. It was difficult to tell. Time was strange and getting stranger. I listened as the low hum of all the noise from the city blended in together and tried to get above the concrete lip of the rooftop, but it just stayed low and comforting as I laid on my bed in the middle of the tar paper and gravel and the dark ocean of the San Francisco winter sky. No stars to be seen, just the low fog that caught the light from below and diffused it into a sickly brownish-gray. I pulled the blanket up under my chin and drifted off to sleep in the cold, humming womb.

↩↬↬↬

The morning was wet and I woke up shivering. The blanket was completely soaked from being so high up in the fog. By the overcast pall of the sky, I could tell it was early. Early enough for the sun to still be stuck behind the clouds, which were far too thick to burn off. I took the blanket off me and stood up, bones creaking and popping under the weight of the smallest movement. I took a short walk around the roof to try and work some of the kinks out of my neck and back and warm up a little bit. It didn't work. I touched the HVAC vents and found one pumping out warm air, so I stood over it and warmed my hands, rubbing them together and blowing into them while holding them over the vent. There was nothing in front of me and so much behind me. So much that I wanted to forget about and make up for. There were people who I would never see again and other people who wouldn't mind never seeing me again. They were all floating out there. Some of them were close by, swimming around somewhere in the ocean of streets and cars and buses down below.

I stepped toward the edge of the roof, which was flush and had no lip to it like the other side did. It was just a flat surface and then empty space. I inched closer and looked over it, craning my aching neck to try and get a good look at how high up I was. Below me, there were about eight stories worth of air and then the solid, flat concrete of the ground. There were stains of all kinds covering the sidewalk under the spot where I stood. Some were fresher than others, but from that high up, they had a kaleidoscopic, mosaic effect, swirling in interesting patterns of hard days and nights led by the people who lived in this neighborhood. I inched closer to the edge, almost putting one toe over it. I heard someone screaming. I could picture them standing in the middle of the street, grasping at their hair and looking to the sky for something. Some answer to their impossible question. They had faith that there was someone listening up there. And I was. I noticed that I was shaking and my heart was pounding in my temples as I inched just a little closer and put my other toe over the edge. The space between me and the ground below felt like a long hallway that led to a place where everything would stop and the journey could end. Where there was nothing but the space above and below, and only the sticky tar paper holding my feet to the surface.

"Matty? Matty, are you up here?"

The sound of my name shocked and confused me.

I looked up to the sky and frowned.

"Matty, hey!"

I turned around on my heels and saw a head pop up over the lip of the rooftop where the ladder was, then some arms, and finally a whole body as Austin struggled up over the last rung and rolled over onto the gravel and tar paper.

"Man, that was scary as fuck," he said, looking back at the ladder. "What are you doing up here? It's freezing."

I tried to answer, but I was shivering and trembling and it came out like air being sucked through my teeth.

"Jesus, man what the hell is going on? You look way worse than usual."

He, on the other hand, looked amazing. It seemed he had put on a couple of pounds at his parents' house and grown out his beard. I recognized him mostly from his drawl.

"Dude, have you been sleeping up here?"

"It was noisy," I said. "How did you know I was up here?"

"I tried calling but you didn't answer and someone was coming out the front gate just as I got here so I was able to get in. You know the door to the space is wide open and there's a bunch of broken plastic and bottles of piss everywhere? I went out on the little fire escape thing and saw the ladder so I figured I would check if you were up here. Are you okay?"

I didn't know how to answer.

"I think so," I said.

"Come here," he said, and he hugged me tightly for a long time, just like he had when he found me on the street in front of The Armstrong, but this time I hugged him back, happy to see him and happy, for a moment, to be standing with solid footing on the rooftop. I started shivering even more, uncontrollably. It was hard to tell if it was from the cold or if what I had just been doing was sinking in. Thinking back on the last couple of minutes, I felt a chill go up my back and it made its way into my arms, escaping in a violent tremble.

"Man, let's get down. It's creepy as fuck up here."

I nodded and let him go down the ladder first.

"Should I grab my stuff?" I yelled down, looking at the cushions and the blanket sitting in the middle of the rooftop.

"Just leave it," he said from the fire escape. "It's ruined, man, you can't sleep on that shit it's gonna be all moldy. We'll figure something else out for you."

I nodded and left it up there to rot, then climbed onto the first rung of the ladder, then the next one, and then the next one, without looking down, until I was back on solid metal. The warehouse was quiet and still now and we walked into the padded room, closing the door to keep the cold air out.

Austin immediately got behind the drums and

started playing. I picked up the little electric guitar and turned on the small amp, cranking it all the way up until it squealed with electric delight. I hadn't turned it on in a long time. I had been spending my days on the couch cushions that were now forever rotting on the roof. I kicked the broken plastic pieces of the radio into the corner and played a few chords as Austin played along with me. He banged on the drums and I tried not to think about how the last time I had sat on that drum stool, I had been completely naked. It would be best not to tell him.

We played together for hours. I tried to remember the chords of songs I knew and eventually just resigned to making noise. That was enough. We filled the halls of the practice space with our sound and laughed when something worked and sounded good. In a lull, while tuning the little electric guitar, he looked up at me.

"What were you doing up there?" he said.

I stopped tuning and raised my eyes to him.

"What do you mean?"

"When I came up. What were you looking at over the ledge?"

I didn't say anything for a long time.

"I was thinking about all the people I've known. How they were so far away and how they were even further away up there."

He nodded at this, understanding.

"You know," he said, "Sometimes sick animals

hide under the porch. But no one wants to find their dog's skeleton when they pull up the deck. That's pretty unfair. Pretty unfair to everyone, including the dog."

I nodded at this, also understanding, and turned up the volume knob on the guitar, letting it scream and take up more space in the room. Austin smiled and counted off the intro with the drumsticks before going into another song, with another beat, and another progression of chords.

As we played, I noticed the blanket that had been stuffed into the big bass drum had started to fall out of the front hole, and along with it, my cell phone had fallen out onto the floor. I picked it up and plugged it in to charge it. It had been dead for quite some time, and it would be nice to turn it on and be connected to somewhere else outside of those padded walls.

When we had sweat through our clothes and run out of chords to play and noise to make, we went and sat out on the fire escape porch, just like we had at The Armstrong. Austin lit a cigarette and pulled a half-pint of Ancient Age out of his back pocket. He opened it, took a sip, and offered it to me.

"I'm good," I said, waving my hand at it.

He shrugged and took another sip before capping it and putting it back in his pocket.

"Well," I said. "What are you going to do now? Are you back for good?"

"I think so," he said. "There's not really

anywhere else to be. My folks' place is great but I do have a master's degree. I should probably get a job. I'll just work at the theater for a while. Are you still there?"

"I'm not too sure, but I don't think so," I said.

"Got it. You know, Kevin's pretty understanding about this kind of stuff. You think you're the first mess he's ever hired? He'd probably hire you back in a second. He just needs warm bodies. And not even that. A vampire works there for God's sake."

We sat for a moment, listening to the sirens and the yelling down on the street below.

"Wait, where are you going to live?" I asked.

"The truck, I guess."

I thought about the weather. It was freezing at night and the metal bed of the truck transferred the cold evenly all the way up to the camper top. It was going to be terrible. Then I thought of the roof again. Standing on the ledge and looking at the only way down until he came up and helped me get on the ladder.

"Take this place," I said.

"It's too small for both of us, man."

"No, no I mean take my spot."

"No, I couldn't. Where are you..."

I was already getting up and running into the hallway.

"Don't move. I'll be right back."

I ran into the padded room, flushed and

breathing heavily. I put a few T-shirts into my backpack and threw my hooded sweatshirt on, then tossed the charged cell phone and the charger in there as well. Looking around, there was nothing else to bring. Everything else was his.

I ran back out onto the fire escape.

"Here," I said, taking the keys out of my pocket and handing them to him. "This one is for the front gate and this one is for the room. There's a dropbox out front for the rent. Just have it in there by the fifth."

He reached toward the keys then drew back.

"I don't understand," he said, standing up to meet my eye line.

"It's fine," I said. "Here, take this."

I took out the envelope with that month's rent in it and pulled out twenty dollars in ones and fives, shoving that into my pocket.

"This is most of the rent for next month, do you have twenty bucks for the rest?"

"Yeah, sure," he said. "Where are you going?"

"I'm going home," I said. "Out from under the porch."

I wrapped him in a hug and when we broke away I put the keys and the envelope in his hand.

"I'll come visit," I said. "We'll play music."

Chapter Twenty

I ran down the hall, leaving Austin standing on the fire escape holding the money and keys. As I passed by the space's open door, I stepped in, grabbing two library books from the corner and tossing them into my bag. I stopped for a moment to look around, then bolted out the door, running down the hall and pushing past a couple of metalheads lighting a joint in the hallway.

"Sorry," I yelled back at them. "Sorry about that."

Running down the steps, I kicked open the front gate, letting it swing wide and bang into the wall next to it. There was a guy leaning against the wall, and he yelped as I kicked it open, jumping quickly out of the way and scowling.

"Sorry, so sorry," I said, as I kicked the gate closed again and nodded to him, running in the direction of the library.

I sprinted down Hyde, brushing past people and apologizing to them as I ran in the other direction, making sure that I looked back and looked them in the eye as they frowned at me and shook their heads. I hadn't eaten in a long time, and as I passed the mirror-like windows of the buildings, I could see that I was gaunt and my hair was long and stringy. The swelling from the broken tooth had gone down and my cheeks were now sunken in and casting a shadow on my face. I usually tried to avoid any kind of prolonged attention to how I was looking. Out here, in the light of the morning though, I could get a full glimpse of my entire self, sprinting along Hyde Street, pulling at my pants as they slipped down my waist. It was me. I could recognize me.

As I ran, I passed the spot where I had been robbed. I hadn't been back since it happened, and I could see a small splotch of blood still on the sidewalk where my face had landed. It was mixed in with all the other small splotches from all the other people who had fallen headfirst in that very spot. There was a piece of me left there now for people to step over and pretend they didn't see. I would know, though, and I was happy to contribute to the collage of bodily fluids that was always changing and always getting thicker, like coats of paint on a wall.

I stopped a couple of blocks away from The Main Branch to catch my breath. My chest was heaving and my heart was beating through my temples. I hadn't had that much exercise in a long time. I bent over and put my hands on my thighs as I tasted a warm, metallic tang in my mouth. The air was cold and burned my lungs as I gasped. Pulling out my little cell phone, I dialed 411 for information. A computerized voice came over the receiver.

"City and State Please"

"San Francisco, California," I said between gasps.

A human voice interjected.

"Okay, what listing in San Francisco?"

"Golden Gate Transit or I don't know, do you have bus schedules?"

"I do," the voice said.

"I need the next bus from San Francisco to Santa Luna. I grew up there. My parents are there. My old school, the church, everything."

"Okay," the voice said, only taking in the pertinent information. "Looks like there's one at 12:30 p.m."

"Where does it pick up?"

"Civic Center."

"That's great," I said. "That's perfect."

There was a small silence on the other end of the

line.

"Is that it?"

"I don't know," I said. "How long does that bus take?"

"It's arriving in Santa Luna at 3:30."

"And how much does it cost?"

"To go all the way, it is..."

I heard some typing in the background.

"...it's eight dollars."

"Okay, I can do that. I can do that. That's really fantastic. I usually don't have eight dollars, but I do today. Have you ever not had eight dollars?"

There was a long pause and for a moment I thought they had hung up.

"Yes," the voice said.

"Well then you know exactly what I'm talking about," I said. "Have you ever had a moment where everything just lines up and makes sense and seems so simple?"

"I have," the voice said.

"I think it's important to jump on that, right?"

There was another pause.

"Is there anything else I can help you with?"

"Oh," I said. "What time is it now?"

"It's 12:10."

"Okay, thank you. Thank you so much. You're amazing."

"No problem. Good luck."

I hung up the phone and caught my breath a little

bit more. This was going to be close. There were still so many things I had to do in such a short period of time. Groaning, I took off again, sprinting down Hyde Street. If I could get to the library in time and then make one more stop, I would be good to go. I could leave town free and clear, not leaving anything behind but what had already been left. There was nothing else to hold onto. I was light and free and finally headed home. I ran harder and ignored the pleas from my heart and lungs.

When I got to the front of the library, I couldn't see straight. My legs were wobbly and barely holding my torso up as I clung to the railing that led up the concrete steps. It felt like my feet were dragging behind me and every organ was screaming for mercy and telling me to sit down. There was no time, though. I had to make all of this quick.

When I finally got to the top of the stairs and up to the heavy glass doors, I pushed with my body weight on the brass handle to get them open. The huge marble entryway was full of people. Some were checking out books, others were chatting and milling around, going about their lives. A couple of the people working behind the counters stopped and looked at me, sweating and wild-eyed in the doorway, holding a collection of some Peanuts cartoons and a copy of *Blood Meridian*. I recognized a few of them and smiled wide. I could feel cool air on the broken tooth and it stung.

"I made it," I said, loud enough that it echoed all around the entryway.

A man about my age with a cardigan and tie behind the counter raised his eyebrows and smiled back.

"Okay," he said. "Sounds good."

I handed him the books, then reached into my back pocket. He backed away for a moment, unsure of where this was headed. I pulled out the piece of paper with Austin's library card copied onto it and handed it to him.

"Will you make sure this gets shredded and thrown away?" I said.

He took it and turned it over, frowning at it.

"You know, you're really not supposed to do this," he said.

"I know," I said. "I know, but I'm leaving, don't worry. Thank you. Thank you so much."

And with that, I pushed through the glass doors and was back out on the street.

Checking my phone, it was now 12:15. Fifteen minutes to run this last errand. I could make it if I sprinted.

My legs had other plans, but I pushed them with all the strength I had left, putting one foot in front of the other and pumping my arms as my backpack bumped and flew behind me. I got to the front of the church at 12:18.

Walking in, I realized that I had only ever gone

down to the basement to eat. Aside from the one time I had been there years earlier as a kid, I hadn't seen the inside. In fact, it had been a long time since I had seen the inside of any church at all. The quiet felt like a punch in the face. I could hear my sucking breaths and the beating of my heart in my ears, but other than that, it was complete silence. A few people sat in the pews with their heads down, deep in prayer, and I wondered if they could hear my heart beating as well, as I walked into the main area and looked around. I was searching for something and as soon as I saw it, I noticed a security guard in the corner, eyeing me, concerned. I pointed to the plastic donation box sitting next to the large display of candles that you could light to say a prayer for someone, like a fast track to God.

"Do you know where this goes?" I asked the security guard, much louder than I had intended.

He shushed me and a couple of the people sitting in the pews turned back to look as well.

"Sorry," I said, whispering now. "Do you know what this goes to?"

"What do you mean?" he said.

"I mean like, does this go to legal defense for priests or does it go to the kitchen downstairs?"

"The kitchen," he whispered back.

"Good," I said. "That's really good."

He smiled.

"Yeah, it's a great program."

"You have no idea," I said, digging into my pocket and counting out twelve dollars, leaving me with the eight I would need for the bus ticket.

"Oh, I do," he said, and he reached into his wallet and took out a couple of singles.

We each put our money in and nodded at each other. I checked the phone. It was 12:20 on the dot. The security guard nodded and sauntered back to his post as I spun around and ran out the door.

When the cold air hit me, the sweat on my back shot down in temperature and I was immediately rejuvenated, like a cold shower of my own filth. It was bracing, and I felt a new strength in my legs and lungs as I sprinted down the sloped grass of the church and back out onto the streets of The Tenderloin.

The sidewalks seemed to be exceptionally full. I tried not to bump into anyone, especially those who were leaned over in a full heroin nod. It sometimes seemed like they could never tip over. Like they were just punching bags with rounded bottoms that always stayed upright no matter what. I knew better, though. They could easily be knocked over and it didn't take much at all.

As I ran, I looked at the phone again. 12:22. It was going to be close, but I had time. Buses were always late. I passed by the practice space again on my way to the Civic Center Plaza and took one last look. The stain where someone had pissed into the keyhole had formed into a large splotch where the paint was fading. I could only imagine what was in the urine that had made it corrode the finish like that. A diet of malt liquor, cheap whiskey or vodka, and whatever someone could eat at the liquor store. My diet.

I got to Civic Center Plaza at 12:27. The trees that lined the walkway were bare and desolate-looking from the winter chill and I wondered how long it took to rake up all the leaves that fell to the ground. I wondered if there was a place where every discarded boot and piece of clothing and empty bottle that was left there ended up, or if it all went to different places, scattered in the wind and left strewn in different landfills and different dumpsters.

I found the Golden Gate Transit stop and sat down on the bench. My chest was heaving now and I thought I could taste blood in my mouth with each expulsion of breath. As soon as I sat down, I could feel that the running and heavy breathing was too much for my stomach and it was starting to flip inside out. I tried to hold it in, but after a few seconds, I stood up and vomited into the street. There wasn't much to it. It was mostly bile and some brown liquid, but thankfully, no blood. I felt clean, then. Purged and happy to leave one last mark on this place. I stood on the curb with vomit dripping down my chin and took one last look around. Cars went past and a few of the drivers stared at me. A cop in his cruiser drove by but he didn't even look once. He just stared straight ahead toward Market Street where there would be more opportunities to meet his ticket quota. Someone vomiting into the street was the least of his concerns and I didn't have anything to take anyway. Up there, he might at least be able to confiscate some drugs that he could sell to his buddies or take himself later.

I looked up McCallister and saw the bus rolling down the hill about five blocks away. It looked like a big blue whale lumbering up the street with the green and red insignia of Golden Gate Transit emblazoned on the front. I took one last moment to remember what this was like and where I had been. The vomit bubbled and fizzed on the ground in front of me and I wiped my chin with the bottom of my hooded sweatshirt. I kissed my hand and blew it into the chilled wind that rushed through the buildings and the barren trees. There would be other places to go and other places to see, but at that moment I only wanted to remember this place and what I had left there on the street, running into the storm drain and out to sea.

When the bus pulled up, I took out my eight dollars and got on when the doors hissed open.

"Where you going?" the driver asked, leaning on the huge steering wheel with his fingerless gloves.

"Santa Luna," I said. "All the way to the end."

"Eight bucks," he said. "That's a long trip."

He looked me up and down in a way I was very familiar and comfortable with.

"You gonna be okay for that long? I don't make

any stops except to pick people up and there's no bathroom on this thing."

Instinctively, I wiped my mouth with the sleeve of my sweatshirt.

"I'm good," I said.

"Okay, come on, I'm gonna hold you to that."

I put the money into the machine and he looked at me, worried, as he closed the doors and I walked back to take my seat.

The bus seats were soft and patterned. I sat down next to a window and breathed in the cool air that was flowing out from the vents underneath the seats. The bus lurched into traffic and I leaned my head on the window, watching as The Tenderloin slowly rolled away. We made several stops within the city and more people got on. Commuters who came into San Francisco by bus instead of driving opened laptops as soon as they sat down, hoping to get a little bit more work done before going home to one of the towns that dotted the coast on the way to Santa Luna. All of them looked at me as they passed, noticing that I was not a regular on this bus, before finding their usual seats.

We went through all the neighborhoods, down Van Ness and Lombard Street, which was the first road in from the Golden Gate Bridge. It was jammed with traffic and I watched tourists try to park their cars at the hotels and motels that lined the entry into San Francisco with names like the Motor Inn and the Carriage House. We passed Mel's Diner and other tourist attractions that I realized I hadn't seen since getting to town. There was no reason to see them, I was down where there were stun guns and piss on the door and people named Fast Eddie waiting around every corner. It alarmed me to see that there was so much going on out here. So much that I had not been a part of in so long. I hadn't been in a sit-down restaurant in months or even years. There were many things that I would have to make sure I did, once I was willing and able to make it happen.

When the bus turned the corner and got onto the 101 freeway, the Golden Gate Bridge came into view. Its big spires shot up into the clouds that hung low over it, and as we rose up over the Presidio, I saw the ocean. My breath immediately quickened and I tried to take it in as it stretched out toward Baker Beach and west into the clouded horizon that covered an endless expanse. There were boats out on the water to the east and Alcatraz peeked out through the December fog. I looked around the bus and saw that all the rest of the people in their seats were looking down at their phones or laptops. They saw this every day on their way home from work. All it meant was that they were a little bit closer to home.

The bus went through the toll booth and the driver punched the gas as we pulled out onto the bridge. Groups of tourists in jackets and plastic parkas passed by, taking pictures of the water and each other, smiling and laughing in the mist that whipped up from the ocean hundreds of feet below. The bus bounced and swayed as it made its way across the bridge and the water under us was deeper than I could imagine and full of things I could never name. There had been many people who had walked halfway across this bridge and decided not to turn back or keep going. They had climbed over the side and taken the only other way, which was down. The open sky above them and the deep, deep water below had squeezed them too tight and I knew what it felt like to be between them, occupying that little, awful space. But the bus didn't stop in the middle. It kept moving and I was just along for the ride. It would get to the other side and it would keep going. It was just like the driver had said. He didn't make any stops. He stepped on the gas and the bus crossed the bridge and passed the Vista Point where tourists stopped to look through coin-operated telescopes and where my father had proposed to my mother years and years ago, which would eventually result in me. Right here. Along for the ride and going wherever it took me. Down the road and through the tunnel that had been carved into a green and brown mountain and out the other side. Sitting in a padded seat, rumbling and bouncing along the highway, with everyone else who had gotten on. All the way to the end.

Acknowledgments

This book would have been impossible without the help of so many incredible people. I'm going to go ahead and start from the beginning:

Thank you so much to Mom for all the books, Dad for not giving up on me, Ian for showing me the power of storytelling, and Leanna for making me a whole person.

Thank you to Noelle Oxenhandler at Sonoma State University, the Creative Lotus writing group, Sarah Lynn Chavez, Aaron Goeth, Jared Horney, and the guy in my memoir class who was always enraged by my work. You all helped me find the right direction.

A very, very, very special thank you to the wonderful Nate Ragolia, who has been a consistent guiding light and a fantastic, supportive friend not only during the writing and publishing of this book but for many years before.

Finally, thank you to everyone who ever gave me a couch to sleep on, bummed me cigarettes, played in a band with me, let me borrow a guitar, didn't get too mad when I drank all their booze or did all their drugs, and didn't let disappointment stop them from being my friend.

About the Author

Michael J. O'Connor is a writer from the San Francisco Bay Area. He is a graduate of Sonoma State University's Creative Writing program and a former prose editor for the Zaum literary magazine as well as a recipient of the Moon Valley Writing Award. He has had short stories published in journals like River River, Flying South, and Hive Avenue. This is his first novel.

About the Publishing Team

Nate Ragolia is a lifelong lover of science fiction and its power to imagine worlds more hopeful and inclusive than the real one. His first book, *There You Feel Free*, was published by 1888's Black Hill Press in 2015. Spaceboy Books reissued it in 2021. He's also the author of *The Retroactivist* (2017). His most recent book, *One Person Can't Make a Difference* (2022), was featured on Tor.com's Can't Miss Indie Press Speculative Fiction list, and was translated into Italian for Ringworld Sci-Fi in 2023. He founded and edited *BONED*, a literary magazine, and also created two webcomics. Nate is also a husband and a dog dad.

Shaunn Grulkowski has been compared to Warren Ellis and Phillip K. Dick and was once described as what a baby conceived by Kurt Vonnegut and Margaret Atwood would turn out to be. He's at least the fifth best Slavic-Latino-American sci-fi writer in the Baltimore metro area. He's the author *Retcontinuum*, and the editor of *A Stalled Ox* and *The Goldfish* for 1888/Black Hill Press.